CHICKEN FOOTS STEW

And Other Humorous Stories

Michael Delphy Hunt

Writers Club Press
New York Lincoln Shanghai

Chicken Foots Stew
And Other Humorous Stories

Writers Club Press
an imprint of iUniverse, Inc.

For information address:
iUniverse, Inc.
2021 Pine Lake Road, Suite 100
Lincoln, NE 68512
www.iuniverse.com

ISBN: 0-595-26019-5

Printed in the United States of America

Contents

For Starters

For starters, let me tell you a little bit about myself. My name is Michael Devin Hughes. Not to worry though, no one ever calls me Devin. I am thirty-three years old, six-foot four, with blond hair, blue eyes, copper-tanned, and a lean one hundred eighty-five pounds. My personal trainer Sven Jefferson makes sure I complete three hundred ab crunches every other day, which contributes to my one percent body fat. My wife is a former Miss California, and my son Dakota, and my daughter Aspen will be starring in their first theatrical release next year. We own a five acre estate in Beverly Hills, complete with an Olympic size pool, twin tennis courts, bowling alley, arcade gameroom with over two hundred diversions, and a home theater that seats seventy-five. We also have homes in Santa Fe, Longboat Key, and Palm Beach. We are on all the *A* plus party lists, and are major sponsors for four theatre groups, three ballets, two symphonies, and a partridge in a pear tree, I mean a poet named Petry.

We are politically-connected, and socially conscious. I have set-up a political action committee and expect to announce my candidacy for governor in the next few weeks. My wife and I belong to the right boards, and contribute to the most visible and popular charities. We are members of the most exclusive clubs, distribute meals to the less fortunate at the downtown soup kitchen, and donate at least once a month to the local blood bank.

And if you believe all that drivel, then I also want to tell you that I, not the United States government, own Yellowstone National Park. For extremely personal reasons, I have decided to sell the Park, lock, stock, and barrel, except for Old Faithful Geyser. My daughter wants a keepsake for her children. The appraised value is over one trillion dollars. But because I'm in an exceptionally good mood, I'll sell it to the first qualified buyer for the paltry sum of, oh let's say fifteen million, in good old United States currency—none of that negotiable paper from countries that I cannot pronounce, or that I am afraid to visit.

If for some incomprehensible reason, you still believe what I have written so far, then you are either a) brain-dead, b) an alien from another galaxy, or c) in terrible need of another life.

The truth is that I am a forty-something, all right, so I am closer to fifty-something. I am somewhere in the neighborhood of six feet tall—try five-foot eight, a smidge over two hundred pounds, give or take one hundred pounds. I have a shiny forehead that extends all the way back to the base of my neck, and I am tanned, though not by the sun. I've been married four times, divorced four times, and my two kids love me, except when they don't, which changes as frequently as a barometer. I believe two of my ex-wives have employed root doctors to make sure that I am eternally unlucky in love, money, work, sports and anything else that I might do.

To give you an idea of how bad things have gotten, this is the tenth time that I have started this book. On one occasion, a neighbor's dog chewed the half-completed manuscript, and buried the computer disk—on another occasion, the manuscript, computer disk, back-up disk, and my car all went up in flames at the local Funky Burgers. As I recall, the Sheriff's Deputy said, "You should have asked for a char-broiled hamburger instead of a char-broiled jalopy." On another occasion, my manuscript and computer disks were abducted by illegal aliens—whether they were from this world or not, I am not sure—On another occasion, well you get the idea.

I could tell you that the names in this book have been changed to protect the innocent. But that would be a lie. Oh yes, I changed virtually every name, community, and landmark in this page-turner. But I did not change names because the individuals depicted are innocent. There are no innocent individuals in this book—especially me. I am guilty, and on occasion, embarrassed by my actions, which are richly detailed throughout. The others are equally as guilty, which brings me to the prime reason I changed their names—to protect me from years of complex, gut-wrenching, money-siphoning litigation. In fact, after my publisher's lawyers read the last draft of the book, they counted at least six hundred forty-two incidents that could have subjected me to various allegations of defamation, slander, libel, and some common law tort known as thuggery. At first blush, I thought being a thugee might not be so bad. But the lawyers strongly suggested, actually held a sharp instrument to my back, and forced me to change names, and delete certain stories. So, I am afraid that as a result of the mandated editing you will not be reading about *My Night in a Mississippi Turkish Bath*, or *Boy, I Thought They Were Just Fireworks*, or *So That's Why Santa Claus Wears Red Suspenders*.

Anyway, I still have a million other stories. Here in no particular order are the first batch.

Convenience Stores

Everyone has certain dislikes. For some it's eating potato chips in bed. For others it's drinking milk directly from the carton. For my father, it's convenience stores. I would say that he detests them, but that would be a grand understatement. He'd rather have open heart surgery without anesthesia, than to have to set one toe in a convenience store. There are over five hundred convenience stores in our hometown, and he avoids them like the plague. I am not certain what single event or chain of events acted as the catalyst for my father's contempt of convenience stores. In fact, as far as I could tell, my father never suffered one bad experience in a convenience store. My mother even states that he used to go to the convenience store and buy diapers for me when I was a wiggly waif. Nevertheless, he could recall and recite isolated circumstance after isolated circumstance occurring after hours at convenience stores across the country. If my father availed himself of the Internet, which he does not (but that is another story as well), then I am positive that he would maintain a website—dontgothere.com that would chronicle real and imagined acts of convenience store mayhem. Even without access to the Internet, there was not one convenience store chain that escaped my father's wrath and vitriolic scorn.

But my past experiences with my father and convenience stores paled in comparison to my encounter with him during spring break of my junior year in college. Instead of heading to the beach for spring break, I thought it might be nice if I spent a few days home—sort of bonding with my father and brother. It seemed like a great idea at the time. And quite frankly it was for the first couple of days. We rehashed the good old days, and participated in guy activities like watching action movies all night, and installing a fence around the flower garden. Everything was percolating just fine until that third night—the night before my scheduled job interview with a public relations firm.

While I did not necessarily want a full-time job, I did want full-time independence. Therefore, I viewed the job interview as an opportunity to achieve my primary objective. For different reasons, my father also viewed the interview as an opportunity to reach one of his primary objectives—which was not having me ask for money every other week. So it was no surprise, that he kept making comments like, "It sure would be nice for you to get that job, so that you can be out on your own, and out of this house," or "If you get that job, and move out, I can turn your room into a nice little library," or "If that public relations firm hires you, then maybe, just maybe, you could pay back some of those emergency loans you've gotten from me over the last four years." Yes, my father wanted me to get the job, to remove another dependent from his tax form—he had always said the deduction wasn't enough and didn't even pay for two months of keeping me fed and in clothes. It was nice to know that my father had my well being at heart.

Anyway, I decided that I would make every effort to dazzle the interview committee at the public relations firm. To that end, I polished my shoes until they shined—so much so that you could see my reflection at ten paces. The crease in my black pants was so sharp that it could cut a frozen stick of butter. My dress shirt was neatly pressed without a single wrinkle.

Everything was in place or so I thought. Then I made a horrifying discovery—a discovery that I was sure would wreck havoc in the family.

I realized that I had left my shaving cream in my dorm room. It was just after nine, and my choices for buying *Creamy Suds* shaving cream were limited. I could either go to PSC Markets or to the Lime Green Store. Both were convenience stores. Either choice required that I journey to the land of the forbidden after sunset—in the dead of night. And as I have already noted, my father would rather that I wrestle a grizzly bear with a wet noodle than visit either convenience store.

I should have stayed home. Day-old stubble would have given me the appearance of an older, wiser man. But of course I was not too smart. So, I reached for a jacket and headed for the door.

My father glanced at his watch. He cocked his head a few degrees and stared at me in a harsh frosty silence. Although no words were spoken, I could tell that he wanted to say, "I know my son has better sense than to go out traipsing about the countryside at this late hour of the night."

I continued walking toward the front door.

"You don't need to go out at this time of night," my father said as though I were still in grammar school.

Avoiding eye contact, I replied, "You said I needed to shave."

"You can use my shaving cream."

"You use soap and water."

"It does the job every bit as well as that fancy shaving cream you buy."

"My face needs more lubrication. The last time I used soap and water, I nearly bled to death from the razor cuts."

"That's because you don't know how to shave."

Actually, there was a crumb of truth to that statement. I held my razor like a hatchet, and I moved it in a zig-zag fashion across my face, instead of gliding it across my face as though it were an ice skate. But whether I shaved correctly or not was not really the issue, because soap and water simply did not provide me with enough lubrication and protection. After a moment, I responded to my father's last statement by saying politely, but firmly, "I need *Creamy Suds*, pops."

"*Creamy Suds?* That's the name of your shaving cream? It sounds like a ladies' beer."

He had a point. Still, I replied, "It's not."

"The world would be a better place if we stuck to the basics, instead of going with fads, like shaving cream."

"Shaving cream has been around for almost fifty years."

"Well, at least wait until tomorrow morning when the supermarkets are open."

"I've got an early appointment. I need to shave tonight. It will only take me ten minutes to go to the convenience store and come back. The Lime and Green Store is right down the street."

"The Lime and Green Store?! Why don't you just drive a stake through my heart and be done with it?"

"Pops, I'll be all right."

"You know you shouldn't go to the Lime and Green Store."

"It's less than a mile away."

"You got a better chance of surviving Russian Roulette, than going to the Lime and Green Store."

"Pops, it's just a convenience store."

"Just a convenience store!" he exclaimed. "Just a convenience store," he repeated in a more animated manner, with the saliva oozing from the corners of his mouth.

I believe I could actually see the blood rushing to my dad's head. His face turned a color that I am certain no paint store could match. His eyes bulged and he trembled, as though he was about to have a seizure. In this instance though, it would have been called a mooligan which is a seizure induced by the irresponsible or irrational acts of a child.

"Just a convenience store!" he repeated for the third time. "What have I told you since you were knee-high to a gnat about convenience stores?"

"You told me never to go to a convenience store before ten in the morning or after five in the afternoon."

"And why did I tell you that?"

There were so many reasons, so many stories, that I honestly did not know which one he was talking about on that night. Out of frustration, I replied, "I don't recall."

"You don't recall?" My father's voice boomed.

I had not been home for quite seventy-two hours, and yet my father was seconds away from giving yet another version of the 'Convenience Store' speech. I prayed for divine intervention, but none was forthcoming. Resigned to my fate, I sighed and replied, "No, I don't recall."

"Remember Omar—Omar—Now what was that boy's last name? It sounded like a dessert."

"You mean Puddinhead?"

"Yeah, Omar Puddinhead. He got shot the last time he went to a convenience store."

"For crying out loud pops, he was trying to rob the convenience store."

"That's not the point, son. The point is that bad things happen when you go to the convenience store."

There was no way that I was going to win this argument. In fact, in an effort to preserve family harmony I even considered not going to the neighborhood Lime and Green Store. But I couldn't let my father have the last word just yet. So, I added in as sincere a tone as possible, "That was an isolated incident pops."

My father gave me that type of gaze that a father gives a son, when he thinks his offspring has gone stark raving mad. If I had been within arm's reach, he would have given me a swift slap to the back of my head. As it was, he stared at me for what seemed like an eternity, then trying to compose himself sputtered, "Isolated incident? Isolated incident? I guess the world is just filled with isolated incidents. Remember Mr. Albert Coats? He died at a convenience store."

"He was ninety-seven years old, pops. He walked around with a mask attached to an oxygen tank, and he wore a pacemaker. He suffered a heart attack and collapsed at the Lime and Green Store after he got too near a microwave that was popping popcorn."

"Need I say more?"

How was I going to prevail with that type of logic? My older brother Tony, who up to that point had kept silent, and watched the verbal fireworks between me and our father with a sort of reserved sibling joy, finally entered the conversation and said, "Look dad, you've got a very good point about those convenience stores. But if it will make you rest any easier, I will accompany Michael to the Lime and Green Store."

My father grunted, rolled his eyes, then said, "All right, but if you're not back in fifteen minutes, I'm calling the police, and asking for a SWAT raid on the store."

"I read you loud and clear. Trust me, we will be back before you know it." Tony grabbed the keys to his car, and said, "Let's go little brother."

Little brother, indeed, I stewed and smoldered like day-old tomatoes in fresh hot chili.

Nothing was said until we got a couple of blocks from the store. Feeling something needed to be said, I finally asked, "So why doesn't pops mind you going out at night?"

"Oh he does. But he knows I carry a loaded streetsweeper."

"I see." I paused for a few seconds in order to fully absorb and appreciate the significance of that fact. Afterward, I requested, "Look, I need you to do me a favor."

"What?"

"In the unlikely event that I become cannon fodder for some crazed homicidal lunatic who decides that tonight is the perfect night to rob the Lime and Green Store, then I want you to move my body out into the street and run over it—make sure that the tire marks cover any bullet holes—so you can tell pops that I died from a car accident as opposed to a shootout in a convenience store."

Now Tony glanced at me like I had lost my mind. "I thought pops had gotten rid of all his crazy children. Never in a million years would he believe a story as preposterous as that."

"He might if you told him. After all, he trusts you more than me."

"Pops wouldn't believe that story even if it were moms who told him."

Of course, Tony was right. I was grasping at straws. Anyway, what did I have to worry about? Up to that point, I had never concerned myself about going to a convenience store at night. It made no sense to consider any one of my father's doomsday scenarios because nothing was going to happen. Nothing at all. I would buy my shaving cream, and be in and out of the store in less than two minutes. It would be simple.

In a couple of minutes, we parked in front of the Lime and Green Store.

There were two other cars parked in the well-lighted lot. But even with the most technologically advanced sodium lamps, placed at every strategic angle of the store, and at key points along the outer perimeter, my father would have moaned that the parking area was too dark, and just begging for chaos and calamity. If I had been smart, I would have told Tony to take me back home. As I noted earlier, the slightly stubbled look was popular back then. But as my pops often told me, everybody else was working with a one-hundred watt bulb, while I was working with at three-quarters capacity with a seventy-five. So I got out of the car and stepped into the Lime and Green Store. Parked directly in front of the entrance, Tony waited for my return.

All Lime and Green Stores were remarkably similar—thirty-seven feet long by twenty feet wide. Each store's design called for seven narrow aisles arranged in a specific order—candy (the money grabber, child pleaser, and dentist's best friend) always occupied aisle one—toiletries, including shaving cream always lined aisle three.

Before that night, I had never really noticed the type of person that frequents a convenience store after dark. But that night was different. My eyes focused on every individual in the Battery Park Lime and Green Store. On aisle seven, a mother placed doughnuts and other sweet treats in a plastic bag. A few feet down the aisle, a man removed a half-gallon of milk from one of the refrigerated coolers. On aisle two, a young couple chose washing powder, and bleach. And on aisle six, a teenager skimmed through the latest magazines. Instead of finding scores of depraved and lonely souls walking aimlessly down the aisles, as my father had suggested, I saw ordinary people, mothers and fathers, and teenage children engaging in the most ordinary of tasks, buying food, and household supplies. Not one of them a crazed lunatic.

"What's up E-mail?"

I spoke too soon. As I walked down aisle three, a young man approached me. He appeared cross-eyed, so I really couldn't tell if he was talking to me, or to another person. But he wore a cheap trench coat, and an even cheaper Aussie-style hat. It appeared he hadn't shaved since puberty, and he reaked of malt liquor and cigarettes.

I tried to ignore him.

He repeated, "What's up E-mail?"

"I believe you have me mistaken for someone else," I replied as nicely as possible.

"Naw, I don't forget faces. You're E-mail, all right. I know you couldn't have forgotten. It's Teddy Boy. What's wrong? You too good to talk to me, now that we're not in the joint."

"Trust me, I've never been in the joint."

"Yeah, right," he responded in an unbelieving tone. His eyes were glued on my face, staring at me as though I had stolen his last peanut butter and jelly sandwich. His eyes unhinged me at the joints. Teddy Boy resembled one of those characters that were featured on some cable documentary discussing the pitfalls of ramming your head into a brick wall without the benefit of a helmet.

Between me and the shaving cream stood Teddy Boy. I tried making an end around old Teddy Boy, but he put out one of those big mitts he called hands, and stopped me dead in my tracks.

"You got fifty dollars for smokes?" Teddy Boy asked, as he placed his left hand in his jacket pocket.

Like the naïve rube I was, I replied, "Smokes don't cost fifty dollars."

"I smoke imports. Now do you have fifty?"

Teddy Boy kept rustling with something in his pocket. I guessed he wanted me to think that it was a gun. I was not fooled by his bluff. However, I suspected that Teddy Boy intended to get fifty dollars from me, by hook or crook. Visions of my father appeared. None of the visions were pleasant. I could hear my father saying, *What did I tell you? You're just asking for trouble by going to a convenience store at night. Only crooks, deranged people, and vampires frequent those type of stores after dark.* I then had a mental image of my father blowing a gasket. I did not think it was possible for a human to blow a gasket. But in my all-too-real vision, my father did exactly that.

Outside, Tony watched the events with me and Teddy Boy unravel. He had promised our father that we would be back safe and in the house in fifteen minutes. I should have been leaving the store by now. But my unexpected conversation with Teddy Boy had thrown us off schedule. So Tony decided it was time to break-up the reunion. As I learned later, Teddy Boy had been a classmate of Tony's. Perhaps Teddy Boy remembered a brief encounter when we were younger.

Because Tony understood the potential volatility of Teddy Boy Scott, he wedged himself between Teddy and me. "Sorry, Teddy, but me and my brother are on a tight schedule. So if you will excuse us." With that Tony grabbed my shoulder, and pushed both of us past Teddy.

The swiftness of my brother's rescue mission caught Teddy completely off guard. Teddy continued to search his jacket pocket for something. Retrieving what appeared to be a lint-covered breath mint, he popped it into his mouth. As we separated from Teddy's immediate grasp, he cracked the mint on one of his two good teeth and exclaimed, "Say, what about my fifty?"

"Some other time, Teddy."

Tony grabbed a small can of Lime-Green Special shaving cream. It was not *Creamy Suds*, but under the circumstances it would have to suffice. He tossed the shaving cream to me, as I passed by the check-out counter.

I hurriedly handed the check-out clerk five dollars for a three dollar and fifty cent, two ounce can of store brand shaving lather. Not waiting for my change, I told the clerk to give what was left over to Teddy Boy.

Once in the car, Tony explained his past association with Teddy Boy.

"Do you have any idea what he was in jail for?" I asked.

"I believe it was aggravated assault with intent to maim and dismember."

I shuddered.

"You know that pops is right," Tony commented, as he drove back to the house.

"Just drive on." I was in no mood to listen to yet another lecture about convenience stores from of all people my brother.

My brother drove on, but continued to talk. "Look, Michael. We all obsess on something. For me, it's the ladies. For you, it's grades. For pops, it's convenience stores."

A minute or so into Tony's comments, I tuned him out, and began to count utility poles. My tally for three blocks was thirteen utility poles—ten wood, two concrete, and one made out of some hard plastic compound.

"I trust you won't say a word about Teddy Boy Scott."

"I won't have to. Pops will know that something happened."

As usual, Tony was right. Our father would believe that we were one second from total obliteration. In this particular case, he would have been correct too. But I was determined not to give him the satisfaction of saying, *"I told you so."*

I entered. The scent of an unpleasant convenience store confrontation assaulted my father's sharpened senses. It did not help matters that I looked guilty.

My father pointed to his watch. "You just made it back in time. Another twenty seconds, and I was going to call the police."

"Relax, dad," Tony said, before sauntering to the kitchen.

I showed my father the shaving cream. "Yeah we're back without one hair out of place," I said confidently, but with just a trace of defiance.

"So why are you perspiring. Something happened at the convenience store. What was it?"

"Nothing out of the ordinary happened," I said, crossing my fingers behind my back.

"And you're telling me that nothing odd happened at the Lime and Green Store?"

Avoiding eye contact, I returned, "Nothing at all."

"You know you're not too old to get a swift slap on the rear, if you're lying to me. I still got some sizzle in my right hand."

"Why would I lie, pops?

My father waved his hands to tell me to stop the charade. He knew that I was being less than honest. If I had been younger, and it had been earlier, my pops would have sent me to bed without dinner. As it stood now, he just said, "Get a good night's sleep." As an afterthought, he added, "I'm glad you and Tony are still in one piece."

"Night, pops."

That night, all my dreams were nightmares about confronting bizarre situations and crazed individuals in endless procession of convenience stores. Aliens, both illegal, and not of this world, beserk clones, stores that vanished, possessed check-out clerks, check-out lines that never moved, and stores that were covered by quicksand were just some of the frightening tales that I dreamt that night. In each nightmare, my father appeared, and said, "What did I tell you, son?"

The next morning, my father walked into the breakfast nook, and shook his head in a disapproving manner.

"What did I tell you?"

I shuddered at the eerie déjà vu. Maybe I was still dreaming. My father tapped me on the forehead. No, I was definitely awake. Composing myself, I asked, "What are you talking about pops?"

My father handed me the front page of the local section of the newspaper. His eyebrows arched, and there was the faint glimmer of a smug smile on his face. I realized that what I was about to read was not good news—and it wasn't. The headline read in bold eighteen point print—**BOTCHED ROBBERY AT LIME AND GREEN**—A quick thinking night clerk at the Battery Park Street Lime and Green store foiled a robbery attempt. Theodore "Teddy Boy" Scott, 21, of 26-G Asa Goodwin Projects was arrested and charged with assault and robbery—

"Didn't I tell you that they might as well put a bullseye sign in front of every Lime and Green Store?"

Actually, I had never heard my father say that. But the sentiment and dislike for convenience stores was unmistakable.

"I guess you're right, pops," I said, as I rubbed my clean-shaven face.

"Tell me, son. Was it worth risking your life for some third-rate shaving cream?"

"I'll tell you after my job interview."

The interview went well, but the firm offered the job to another applicant, someone who had some experience in biometrics. Under the circumstances, I concluded that going to the convenience store the night before had been unnecessary. I shared the observation with my father who agreed whole-heartedly. Yet, out of that incident, my father and I brokered a compromise concerning convenience stores. My father still loathed convenience stores, and thought anyone who patronized convenience stores on a regular basis was either desperate, deranged, or a crook. However, if regular stores were closed, and the end of the world were imminent, and the cow was about to jump over the moon, and I absolutely, positively had no other choice, then I could to go a convenience store after hours in order to buy end-of-the-world supplies, but only from midnight to twelve seventeen a.m.

Okay, so maybe it wasn't much of a compromise.

Where the Hell is Bootsy Devlin

The summer before my parents shipped me off to college, I worked as an intern at a local advertising agency. Although I had absolutely no experience, and no interest in research and development, I was promptly placed in that department.

My boss' name was Lincoln Nebraska Hayes, LN for short, though some of the staff called him Ellen behind his back. LN was in charge of company publicity and promotions. It was his job to develop the most outrageous marketing campaigns, in order to introduce new products into a demographically suitable region, and ultimately fatten the already fat wallets of the corporate executives. In the advertising world, LN was known as a *feel good* representative. He made the corporate brass *feel good* that they were blowing their year's advertising budget on a campaign that the average eight-year-old could develop. Indeed it was a gift. But initially, I did not grasp the true nature of LN's gift and considerable ability.

When I first met LN, I thought he was a rotund, profane huckster with all the charm of a pit bull. After I got to know him, I still thought he was a profane pit bull. However, I also recognized that he was perhaps one of the most brilliant salesmen I had ever met. I mean I'll never forget the campaign he launched that summer—the exhaustive search for one Bootsy Devlin. I'm sure that anyone who lived in my hometown during that summer recalls with a fond bit of nostalgia the Bootsy Devlin craze. And for those too young to remember, and who have no idea what I am talking about, then let me travel down memory lane, and relate with a bit of poetic license the origin and evolution of the Bootsy Devlin frenzy.

It was my second week on the job, and I was bored beyond belief. But in the span of a couple of days, my impression of LN, promotion, and the gullibility of the American public changed forever. On what I later called BD Day, LN summoned me to his office. Figuring that he wanted me to make copies, or refill his coffee mug, I took the scenic route to his corner think-tank. When I entered, he was impatiently tapping his eraser on his computer keyboard. Other interns and entry-level staff were seated around him.

"What took you so long?" he bellowed.

"Sorry," I replied apologetically.

"Well remember kid, in this business, millions can be made and lost in minutes. So it definitely does not pay to be an unmotivated slaggard."

The others in the room cast disparaging glances at me.

By their looks, and LN's tone it was quite apparent, that my standing in the firm had already become quite tenuous. Not wanting to be considered a slaggard of any kind, I replied, "I'll keep that in mind."

After that exchange, LN explained the task at hand. The firm had secured a new client—a reclusive multi-millionaire, who wanted our department to develop the next national fad—in the same tradition as the hula hoop, mood rings, and portable video game players.

"Are we ready to succeed?" LN asked, certain of our response.

Collectively we nodded.

LN asked for suggestions. Each one was dismissed, though not before LN explained his reasoning. LN quickly ruled out trinkets and keepsakes because while cheap to produce, the cost to market was substantial, and the margin for error was too great. He considered, but rejected objects or campaigns that would take weeks to roll-out and generate market buzz because the pay-off would be too slow. He pondered, but ultimately passed on daredevil stunts or tricks because of the potential legal ramifications, as well as, the relative short shelf life of such stunts or tricks. He discussed, but dismissed marketing schemes that were built around a holiday, or designed for some segment of the country because the timing and appeal would be self-limiting.

LN tossed dozens of wads of paper into a brown plastic wastebasket. He talked about former ad campaigns in order to gather a common thread among them. As part of that process, he turned toward me and asked, "You know what the public wants, kid?"

"Money."

"Money? Tell me, kid. How old are you?"

"Eighteen."

"Eighteen, ah I remember when I was eighteen, just like it was yesterday. I didn't know a damn thing either."

LN's response caught me by surprise. I could not fathom what the public could want besides money.

"What are you talking about?" I asked like a know-it-all teenager.

"Now don't get me wrong kid, money is nice and needed. But it's not a universal cure-all because some people will never have enough."

"So tell me what the public wants."

"It's simple. The public wants lies."

"Lies?"

"Yes, lies."

"But why?"

"The truth is too damn depressing."

"That's crazy."

"Crazy, you say? All right, let me give you an example—Your doctor finds out that you have an incurable disease—a disease so powerful that he or she determines that you have one day left to live. The doctor wrestles with whether he or she should tell you about the results of the lab tests. Tell me, under the circumstances, would you rather that the doctor tell you the truth that you have a day left to live, or lie to you, and say that everything is fine and wonderful?"

In an instant, I recognized the brilliance of the man called LN Hayes. Because, in an instant I understood the essence of the human spirit—given the choice of the cruel truth, or pleasant deception—a person will almost always opt for the pleasant deception. It is a philosophy that I embrace even today. At any rate, I am certain that I answered for the majority when I replied, "I'd rather that the doctor tell me everything is fine and wonderful."

"My point exactly. And so it makes no difference if the campaign we design is truthful or not, so long as it is simple, and presents a memorable image."

"Do you have any ideas on what might accomplish those bottom-line objectives."

"As a matter of fact I do. We create a campaign around the search for a completely fictitious character."

"How will creating a completely fictitious character work? People will have no idea who the character is—consequently, there will be no reason for them to get excited about the character."

"But you see kid, the key is to make sure that in creating the character, you give just enough details, and provide just enough life experiences, so that the average person can either relate to the character, or believe that at one time he or she knew the character."

I couldn't quite grasp how LN was going to create the groundswell and interest for a fictional character. But I was certain that LN was several steps ahead of me in developing the character.

"First," LN said, as he tapped a pencil eraser on a styrofoam cup, "We need a simple, yet catchy name."

We considered and rejected approximately a hundred names, including Steuben Ewing, Jedidiah Moss, and Riley Johnson. But none of them grabbed me, or more importantly, LN. Then in the span of a nano-second, the search for a name ended—LN settled on Bootsy Devlin.

When I asked LN why he chose Bootsy Devlin, he explained that the name would be a marketer's dream. Six letters in each name, so that it could be placed on wide array of merchandise from T-shirts to candy bars to beach towels. The name was easy to remember, easy to pronounce, and easy to spell.

LN smiled in such a way that the corners of his mouth curled, and his cheeks glowed. As he rubbed his hands together, LN said, "We'll spend a few days generating buzz and anticipation for Bootsy Devlin on the local level. Specifically, we're going to use the cable system's local origination channel to create, promote, and evolve the legend of Bootsy Devlin. Just watch. Within a week, everyone in town will be caught up in the story. Everyone will be talking about Bootsy Devlin. Then with the help of the media, we'll launch Bootsy nationally. Bootsy Devlin will be on everyone's lips. And when Bootsy Devlin hysteria is at a fever pitch, we will introduce and market merchandise associated with the return of the great Bootsy Devlin."

"Who the hell is Bootsy Devlin?" Bartholomew asked, not really wanting the answer.

"Don't you see?" he returned, in an almost disbelieving tone. "That's the beauty of this marketing campaign. Since there is no Bootsy Devlin, he can be whatever we want him to be. By creating a totally believable fictional character, the public fills in most of the details. We'll create just a skeleton of his life. Just enough to get the story moving. He'll be a mystery man, and yet be everyone's best friend."

"And what will get the story moving?"

LN scratched his forehead. "Yes, we need a hook. Something that will draw the young and the old, the rich and the poor, the city dweller and the country farmer."

Jeff Sampson, another summer intern chose that moment to enter LN's office. "What's going on?" he asked.

LN quickly reviewed the essential elements of the quickly developing Bootsy Devlin campaign.

"It'll never work."

"Kid, I've got ad campaigns older than you. So trust me when I say, I do not care what you think because I know what I know. And Bootsy Devlin will be the biggest, most successful marketing campaign since the hula hoop. When all is said and done, Bootsy Devlin will be more famous than Elvis."

"But Elvis was a real person."

"That's nothing more than a technicality."

"Elvis had countless hit records."

"Hell, that's not an obstacle, that's a challenge. Maybe we'll market Bootsy Devlin's Lost Christmas album. By the way, can anyone of you sing *White Christmas?*"

LN dismissed everyone in order to let his creative juices flow. Thirty minutes later, he triumphantly emerged from his office with the biographical skeleton on the life, times, and mysterious disappearance of Bootsy Devlin. Before the end of the day, LN had disseminated a press release to local media outlets, and the national wire, web, and cable services. Bootsy Devlin had been sighted. But the real question was whether it was another false report. And if Bootsy had returned after all these years, then why?

By six that evening, LN was at the local cable access channel discussing various aspects of the return of Bootsy Devlin.

After LN laid out the marketing blitz associated with Bootsy, the cable system manager turned over the plum eight o'clock slot on the origination channel to the *In Search of Bootsy Devlin Show.*

Sara Stone, an entertainment columnist for one of the local weekly papers, jumped at the chance to host the show. She believed that the Bootsy phenomenon would propel her to a national cable network show. Sara embraced the concept of Bootsy from the beginning. In a calm tone, she briefed the audience on the supposed origins of Bootsy Devlin, and his claim to fame. He was a blues singer extraordinaire. He had a hit tune, *If I am So Sad, then Why is She So Glad, that I am So Bad?* Sara played a bit of the recording. Actually LN had paid a homeless person, to record the song in one session.

The grovely tone of the homeless person, and the cheap acoustics lent an oldies quality to the song, that was a marketing stroke of genius.

Anyway, Bootsy Devlin dropped off the face of the earth some twenty-five years ago, for reasons unknown. Perhaps he had died penniliess in some gin joint. Then again, maybe fame had been too overwhelming for him, and he just decided to go underground.

"—And so Bootsy Devlin would have just become another trivia question, if it hadn't been for a fan, a Mr. LN Hayes, recently asking the question, *Where is Bootsy Devlin?* And that is what I am asking tonight—has anyone seen Bootsy Devlin in the last twenty-five years. If you have, then please contact us on our open line—"

Sara noted the phone number. Afterward, she discussed other bits and pieces of *common* knowledge from Bootsy's sparse biography. LN was off camera, smiling at her in an approving manner.

"Do you expect anyone to call into the show?" I asked LN, still naieve to the secret rules of marketing.

"Just wait," LN said, as he glanced at his watch.

As if on cue, the phone rang. Sara remarked, "Well we have our first call of the evening." She answered the phone and asked, "And to whom am I speaking?"

Instead of a human voice, there was a long and obscenely loud belch or warble of indeterminent origin. Finally after twenty or thirty seconds, a man obviously drunk answered, "Billy Jackson, but everybody calls me Mule."

"Mule?"

"That's right, Mule."

LN smiled, as his brain churned out hundreds of potential promotional opportunities for Bootsy Devlin.

Sara asked, "So what can I do for you, Mule?"

"You've been talking about Bootsy Devlin, and where he is."

"That's right."

"Yeah, yeah. Well, I saw him just the other day. He was at a Lime Green Store over near Battery Park. He was buying a forty-eight ounce brew and a pack of smokes."

"Really?"

"Yeah, yeah. He stops over there about twice a week. Sometimes he kicks back and we talk for awhile."

"About what?"

"Stuff."

"Just stuff?"

"Yeah, stuff mostly. Sometimes politics. But mostly just stuff."

Stuff indeed. The Bootsy Devlin craze officially started that evening. I shook LN's hand. "Just listen to Sara," he whispered.

Sara continued her over-the-air interview with Mule. "Has Bootsy ever discussed why he disappeared at the peak of his popularity?"

"That's just it. He never really wanted to be famous. 'Presidents of countries are famous,' Bootsy would say. 'Not blues singers.'"

"Has anyone else at the Lime Green store recognized Bootsy Devlin?"

"Not a soul. And that's the way he likes it. After tonight, I suspect that he won't be dropping by the Lime Green Store anymore. But that's okay. Everyone has to move at one point or another. And I'm sure that someday, I'll see him again."

At the time I was not aware that Mule was another person paid to expand the legend and the myth of Bootsy Devlin. LN had promised the unemployed actor some voice-over work on another ad campaign he was developing. Again, the promotional tool was a stroke of genius. That one set-up phone call unleashed a wave of other would-be Bootsy confidants. They contradicted Mule's assessment of Bootsy's reasons for running from the spotlight. That actually was okay. The more opinions on the origins of Bootsy, the more ways to mine the quickly evolving Bootsy Devlin story. The next day the local radio stations were flooded with calls requesting Bootsy Devlin's number one hit.

I expected that Bootsy Devlin would create a ripple among the local media. But, in my wildest dreams, I never imagined the nation becoming obsessed with the quest to find Bootsy Devlin. As LN had predicted, the wire and Internet news services jumped on the story. Within two weeks, Bootsy Devlin was page one, above-the-fold material. From Singapore to San Antonio to Sarasota, thousands of people claimed to have seen Bootsy Devlin. But everyone's description of Bootsy was a bit different, and no one seemed to have a photograph of the *real, genuine, Bootsy Devlin.*

LN jetted back and forth across the country to promote more than a dozen campaigns associated with Bootsy Devlin. In Topeka, he kicked off the Last Place on the Earth Where Bootsy Would Visit Contest. Followers of Bootsy voted on the community that appeared least Bootsy-like. Montpelier, Vermont won that dubious distinction handily. Of course, there were the obligatory Bootsy-sightings with Elvis, Abraham Lincoln, Butch Cassidy, and D.B. Cooper. From Auckland, New Zealand to Nome, Alaska there were signs and placards that read *Bootsy Slept Here* or *Bootsy's My Bud!*

Bootsy was a bona fide celebrity without ever having set so much as a foot inside a recording studio or music theater. He transcended cultural and ethnic differences. He was an everyman for everywhere and everytime.

It seemed as though everyone was wearing a *Where the Hell is Bootsy Devlin* T-Shirt. And if it wasn't a T-shirt, then there were posters and placards proclaiming *Free Bootsy Devlin* and *Bootsy Devlin was last seen at the Lime and Green Store.* In every store, on every sidewalk, entrepreneurs from across the country hawked Bootsy Devlin merchandise. One enterprising vendor told me that he had grossed more than twenty thousand dollars in less than three days of sales. As a commodity, Bootsy was better than gold, and approaching the status of platinum.

However, no one was as successful as LN at capturing the essence of Bootsy, and in the process capturing the lionshare of the revenue and publicity. LN tapped into all media, all senses, all markets. Nothing, and I mean nothing was too crass to be sold. LN's personal favorite was the Bootsy Devlin potato peeler that sold for $1.98 at the Lime and Green Store.

As part of my duties that summer, I co-ordinated the one and only official Bootsy Devlin web site. There were literally hundreds of other so-called official sites. But whosbootsy.com was the only site that contained the "factual" bits and pieces of the strange and mysterious life and times of Bootsy Devlin. The web site averaged a million hits per day. The revenues garnered from advertisers on the web site, could have fed a community of twenty thousand residents for an entire year.

Through the web site, LN provided a virtual Internet catalog of Bootsy Devlin merchandise. For a cool grand, a person could purchase an exceptionally rare authentic autograph of Bootsy. There were two staffers who worked overtime filling all the orders for the rare autograph. Other merchandise included Bootsy's shoes, and his first car. The vehicle carried a sticker price of over one hundred thousand dollars. It was actually a car that LN had bought years ago from a widow from Modesto. He applied a few well placed dents, and spilled dark coffee on the cloth seats. An antique car dealer from Vancouver snapped up the car in less than a week.

As host of The Bootsy Devlin Show, Sara Stone was an instant hit. In just over a week, the Bootsy Devlin Show generated the highest national ratings ever for a locally-produced cable show. In less than two weeks, the Bootsy Devlin Show was satellite-delivered to cable systems across the country. In that time span, LN secured an impressive array of advertisers, both national and regional. Again, the advertisers paid record sums to showcase their products and services on The Bootsy Devlin Show.

By the end of the third week, one of the local radio stations sponsored a Where is Bootsy Devlin Rally. To my utter amazement, over twenty thousand people crowded into the makeshift ampitheater at

McGregor Park. With amusement rides, and funnel cakes, there was a carnival atmosphere to the Rally. The hottest selling item on that windswept afternoon was the *Official Unauthorized Biography of Bootsy Devlin*. The book, all one hundred twenty-six pages of it, delved into every conceivable aspect of Bootsy Devlin's supposed life. The superband Trillitious sang *The Ballad of Bootsy Devlin*.

In no time, the tabloids exposed and exploited new revelations from Bootsy's stormy past. There were allegations that Bootsy was the last person to see Elvis alive. There was a claim that Bootsy Devlin fathered a child with K Sara the supermodel. K Sara, for her part, would neither confirm, nor deny the claim. Certainly, K Sara was not above riding the enormous wave of publicity that the Bootsy phenomenon generated. However, the most outrageous fabrication had to be that Bootsy Devlin was an alien from Mars. According to the article, Bootsy had lived off and on in notorious Area 51 for the last twelve years.

Not far behind were the other news and entertainment magazines. Spending considerable manpower and financial resources, every major news organization combed the backwoods for interesting tidbits on Bootsy's rise to glory, and inglorious fall into oblivion. More than one journalist remarked that the Pulitzer competition should create a new category for Bootsy Devlin coverage. Of course there was an official media corps that staked the Battery Park Lime and Green Store. But as Mule had predicted, Bootsy Devlin never returned.

Everyone wanted a piece of the action. The licensing and marketing rights for Bootsy apparel and trinkets grew each day for several weeks. The public's appetite for Bootsy wear was insatiable.

There were Bootsy groupies and wannabes and possiblees at every turn. Even Hollywood embraced the craze. Stars discussed their not so brief encounters with Bootsy Devlin. Some accused Bootsy of being temperamental. However, most shared touching, but fabricated, memories and vignettes of a man without a history or past. There was the obligatory movie deal.

Like all fads however, this one ran its course, and was over in less than six months. In less than a half of a year however, the quest to find Bootsy Devlin made LN Hayes a millionaire several times over. I received no glory, and just a fraction of the money. But, with my bonus check, I bought my first convertible. The roadster was fire red, and faster than warp speed seven.

Every now and then I run across someone who remembers the Bootsy Devlin craze. Hell, I even met a couple of lost souls who claimed *to be* Bootsy.

But Bootsy was fiction pure and simple.

And if anyone asks me "Where is Bootsy Devlin now?"

I simply respond, "The hell if I know."

Food Poisoning

To anyone who has suffered through food poisoning, I offer my heartfelt condolences. There are few experiences in a person's life that are more gut-wrenching, or cause as much physical upheaval. The year after my college graduation, as I enjoyed the fruits of true batchelorhood, I contracted food poisoning. About the fifth time to the bathroom, I swore off food—forever.

Anyway, the next day, I truly felt as though the end of the world, at least my world, was near. It was a bright sunny, summery day outside, but through my bloodshot eyes, I could not see past the toilet.

My stomach had succumbed to the revolution long ago, there should not have been anything left in it. Yet, it still griped, and churned, and did somersaults. When I thought that it could not get any worse, it did—the phone rang. I should have let it ring, and let the voice mail record the message. But somewhere in my food-deprived delirium, I chose to answer the phone. It was then, and continues to be one of my all time biggest mistakes.

"Hello," I said in a drained, dehydrated voice.

"Michael, is that you? Are you all right?"

It figured that my father, the one person that I absolutely did not want to talk to during a gastro-intestinal episode, would be the one person that would call me to see how I was doing.

"Afternoon, pops," I returned, trying to mask my illness.

My father was not fooled. "What's wrong, son?"

"Nothing."

"Nothing. You sound like that time you ate that cleanser by mistake."

Well, I should not have been surprised. It had been almost two months since my father had mentioned the *cleanser* incident. Never mind that it happened when I was five. Never mind that I mistook cleanser for sugar and placed a pinch in my mouth. Nevermind that it was the last time that I made such a mistake. Nevermind all of that. For my father, it was a defining moment—that from time to time, I made wrong decisions with respect to food. Anyway, that's another story.

"I'm not feeling too well, pops," I confessed.

"You got the flu?"

"No, I don't have the flu."

"That's good. You shouldn't have the flu since you take a flu shot every year." My father paused, then asked, "By the way, you did take your flu shot this year, didn't you?"

"Yes."

"And you're drinking enough water everyday?"

"I'm doing my best." Actually, my father believed it was absolutely essential to drink sixty-four ounces of water a day. I on the other hand, did not want to drink sixty-four ounces of any liquid in a day, especially water. When I drank, I craved taste, carbonation, and caffeine. So when I informed pops that *I was doing my best*, I actually meant that I had consumed at least one five-ounce toddler cup of water in the past forty-eight hours.

"Maybe you got a bad cold. I hear that's been going around. Have you been coughing lately? Because if you have been coughing, I can recommend a new cough syrup that really works."

"No cough, and no cold, pops."

"Then is it your hay fever? You know that you haven't had that for a while—you're probably overdue."

"No, it's not hay fever. I don't have any congestion or watery eyes."

My father intended grilling me on every ailment, and malady known and unknown until he discovered what was causing my illness. I could play twenty questions with him, or cut to the chase and tell him the cause of my illness. In the interest of time and energy, I chose the latter. "No, I think I got food poisoning."

"Food poisoning?"

"Yeah."

"When did you get it?"

"Last night."

"What did you eat?"

I did not want to talk about food in general, or in particular what I had eaten the day before. Yet, I realized that my father would continue to ask, until I answered him. So, I wet my chapped lips and replied, "I had steak with zucchini squash."

"Did the steak have any sauce on it?"

"Any sauce?" I gasped. To my horror, I realized that I had just opened a pandora's box for my father to explore.

"Yeah, did the food have any sauce on it?"

"I don't recall," I replied both weakly and unconvincingly.

"Come on son, this is your pops. You ate steak less than twenty-four hours ago, and you don't remember if the steak was smothered in sauce."

"My steak wasn't smothered in sauce."

"Aha! So you admit that you had steak with sauce on it."

"No."

"No?"

"No. What I was saying was that when I have had steak with sauce on it, the sauce was light and on the sauce."

"So there was no sauce on the steak."

"There was no sauce on the steak."

"Are you sure?"

"Yes, I'm sure."

"Now you know better than to eat food with any sauce on it."

"I know now," I mumbled. Actually, I always knew. But in a moment of post-gastric distress, I gave my father yet another forum to vent, rant, rave, and complain about foreign foods. For my pops considered a sauce as anything that was added to a dish, other than salt and pepper. He was a food traditionalist—one who believed that mustard could wreck a person's stomach as much as a curried pepper sauce.

"So you're sure you didn't have any sauce on your steak?"

My father was relentless. He was single-minded. But above all, he was retired, with nothing but time on his hands, which meant he could grill me like hamburger over an open flame until I was well done. I felt a warm surge envelope me—either I had a fever, or my father's questions were starting to affect me. "I'm sure I didn't have any sauce on my steak, pops."

"Did you have any dessert?"

"I had pineapple upside down cake."

"Was the pineapple fresh or canned?"

"The pineapple was fresh, pops."

"I hope the pineapple was fresh because if the pineapple was not fresh, it could do a number on your stomach."

"Pops, I said the pineapple was fresh." I wasn't sure how much longer I could withstand my father's persistent interrogation. I was weakening, and he knew it.

My father pressed forward with his questions. "How about the juice? Was the pineapple juice fresh?"

I assumed that the pineapple juice was fresh. My father assumed nothing. He was a skeptic's skeptic who took nothing for granted.

"Sometimes," he began, "they use fresh pineapple, but day-old juice. That can cause problems too. You never can be too careful, son."

"It wasn't the pineapple juice, pops. The juice was fresh. The pineapple was fresh. The icing was fresh. All the ingredients in the cake were fresh. And the cake itself was fresh and quite delicious. I'm sorry I lost it in last night's marathon session in the bathroom."

"So you're sure it wasn't the pineapple?"

"I'm sure."

"And you're sure it wasn't sauce on your steak?"

Again, he was asking questions about the steak.

"There was no sauce on the steak."

"Because if there was any kind of sauce on your steak, it could cause problems with your stomach later. I remember your Uncle Al. He had steak with some sort of creamed onion sauce on it. That sauce tore up his stomach. He ended up in the emergency room at County Hospital. They had to pump his stomach. Now his stomach gets queasy, if he even sees an onion sauce. It's because of incidents like that—that I always ask you if any of your meals are served with a sauce of any type on it. So you didn't, did you?"

"Didn't what pops?"

"Have sauce on your steak. It's a losing proposition son. The sauce wins almost always. And what do you have to show for it—a long, fitful night in a bathroom. So you didn't, did you?"

"All right, all right," I finally confessed. "The steak had a wild mushroom sauce on it."

"Why didn't you just eat beach sand and be done with it? It would have had the same effect."

"Pops."

"I'm serious, son. What would possess you to do a thing like that? Don't I send you articles once a month on food poisoning, and ways to avoid it."

Not only did my father send me articles on food poisoning, but he taped television news segments on food poisoning for my later review, and even bought me a book entitled, *Don't Touch that Sauce—Ways to Avoid Food Poisoning*. At that moment, I didn't have the nerve to tell him that I had trashed, and thrown away almost every bit of information he had provided me over the years. If I had

read chapter five of that book, I would have read in big bold letters—**UNDER NO CIRCUMSTANCES SHOULD YOU EAT STEAK
WITH WILD MUSHROOM SAUCE.** But of course, I hadn't read
chapter five, and my stomach couldn't read, so I suffered for my
trangressions. But I couldn't admit to my father that he had been
right—at least not just yet. "I've had wild mushroom sauce on steak
before, pops. This is the first time that I have had any problems."

"It only takes one time, doesn't it son?"

Having no choice but to be contrite, I said, "Right, pops."

"Well let me ask you this son. Have you finally learned your lesson?"

"I sure have pops. No more sauces for me."

"Well as a reminder I want you to watch a documentary on cable
tonight entitled *Restaurant Nightmares—Sauces Run Wild.* After that
I doubt you'll ever order another sauce."

I watched the documentary, and must admit that it scared the living sauce out of me. I was finally a believer, and vowed never to eat
another sauce. But I didn't stop there. I started a petition to rid the
world of sauces—of all kinds. No sauce could be trusted. My father
signed the petition. I stopped unsuspecting shoppers in front of the
Sliver Produce Market, and asked them to join in my universal campaign. There were some true believers among the group—those that
had seen the documentary, and felt that the erradication of sauces
was the only sensible goal. But most people thought I was crazy, and
walked away from me, or tossed fruits and vegetables at me. I was a
reformed sauce person for an extended period of time—almost two
weeks. But the spirit grew weak, and I indulged in an Asian hazelnut
sauce.

For once I triumphed over the sauce. There was no night of or
morning after suffering or distress.

Upon hearing of my latest sauce escapade, my father shook his
head. Without question he thought I was nuts.

I wasn't nuts, just hungry. Oh well, until the next time.

Gifts 1

In my younger years, I was the poster person for last minute shoppers. I ridiculed anyone who dared to buy gifts before the last minute. Why expend any energy or effort buying a gift several weeks before a birthday, anniversary, or other festive occasion, when the day of the special event would be more than adequate. I pitied those poor souls who agonized for weeks over whether their gift was the perfect gift.

Having children however, taught me the value of shopping early for Christmas—like no later than New Year's for the following Christmas. There was always a problem with securing the hot toy or gadget in any given year. Santa and his elves did their best, but sometimes, even Santa could not meet the laws of supply and demand.

But I digress. Malcolm had already E-mailed Santa an extensive Christmas list complete with charts, graphics, notations, and alternatives. However, he needed to save a few items for family members to purchase. So I wasn't surprised when Malcolm sat beside me to discuss what he wanted for Christmas.

"I've been extra good this year, dad."

"You don't need to butter me up, son. It's Christmas. Is there something special that you want dad to get you for Christmas?"

"There certainly is dad. I want a Clogster."

"Sure son, if you want a Clogster for Christmas, I'll make sure you'll have one."

"Thanks dad." Malcolm hugged me as if I was the most special dad on earth—then he trotted off to his bedroom.

A Clogster? What on earth was a Clogster? I thought it might be a plumbing devise disguised as a toy. My brother Tony informed me that the Clogster was just the hottest toy to be marketed in the last hundred years. I found that hard to believe. He handed me an article straight from the Internet. The story noted that in the span of just one year, the TB Tickler Toy Company had risen from complete obscurity to the hottest toy company in the universe based on the strength of the Clogster.

The article contained a photograph of the Clogster. After staring at the photo for at least a couple of minutes, I re-iterated my earlier question—What on earth was a Clogster? It appeared to be a large ball of twine wrapped in a red bandana. I could not imagine that the Clogster cost more than fifty cents to produce. The list price however was twenty-two dollars and seventy-five cents. At that price, I seriously considered setting up my own sweatshop and manufacturing the almost identical *Bogster* for just twenty dollars even. But as Tony pointed out, each Clogster came with its own certificate of authenticity that was supposedly priceless.

With precisely five shopping days left before Christmas, I realized that under the best of circumstances, it would be difficult to find a Clogster. I decided that it would be in my best interest if I made a few preliminary calls to determine the availability of the Clogster. I called the manufacturer, and was told that they did not sell to individuals. I implied that it was for someone who was in real need. The receptionist told me that she had heard every sad story at least once an hour, and that my story was neither particularly sad nor believable. She wished me a Merry Christmas before slamming down the receiver. Rebuffed in my initial approach, I tried a different tactic. I called two super warehouse stores, three specialty toy stores, and a discount department store. None had the Clogster. None expected to receive another shipment of Clogsters before Christmas. None knew where I might find a Clogster, though three stores said I might try Jungle Mall. I winced. So I would have to fight the holiday throngs at Jungle Mall. I'd sooner wrestle an alligator over a side of beef, than visit Jungle Mall during the last six weeks of the year. But with virtually no other choices available, I fortified myself with a double dose of warm apple cider, then drove to Jungle Mall.

Jungle Mall had a four level parking deck with over two thousand parking spaces, and open parking for another three thousand cars. On that day, five days before Christmas, assorted sedans, mini-vans, sport utility vehicles, and pick-ups of every color size, and shape filled every available space. There were both local police, and mall police directing traffic to outlying parking areas. In the end, I parked in remote lot #6, and took two shuttle buses to reach the western drop-off point for the mall. That left me still a half mile from the mall, so I walked with a wall of other shoppers to the mall's western entrance.

Before I entered Jungle Mall, I said a silent prayer to Saint Jerry, patron saint of fools and last minute shoppers. I was pretty sure that Saint Jerry answered my prayer by telling me that I should go home, drink some non-alcoholic egg nog, and reconsider my obviously irrational actions. But like always, I didn't listen, and pressed forward.

Jungle Mall provided a fitting testament to the grand excesses of capitalism. Four hundred twenty-one stores were cramped into a four-story urban mall. Internet on-line shopping might be convenient. But Jungle Mall billed itself as a total entertainment experience. Its brochures boasted that a person could walk the equivalent of five miles if each store was visited. Moreover, as Jungle Mall's ads were so fond of saying, *If you can't buy it at Jungle Mall, then you can't buy it anywhere.* Perhaps you couldn't buy an island at Jungle Mall, but you could buy an airplane ticket, or a cruise package to travel to one of three thousand islands. To put the mall's buying options in perspective, with three million six hundred thousand square feet of retail space under one roof, and another four hundred thousand square feet of shops housed in the adjoining power center, there were eight department stores, twenty-nine shoe stores, a forty-screen movie complex, and four separate food concourses providing over eighty different restaurants. There was a store that sold antique swords, and another shop that offered hand-me-downs from yesterday's stars and disgraced politicians. Most importantly for my purposes, Jungle Mall contained a dozen toy and game stores.

I thought it would be so easy. In retrospect, it was one of the biggest mistakes that I had ever made.

Nothing But Toys had Clogsters yesterday, but not today. The staff at Madhouse Toys said that they had sold out of Clogsters two weeks ago and did not expect to get another shipment before Christmas. Each store that I visited gave me the same sad story.

An hour later, I was down to my last option. The Clogster had to be at The Murphs Toys. At twenty-five thousand square feet, The Murphs Toys was large for a mall-based toy store.

I stopped by the information counter. It wasn't even Christmas yet, and frazzled parents and relatives were exchanging toys, gifts, and other holiday-related merchandise.

"What do you mean, that this coupon for the Super Secret Spy Plane has expired?" a father with bulging eyes, and a receding hairline asked.

A small child waved a cloth doll and said, "This dolly is coming apart at the seams. Do you have any more?"

A woman dressed in a business outfit, talked to the second assistant manager. "I will not take no for an answer," she said. "I know that all toy stores hold back a few of the hottest toys for VIPs. So I know that you have the Alberta Doll. If you bring it out now, I won't make a scene."

"But I want the Creepy Blocks," a young boy whined.

A woman with hair pointing north, south, east, west, and all routes in between, grabbed the boy by the scuff of the neck and said,

"You'll just have to see if Santa brings you any Creepy Blocks, although I don't know why. Santa knows that you have been naughty this past week."

"But I'll be extra good until Christmas," the boy whimpered.

"It might be too late," the woman said, as she ushered the boy out of the store.

Like a child lost in a maze, I wandered aimlessly, searching for a stock clerk. Finally, I spotted one between aisle three and four. I tapped her shoulder. "Excuse me," I said, frazzled, but trying to remain in the Christmas spirit. "Do you have the Clogster?"

The young woman turned and snarled. Clearly she was offended by my actions. "Say, you don't know me well enough to touch me," she replied with an accent and an attitude.

"I'm sorry. It was a mistake. I was just trying to get your attention."

The store clerk rolled her eyes, then closed them and sighed in an agitated fashion. "Just make sure that you don't touch me." She paused, then asked, "Now what do you want?"

"I wanted to know if you had the Clogster?"

"What kind of parent are you?" she asked, her neck rotating as if it were on a swivel stool.

Surprised and upset at her question, I replied, "Excuse me?"

"You wait until the last minute to go Christmas shopping for your kids, and then have the brazen audacity to ask me if we still have the Clogster—a toy that just happens to be the most popular toy of all time. You must be one of those part-time dads."

"Look, do you have the Clogster or not?"

"We got our last shipment before Christmas this morning. But all two hundred fifty of them were grabbed within minutes."

"Well where were they?"

"They were on a table at the end of aisle seventeen. But like I said, they were all sold hours ago."

The clerk was probably right, but I had nothing to lose. So I rushed to aisle seventeen. At the far end of the aisle, I saw the 'Today's hot item table.' From my vantage point, I could not tell whether there were any Clogsters buried in a mountain of stuffed animals, jigsaw puzzles, and video games.

Some child removed a cuddly stuffed bunny from the table. The removal of the bunny revealed a Clogster. It was mine for the taking, or so I thought. About ten feet from the Clogster, I spied another individual racing toward the table. It was an elderly woman, no doubt a grandmother intent on buying the Clogster for her own grandtyke.

Granny and I froze just a few feet from the table. In a scene reminiscent from a 1950's era black and white western movie, we stared at one another while we slowly circled the table. Maybe it was my imagination, but I could have sworn that I heard the faint din of the climatic music from *High Noon*. No matter. I figured that it was only a matter of time before the Clogster was in my control. After all, Grandma stood no chance of retrieving the one remaining Clogster in the free world.

Grandma lunged for the Clogster. She was quick and wily, but not nimble enough. I leapt for the toy a half-second later and landed directly on top her. She wheezed. At that time, I made an important discovery. She might have been short and thin, but by no means was she frail. She gave me the heave-ho, and I ended up on the floor. She laughed, and said derisively, "Lightweight."

Having a ninety-something great-great-grandmother made me look like an out-of-shape, emasculated wimp, made my blood boil. Unfortunately, that did not change the fact that she currently possessed what in all likelihood was the last Clogster in the entire universe.

I dove toward the old lady, and tackled her near the antique doll display case. We rolled over and over like loose tops. She clutched the Clogster as though her life depended on keeping possession of that treasured toy. But I was relentless. I was determined. I was in a half-nelson. Grandma applied a head-lock on me, and demanded that I cry, "Uncle."

It would be a cold day in Honolulu before I would subject myself to such an indignity. That day came twenty seconds later. As Grandma's applied pressure on my neck caused me to nearly black out, I shouted, "Uncle, Aunt, Mommy, and Daddy!"

Grandma loosened her death grip, and slowly my vision returned. I sighed in utter despair. I had been soundly defeated by a woman who wore a pacemaker, and appeared so frail, that a strong wind might break her in two. But there she was standing over me, gloating with a winner's disdain for the defeated. "The Clogster is mine," she remarked, as she claimed her reward.

I gathered that Grandma would not listen to reason, or sad stories, or threats now. Grandma was from the old school which meant that I had to entice her with something that carried a sentimental value. So I asked, "How much will it take to buy the Clogster from you?"

"You making a monetary offer, chump?"

Grandma had a bad attitude, and a bad mouth. I briefly considered sucker-punching her and running off with the Clogster. But my conscience, or perhaps the fear of being humiliated again prevailed. And so, I replied as any chump would, "Yes, I am making a monetary offer."

"I'm not interested," she snarled.

"I'll give you forty-five dollars for that toy. That's more than twice the list price."

Grandma returned with a surly venom in her voice, "Not only are you a chump, but you're also cheap."

"How about sixty dollars? You can buy another Clogster, and have enough left over to buy a padded bra for your sagging breasts."

"Don't make me have to jack-hammer you into next week," Grandma returned as she grabbed my collar.

All right, all right, I shouldn't have thrown in the comment about her breasts. But having been so thoroughly humiliated on the field of battle, I saw it as perhaps my only chance at redeeming what small shreds of dignity that remained. I stepped back from the old lady (far enough, so that she could not lunge at me). "Okay," I said, "Forget the last comment. I'll give you a hundred dollars for that Clogster."

"What did you say, son? You must be talking a foreign language, because I didn't understand a word you said."

Grandma was really starting to irritate me. Under no circumstances was I going to pay more than a hundred dollars for a piece of fluff that probably cost ten cents to make. I'd buy my son a motorbike or a sports-team, or an Internet company, or anything other than a Clogster. He might be upset for a minute or two, but I know he would appreciate the substitute gift. Sure—and Richard Nixon was innocent, right?

Grandma clutched the Clogster and said, "I knew you didn't have the money. You probably couldn't have even paid retail for this toy."

Didn't have the money? Didn't have the money? I know I didn't hear that from the poster girl for Wrinkles Anonymous. Okay so maybe I wouldn't have had the money, if I hadn't received my paycheck the day before. But I had the money now, and I resented any implication to the contrary. I pulled out my wallet, and removed every bit of paper currency from it. I held two hundred fifty dollars in my left hand, and waved it in front of Grandma. "What do you think about that? I've got plenty of money."

Apparently, Grandma felt the same way because in one fluid motion, she grabbed the money from my hand, and tossed me the Clogster. She stuffed the ten twenties and five tens in her bra, then walked away, muttering about what an idiot I was for paying two hundred fifty dollars for a ten-cent notion.

At that point she could have called me anything but late for dinner because I finally had what I had set out for—a genuine Clogster.

I stood in the checkout line for another hour, and paid for the Clogster with everyone's favorite currency, plastic.

Back in the mall, I clutched my shopping bag as though it contained national security secrets. I made sure that no one got within snatching distance of me. I had fought tooth and nail, but now I had the Clogster in my possession, and I had no intention of anyone else taking it away from me.

On my way home, I stopped by a self-serve wrapping booth and paid five dollars for a box, wrapping paper and bows. In just under thirty minutes I taped pieces of festive paper around a much too large box. I wasn't much on wrapping, but I was sure that contents of the box would make up for the wrinkled and torn paper.

I placed the gift box under our seven-foot Fraiser fir. Even with almost a hundred boxes under the tree, my tattered box stood out. Millicent told Malcolm that there was a special gift under the tree from daddy. Malcolm shrugged his shoulders, but made no attempt to inspect or shake the box.

As is tradition in my family, we opened gifts at the crack of dawn on Christmas. Malcolm opened his presents first and received the obligatory tie from the Womacks, and handkerchiefs for any occasion from the Andersons. The last box he opened was mine. He smiled at me, as though he knew what was in the box. But he took his own sweet time opening it. Finally, he removed the Clogster from the box. He smiled again and took the Clogster into another room.

Funny. I was expecting Malcolm to exhibit more outright joy when he pulled the Clogster out of the gift box. But he didn't. He just started playing with the Clogster. I somehow felt cheated by Malcolm's reserved reaction. I wanted, and quite frankly I believed, I deserved a two hundred fifty dollar yell of appreciation from Malcolm.

Unlike video games, and mechanical toys, the Clogster was a quiet toy.

Malcolm played with the Clogster for the better part of an hour. Suddenly the expected happened, the Clogster broke—I guess it would be more accurate to state that the Clogster just sort of separated into seemingly a thousand pieces. I moaned. I was certain that Malcolm would be upset and cry and pitch a fit because his prize toy and possession had not lasted even one hour before becoming worn and torn like so much used Christmas wrapping paper.

But the untimely and premature demise of the Clogster did not seem to phase Malcolm in the least. He placed what was left of the Clogster back in the gift box and moved on to another toy.

"You're not upset with the Clogster breaking up?"

"Not really."

"Oh."

Malcolm sensed my bewilderment. He stopped, and said, "Pops, what did you expect? It was a Christmas toy, for goodness sake. A turtle crossing a fourteen lane superhighway at rush hour has a longer life expectancy than the Clogster had."

While Malcolm's observation was correct, I somehow felt cheated that the Clogster did not last a full day, and that Malcolm did not show more appreciation for the toy. After all I went through to acquire an over-priced piece of fluff, I had wanted the Clogster to last long enough for Malcolm to give it to his first-born. And I wanted Malcolm to shout from the rafters at his good fortune for receiving a Clogster as a Christmas gift.

But as I said, Malcolm was right. Toys were not supposed to last nowadays.

Gifts 2

During junior high school I handcrafted a ceramic ashtray for my mother. Not just any ceramic ashtray mind you. My ash tray was a brown square face, with two dots for eyes, a flat clay attachment for a nose, a long, hardened clay cylinder that in some primitive countries resembled a tongue, and a sort of round opening that doubled as a mouth and repository for ashes. I remember my art teacher gave me sort of a quizzical look, as if to say—why would I waste good clay on such a monstrosity. But I was artistically ignorant, and believed that my ashtray was not only an exquisite work of art, but also an ashtray worthy of an entire room in one of the most exclusive museums.

That other souls did not see or comprehend the genius of my artistic expression did not bother me. For this ceramic ashtray was not necessarily for the masses. Rather, this ceramic ashtray was for my mother. Though she did not smoke, I was certain that she would appreciate the simple texture, and universal theme. And I was certain that my mother would display the ashtray in the living room. I could remember several homes where ashtrays were displayed, but never used. It was an unwritten law of household etiquette I supposed that large, antique, or artistically impressive ashtrays should be seen, but not used. Obviously, my ashtray qualified under the last standard—artistically impressive.

After carefully wrapping the ashtray in bubble wrap, I rushed home to present my mother with my latest gift.

"So how was your day, darling?"

My mother often called me *darling*. To this day, it warms my heart to hear those words from her. On that day however, I hugged my mother, then said, "Close your eyes, moms. I have a surprise for you."

"All right, baby," my mother said, as she complied with my request.

I removed the bubble wrap. "Now hold out your hands."

Again she complied with my instructions. I placed the ashtray in her cupped hands.

"Now open your eyes."

My mother opened her eyes. There was this curious look on her face that seemed to convey a sense of confusion. "You made this for me?" she asked, not knowing whether to smile politely, laugh, cry, or recoil in horror.

"Yes, moms. Just for you."

She patted my forehead, then embraced me as only a mother could.

"Do you know what it is?"

"I certainly do, Michael."

From my mother's still quizzical look, I should have guessed that that she had no clue as to what I had given to her as a gift. But I was so excited about my creation, that I let her off the hook by saying, "Isn't it a great ashtray?"

"It is the most special ashtray I have ever received," she replied sincerely.

"So where are you going to place it, moms?"

"I'll have to find, just the special place for it, darling." With that, my mother left the ceramic ashtray on the living room coffee table.

At the end of the evening, the cigarette ashtray was still on the living room coffee table. Moms had not smashed the ashtray into a thousand million pieces, and then ground those pieces into ceramic dust in order to sprinkle over the flowers in the planter. She had accepted my ashtray as a work of art.

I thought my mother would designate and reserve the coffee table as the permanent repository of the cigarette ashtray. I fell asleep pleased at the thought that my gift to my mother had been so honored. As it turned out, it was a short-lived honor. For the next morning I woke up early and tip-toed downstairs to the living room to admire my artistic masterpiece. I expected that the morning sunlight would cast an aura around my ashtray. But the coffee table was clean as a blank slate, and there was neither a sign nor trace of my beautiful gift. My first thought was that someone had stolen my ashtray. That had to be the answer. Some heartless crook must have broken into our house, and searched the entire house before deciding to take just one item, my award winning ashtray. In my mind that was the only logical explanation.

My next thought was that we had to report the theft to the police, so that law enforcement officials could exert their considerable skills in capturing the despicable lowlife who stole the most valuable piece of artwork in the house. On my way to my parent's bedroom, however, I found the ashtray, partially hidden under two-week-old newspapers. I was relieved to have located the missing ashtray, especially since it could have been accidentally placed in the recycling bin with the other paper products.

After a few minutes, I wondered who placed the ashtray under the newspapers. It was a mystery that was worth unraveling.

But there was another task that required my immediate attention. Convinced that I would be fulfilling my mother's wishes, I returned the ashtray to the living room coffee table, where it belonged.

Before breakfast my mother spied the ashtray. In between mixing batter for pancakes, and pouring fresh-squeezed orange juice, she asked, "Who put Michael's ashtray back on the living room coffee table?"

I returned with innocent charm, "That would be me, mom."

My mother forced a faint smile. "I thought I told you that I wanted to place your ashtray someplace truly special."

"You did, mom. And when you placed it on the living room coffee table, I could think of no more special place in the house, right?"

My mother brushed my forehead in that special motherly way. I should have known then that she had no intention of keeping my ashtray in a prominent location in the house. But I loved my mother and believed her when she said, "There is an even more important place than the living room coffee table."

"And where would that be, mom?"

"In my bedroom."

My eyes grew wide with anticipation. Of course her bedroom was the best place to place the ashtray. She could see it everyday, and every time she saw it, the ashtray would remind mom of her youngest son. I smiled and said, "So you're going to put the ashtray on your table with all your special trinkets?"

"Not exactly."

Mothers are supposed to be reassuring—and my mother was 99.99% of the time—but this time was different, this time my mother sounded—well she sounded a little bit like my father—just before he told me that there really was no pot of gold at the end of the rainbow. I started to worry. "What do you mean, 'Not exactly', mom?"

"I am going to place it near the bathroom vanity mirror."

"How near the vanity mirror?"

"I'll place it in the middle of the perfume."

"But you've got over a hundred bottles of perfume. Not only will no one else see it. But you won't either. It'll get lost in that sea of scent."

"No it won't. I will see it every morning, and it will remind me what a special son I have. By seeing the ashtray in the morning, I will start my day with a smile, and thoughts of you." She hugged me again. At that moment, I was the happiest child on earth.

Many years have passed since I presented my mother with that most special ashtray. The paintings and scribblings of my youth have long since been discarded. The cards and dime-store jewelry given for Mother's Day and other special occasions have been lost or tossed aside.

Even now when I visit home, mom has my ashtray adorning her vanity room. The perfume bottles still surround my ceramic master-piece. I doubt that my mother has ever mentioned my ashtray to another living soul. It doesn't matter. For some, gifts have a senti-mental attachment that is far greater than words can express, or riches can buy. For my mother, the ashtray was indeed special, and for no one else to cherish, but her. And I believe that was the way it should have been.

Airplanes

Without question, without doubt, I hate anyone and everyone who has flown, currently flies, or will ever fly first class on an airplane. By all rights, I should fly in first class. I deserve to fly in first class. But I will never fly in first class. And why won't I? Because my boss is a tightwad of the first order. He'd rather have wooden splints inserted under his fingernails than pay for a first class ticket for his number one employee. So for yet another flight, I was destined to the cheapest seat available. That in turn meant that I would be in back of the plane. But as I found out, *back of the plane* is a relative term that means different things to different people and airlines.

It didn't help matters that on that day I was scheduled to go cross country on Flying Squirrel Airlines. To put it bluntly, I was not particularly reassured by an airline whose corporate symbol was a squirrel wearing an aviator's jacket and blue-tinted goggles.

I handed the check-in attendant my ticket, in order to secure a boarding pass.

The check-in attendant squinted her eyes in disbelief. She held my ticket for well over a minute, then called for her supervisor.

She whispered something into his ear. The supervisor scribbled a few symbols on the ticket, then said, "Yes, yes, that's the correct class of service." He handed me the ticket, then explained the attendant's confusion. "You'll have to excuse Mrs. Huffington," the supervisor began. "She's a trainee, and was not familiar with the class of service noted on your ticket."

"And just what kind of ticket do I have?"

"You have what's known as an XYZ ticket. Quite frankly, this is our least publicized, and offered service. In fact, we have only about ten routes where the XYZ ticket and service is available. However, for those lucky few who can take advantage of this service, the savings are quite substantial, up to ninety percent off our regular published fares."

"And what do I get with an XYZ ticket?"

"A seat, and the eternal gratitude of Flying Squirrel Airlines."

So my boss had purchased an XYZ ticket. As I learned that afternoon, Flying Squirrel Airlines had seventy-six different fare classes, and my boss had purchased the cheapest ticket possible—a true no frills fare—with few perks available.

On most airlines, after children, the elderly, and first class are seated, the plane is boarded from the rear. That was not the case however with an XYZ fare. Every other class was called to board before XYZ ticket holders. When I learned that I would have to wait up to thirty minutes before I could be seated, I decided to go to the bar, order a ginger ale, and watch TV. The ginger ale was flat, the bar was crowded, and my team was losing as usual. But I preferred that than waiting in an interminable line to board a plane that had a XYZ class of service.

I returned to the boarding area, and was informed that though I had a guaranteed seat, I could be bumped by anyone who was flying standby, and wanted a seat in the XYZ class. I waited another fifteen minutes, as standby passengers were asked if they wanted to fly in one of the XYZ seats. Apparently all of them at one time or another had flown in the XYZ seats because all emphatically declined. In fact, one of the standbys said that she would rather be swept away in a torrent of volcanic lava, than be subjected to even one moment of the humiliation and pain associated with XYZ seats. I had been on some memorably bad flights in my day, but I could not envision any flight being so awful that I would prefer physical torture. But then again, I had never flown in the XYZ class of Flying Squirrel Airlines. I was about to discover why people wanted to avoid XYZ service at all costs.

I entered the plane and trudged past the first class cabin. The seats were wide, soft-polished leather. There were foot rests, and the seats reclined to any desired level. In first class, the lighting above every seat adjusted to the needs of every privileged passenger. Each seat had its own entertainment system, complete with numerous movie and music choices. There were unlimited drinks and snacks prior to lift-off in first class. I, however, was not first class material. Most of the first class snobs awkwardly twisted their necks in an obvious attempt to avoid me and other commoners. Those who reluctantly glanced at me, curled their lips in utter disdain. It was as if they knew that I possessed an XYZ ticket. As I carried my tattered overcoat down the wide aisle, my overcoat nevertheless accidentally brushed against one of the first class passengers. The woman with whom I had the brief encounter almost fainted. She was appalled that I had the unmitigated audacity to have any contact with a first class passenger—especially her. There was collective applause as I slipped past the curtain in first class.

I trudged past business class. The seats were not as plush, and not as wide. But they were fresh-scented cloth, and comfortable. The passengers in business class received one complimentary glass of wine or juice. Each seat was equipped with a phone/data port. There were business executives seated smartly, handling a vast array of business activities prior to pushback from the jetway. The gent in 10-C entered expense information in his personal desk assistant (PDA). The lady in 12-B reviewed a contract of some sort. Most ignored me. Some however, stared at me for a second or two, then shuddered. They were the business class elite. It was obvious to them that while I might have been a manager or supervisor, I was not business class material, and did not deserve to be seated near them. I suspect they guessed that I was some poor slob employed by a third rate, struggling company that had no appreciable travel budget, and offered its employees absolutely no perks. The thought that they guessed I was a slob irritated me to no end. But of course it was true, as were all the other observations they made as I sort of shuffled past them. There was a collective sigh of relief, as I slipped past the curtain in business class.

I trudged past economy class. The seats were chewed-up, drooled-on, juice-stained cloth. The smell in economy class was reminiscent of baby food—specifically strained peas, and apricot delight. The lights above the seats were partially obscured by dried milk, bubble gum, or crayons. The seats were mostly occupied by families with children, mostly infants, with a few toddlers, and a couple of teenagers. I had no business being in economy class because I was not traveling with children. They watched me walk past them. Unlike first and business class however, both parents and teenagers were sad that I was not joining them. The parents were sad because I could have provided a momentary diversion for their toddlers, and inquisitive, primary-grade children. The teens groaned because I suspected that they needed a sacrifice for some ritual they were going to perform on the flight. But since there was nothing of worth to sacrifice, I would do. But of course I wouldn't, because as I have said, I trudged past them.

I trudged past some class called cheapskate class. No two seats matched. They appeared to have been salvaged from abandoned planes. Covered in garish green and red cloth, the seats did not recline. There were only two lights that lit the entire area. Yet, there were no empty seats. The seats were occupied by the largest group of clowns I had ever seen. I mean honest to goodness red-nosed, big-shoed, seltzer-spritzing clowns. As I learned later, the clowns were a contingent of amateur clowns headed to San Diego for a convention. I believe that every one of them either honked a horn at me, or hit me on the rear with a rubber chicken. Not even the clowns in cheapskate class wanted me. They waved good riddance. It didn't seem that I could endure any more humiliation. But as I discovered, the trip was young, and the worse was yet to come.

At the very back of the plane, behind a rigid, stained wall, practically in the tail cone, were four seats in one row. Finally, I had arrived at XYZ class. The seats were narrow and dirty, with no underseat storage area available. If there was carpet on the floor, then it escaped me. XYZ class was dingy, and poorly lit, and without the benefit of adequate circulation. For a moment, I considered asking one of the flight attendants if I could upgrade my accommodations to the cargo hold. But it appeared that the flight attendants avoided XYZ class as though it were the Plague or some other infectious disease. I opened the overhead storage compartment and discovered that it was filled with Flying Squirrel canisters of some sort. I rearranged the canisters in order to wedge my brief case into the compartment. The compartment latch did not seem particularly secure as I closed it.

In the middle left seat sat a man with glasses, and a bright teflon smile. The closer I got to him, the broader his smile became. His smile was so wide, and his teeth were so bright that he could have warned fog-bound ships of the dangers that lay ahead.

I sat next to him.

"I'm sorry, I should have put in my teeth tinter."

"Teeth tinter?"

"Yes. As you can see, my teeth are so bright, they seem to glow."

"Well yes, now that you mention it—"

He whipped out a dental device from his shirtpocket—actually it looked more like two thin light blue flimstrips and covered his teeth. I had to admit that the so-called tinter did dampen the blinding brightness of his teeth.

"Afternoon." He extended his hand to shake mine. "My name is Buddy Carvell."

"I'm Michael Hughes," I replied trying to get comfortable in the undersized seat with roughly a couple inches of leg room."

"I've been trying for years to find the right position for my legs. So far, I've been quite unsuccessful."

Surprised that anyone would knowingly subject themselves to this type of airline torture, I asked, "You regularly fly XYZ class?"

"Every week."

"Really?"

"Yeah. You know most people call this the Your Boss Must Hate Your Guts Class."

It figures, I mumbled to myself.

"I bet you can't guess why my boss hates my guts."

"I don't really want to guess," I replied.

"No, go ahead and guess. You'll never guess in a billion years."

"You lost your company's largest account."

"No, if only it were that simple," he replied with a contented smile. "Take another guess."

"I'm not really very good at this. Why don't you just tell me, why your boss banished you to a location that's worse than hell?"

"Go ahead, take another guess. If you don't get it on this try, then I'll tell you."

Buddy seemed a bit too happy for my tastes. Why would any sane person seem content, indeed ecstatic about being forced to travel in such a horrid class—and then be willing to share the story that explains the reason or reasons for the permanent exile?

He nudged me, and I realized that I had better humor him by offering another guess. "You wrecked a company vehicle?"

"Not even close."

"Then what?" I asked.

"I had an affair with my boss' mother."

There are some things in life that a person should ponder. I assure you that this was not one of them.

"Well, under the circumstances, I guess you're lucky to still have a job."

"That's what everyone says. But then you'd have to know my boss' mother." He jabbed me between the third and fifth ribs, and began to laugh so hard that he nearly convulsed. He laughed longer than anyone—man or woman—should laugh about a sordid tale like that. Old Buddy laughed so long that I thought he just might wet his pants. After a good two or three minutes, he replaced the belly-busting laughter with a nasal snort that sounded like a bull moose in heat. He alternated between the laugh and the snort for another minute or so, then excused himself to regroup in the restroom.

It was then that I noticed a gloved hand extended in my direction. I turned and was startled to see a mime. Statistically, I was certain that I had better odds of winning the lottery than sitting next to a mime. And yet, there was a mime doing all those irritating things that mimes do like propping up against an imaginary wall, or blowing bubbles, or laughing silently.

There are few things more irritating than having a mime sit beside you on the last row of an airplane that has the interminable XYZ class. I was hoping against all hope that I would be shot by a tranquilizer dart, and wake up in Kansas, or Arizona, or Timbuktu, or anywhere, just as long as I could get off the plane, and never again see anyone from Flight 219. But my own personal private hell was just beginning. And there would be no reprieve from the governor.

The mime smiled at me, then pretended to drink coffee.

I pretended to make a hangman's noose. If I had had rope, I would have made a real one.

The mime dabbed the corners of his mouth with an imaginary napkin.

I turned away from the mime, just in time for Buddy Carvell to reclaim his seat. Realizing that I had interacted in some way with the mime, Buddy said, "Pierre's a real hoot, isn't he?"

"You know the mime's name?" I asked in disbelief.

"Sure."

"How?"

"He told me."

"What?"

"Oh I see. You thought that I meant that he spoke. Now what sense would that make? After all, mimes don't speak—at least not in public. No, Pierre printed his name in the air."

I realized that I had momentarily been caught up in the shenanigans of Buddy and Pierre. It hit me all at once, that this was going to be an extremely long flight—one that I would not soon forget. I closed my eyes, hoping that when I opened them again, I would realize that it had been nothing more than a nightmare. But it wasn't.

Buddy nudged me. "Aren't you curious to know how I found out what Pierre's first name was?"

"Not really."

"Sure you are. Anyway, the story's a riot."

"Look, I'm sure, I would bust a gut laughing. But really, I just need some quiet time, I've got a grade ten headache."

Pierre the mime pretended to place a cold compress on my forehead. I would have traded all my wealth, which admittedly was not much, for a stun gun to send Pierre to the Island of Immobilized Mimes.

The final seat in the XYZ class was taken by none other than a pilot for Flying Squirrel Airlines. To put it mildly, he was not a happy camper. In fact, I had seen people in the hospital awaiting quintuple by-pass surgery who were happier. He kept mumbling, "Dirty, cheap blast cards. I'll get those dirty, cheap blast cards, if it is the last thing that I do." At least that's what I think he was saying.

Pierre gave the pilot a pretend balloon.

The pilot promptly popped it, and sneered at Pierre. "Get away from me mime, or I swear, I'll squeeze you in the tailcone, and no one will be the wiser."

Even the mime could appreciate that threat. Pierre returned to his seat and read an imaginary book.

A video provided safety instructions and other information about the plane. But there were no video screens in XYZ class. Moreover, no flight attendants strolled back to XYZ class to check on our condition. I checked for the plastic folder that contained information on the type of plane and emergency instructions, but of course, there were no such folders in XYZ class. I believe prisoners in transit were treated with more dignity.

I attempted to fasten my seat belt, only to discover that there were no standard issue seat belts in XYZ class. Rather, the seat belts were made of nothing more than hemp that was attached together by small strips of velcro. If there were a sudden jolt, I could not imagine the seat belts providing any resistance or safety.

So there I was, sitting in the bowels of a plane, with a mime, a surly pilot, and a womanizer. If hell could have been any worse than the moment that we took off, I could not envision it—or so I thought—forty-five minutes into the flight it got worse. We were over a cornfield or a mountain—at that altitude, I could not tell which, when a flight attendant stopped by with a beverage cart.

"We ordinarily don't serve XYZ class passengers. But since Captain Marshall is back here, we're making an exception. What'll you gentlemen have?"

The pilot said in a harsh voice, "The blackest, hottest coffee that you've got."

Pierre and Buddy passed on the beverage service.

The flight attendant turned to me and asked, "Do you want anything?"

"Ginger ale, if you have it."

"Of course we have it," she replied. "I'll be back in a minute."

The flight attendant returned and handed me a dusty bottle of Blackberry Hills ginger ale. It was without a doubt, the darkest, and most bitter ginger ale, I had ever tasted. With a flavor reminiscent of bleach, the carbonated cleaner deadened my taste buds for over three months.

Pierre rested his eyes, though for a mime even a common action appeared bizarre and exaggerated. Buddy deciphered a cryptogram of some sort. I felt claustrophobic. People trapped in an over-crowded elevator had more room than we had in XYZ class. I checked my watch and realized that we had not even reached the one-quarter point of the flight.

A few minutes later, one of the flight attendants addressed the passengers over the PA system. *For our passengers in first and business class, please note that video and audio selections are available through the entertainment monitors. In economy and extremely thrifty classes, we will be showing a series of film shorts on the overhead monitors. If you would like a headset, please notify a flight attendant as he or she passes your seat. Now sit back and enjoy the flight.*

No one mentioned XYZ class. It was as if we didn't exist.

Because I flew every week, I learned to ignore most bumps and shakes that occur during a flight. As my first father-in-law said, "As long as the airline crew remained calm, and showed no outward emotion, then there was nothing to worry about."

I contemplated whether I should open a pack of imitation, salt-free, pretzels. Checking for an expiration date, I could find none. Based on my earlier experience with the ginger ale I wondered if I should tempt fate twice. I didn't have to—without warning, the plane vibrated in a way and manner that I had never experienced. I would have overlooked it, except for the fact that our guest pilot's eyes widened as big as saucers.

"Uh-oh," the pilot remarked, "I didn't like that shimmy."

So that was a shimmy. Okay, I ignored bumps and shakes. But a shimmy, now that was something different. And when an airplane pilot comments that there might be a problem, then I listen.

"What don't you like about a shimmy?"

The plane repeated the odd vibration.

"A shimmy is an unexpected, and typically unexplained, at least initially, vibration. It can be soft or hard. But it is something that indicates something negatively affecting the stability of the plane. And anything that is negatively affecting the stability of the plane, I don't like."

I had to agree with the pilot whole-heartedly on that analysis. The plane's stability was of paramount importance to me.

For the next couple of minutes the plane flew smoothly and without incident. I would have thought the worst was over, but I noticed the pilot's eyes gazing through a peephole to the skies outside. His face was intense, and his hands were rigid and gripping the arm rest as if he was expecting another shimmy.

A minute or so later, the plane experienced its third shimmy.

Our XYZ class pilot said something under his breath, that was either a curse or a prayer. In any event, I noticed that even Pierre the mime was sitting silently in his seat.

After the third shimmy, the plane's pilot spoke over the intercom. "Ladies and gentlemen. You may have noticed a wobble in the plane. We're experiencing a slight, but constant vibration of undetermined origin. I'm going to ask the flight attendants to take their seats at this time, until we can correct this situation. This is simply a precaution."

Then, in no particular order or sequence, the following events occurred: 1) I smelled smoke; 2) the plane shimmied again; 3) one of the flight attendants uttered a profanity which was overheard on the intercom; 4) one flight attendant rushed back to our section, and said everything was going to be all right, to which our XYZ class pilot rolled his eyes; 5) in the clown section four or five balloons popped in rapid succession; and 6) there was the high-pitched squeal of an alarm of some sort.

In spite of all that happened, I didn't really think that we were going to crash—at least not until—well—have you ever been at the pinnacle of roller coaster—at the highest point of the ride—when for that brief micro-second, you can see the world, when you are suspended above all that is around you—just before the track and your stomach disappears—as you then plummet in a free fall back to earth—well that is what happened to the plane—it hit an air pocket and dropped like an egg tossed off the top of the Empire State Building.

I am not sure if the seat belts remained fastened in the other service classes—in XYZ class however, they did not. The seat belts separated with suspicious ease. As a result, everyone lurched.

During the plane's free fall, each person in XYZ class reacted differently. The pilot kept muttering to himself. It sounded as if he were giving commands, only no one could follow them. Pierre the mime suffered air sickness and that was no act. For some inexplicable reason, I wondered who would replace me on the development team. And then there was Buddy Carvell. Unlike the rest of us, Buddy was calm and unconcerned. Somehow, in spite of impending doom, he read a mystery novel. "I'm just a few pages from the end," he remarked. Even with his teeth tinter, I was amazed at the brightness of his teeth.

I couldn't understand, and quite frankly resented Buddy's cool, calm demeanor. When you're facing one of those end-of-life events, then you should at least show some emotion. As the plane dropped closer to the ground, I asked, "Aren't you the least bit afraid?"

"Would you believe it if I told you, this is the third time that something like this has happened to me. The first time I wet my pants. The second time, I passed out. In both instances, the situation was corrected. So I'm not worried this time. I know that everything will be all right."

Somehow, Buddy's comments did not reassure me. My ex-wife Marcia often talked about bad karma, and bad vibes. Well the vibes had been bad on the plane from the first moment I had stepped on board. And now, as we plunged from the stratosphere to that patch of dirt called Earth, I discovered that I was seated next to the eternal king of bad karma. I momentarily forgot about my own mortality, and wondered aloud, what kind of individual continues to fly after escaping certain disaster twice before. The answer to that question was none other than Buddy Carvel, a man banished to the bowels of a plane because he had been carrying on an affair with his boss' mother.

I am not sure how long the plane had been on its downward descent—to me it seemed as though it were almost a minute —though it might have been only several seconds. Anyway, I thought about my kids, my ex-wives, butterflies, and peanut butter sandwiches—can you imagine that my life might end in the next minute, and of all things in the world, some of my last thoughts concerned peanut butter sandwiches.

As suddenly as the rapid descent, and with absolutely no advance warning, the plane leveled. From my limited vantage point, I guess that our altitude was approximately twenty-five hundred feet. Instead of cheers and celebrating, there was silence, a morbid, anxious silence from those on board. It was as if the passengers were waiting for the plane to plummet once more for earth—it appeared that they could not accept their miraculous good fortune.

After several moments of silence, the captain addressed everyone on the plane, "We do apologize for that unexpected descent. Fortunately, it was brief, and we were able to correct the situation without suffering permanent damage to the plane or controls. However, in an abundance of caution, we will be landing in Omaha. We ask that you remain in your seats for the duration of our flight. Thank you for your understanding and co-operation."

It took a near death experience for me to truly appreciate life. All of a sudden, XYZ class didn't seem as wretched as before. After all, I had a seat with a quarter-inch more room than I needed, and the seat belt detached easily which could provide that extra second needed to get to an emergency exit. Plus, XYZ class was away from all the hubub and distractions that were commonplace in other classes of service.

For the rest of the trip, Pierre pretended to drink vodka, straight. By the time we de-planed I could have sworn he was drunk. Oh well.

The plane landed in Omaha without further incident. A reporter from the local paper interviewed a couple of passengers from first and business classes about the harrowing flight. A television crew gathered video impressions of other passengers. But the media did not ask the passengers of XYZ class for their observations on the flight. That was okay.

Hotels 1

I almost always make it a point to check my hotel laundry as soon as it is returned in order to determine whether I have been short-changed one white sock, or a pair of crème-colored handkerchiefs. But for some inexplicable reason, I did not on my thirty-second visit to the Pilmoor Hotel in Braxton Beach, South Carolina. As it turned out, that was a big mistake on my part.

I needed a pair of socks. So I ripped open the plastic bag containing the underwear. I stuck my hand down into the middle of the bag and retrieved what I was sure was a navy blue sock. However, I could not seem to find the mouth of the sock. It was at this time that I made a disheartening discovery. What I thought was a navy blue sock was in reality a silk, navy blue bra. And it was no ordinary, run-of-the-mill bra. It was huge. Why if a person dipped just one of the cups into a punchbowl, it could fill six ten-ounce glasses.

I recoiled. My first thought was to deep-six the bra in the nearest trash receptacle. However, the bra obviously belonged to some well-endowed woman. Besides, upon a further search of the laundry bag, I could not find my socks, and they were the only pair of socks that matched my suit. So I swallowed my pride, and tucked the bra under my jacket and marched down to the front desk.

At the front desk, the assistant Manager, Jeff Simpson greeted me. "May I help you?"

I explained my dilemma to Simpson, and he reacted so calmly that I got the distinct impression that this sort of thing must have happened more times that I might have imagined. After asking a couple of follow-up questions, Simpson contacted the on-duty Manager.

"What is it Simpson?" the on-duty Manager asked.

"Sir, it seems that our guest Mr. Hughes of Suite 606 received the wrong laundry package. Instead of receiving a package containing socks, underwear, and a casual shirt, Mr. Hughes, received a package containing—well containing—" Unable to say, *bra* out loud, Simpson whispered it to the Manager.

"I see," the Manager said, as he arched his eyebrows. "Mr. Hughes, is it?"

"Yes."

"Well follow me." He ushered me into his rather small office. I immediately felt uncomfortable.

"Mr. Hughes, I am Daniel Abbot, the on-duty manager."

I was expecting Abbot to say that he was sorry for the mix-up, and that he would take immediate steps to correct the situation. But Abbot didn't apologize. Rather, he said something that made the hair on my arms stand on end.

Abbot nodded at me, as if I were some kindred soul, and then said, "Mr. Hughes, I understand."

Understand? Never had four words sounded so ominous. As I viewed the situation, it required no understanding. Just take the bra, find my socks, and we could all call it a day.

"Look it's been a long day, so I'll just—"

Abbot placed his right hand on my shoulder. "Really, I understand."

Those words again. I started feeling uneasy and claustrophobic. I prepared to leave.

Abbot moved closer to me and whispered, "Your secret is safe with me. I've been wearing them for years."

At this point, I was hoping Abbot was talking about wearing candy cane boxers. But I had a feeling that he wasn't. For the first time during our encounter, I stared at Abbot. He was just a shade over six feet with thin strands of blond hair brushed to the side. He was clean shaven with grey eyes and proportionate ears with lobes. I figured that he must have been in his early thirties. And then I stopped, and asked myself, why in the hell am I staring at this man. Unlike Abbot, I did not understand. I started to hyperventilate.

Just as Abbot moved a bit closer, one of the assistant managers knocked on his door. Startled, Abbot jumped back and ran his hand through his hair. "Yes, who is it?"

"It's Jacquanda."

"I'm in a meeting, Jacquanda," Abbot answered.

"Then I'll only be a minute," Jacquanda said, as she opened the door.

One look, that was all it took for me to know positively that the bra belonged to Jacquanda.

"What are you doing with my bra?" she asked in a huffy tone.

"I can explain."

"I mean, what kind of man would take a woman's bra from her laundry bag? I should contact the police, and press charges against you—to protect other women from your depravity."

"You've got it all wrong. Your bra was misplaced in my laundry."

Jacquanda rolled her eyes and swiveled her neck in a manner that left no doubt that she didn't believe me at all. She grabbed the bra, flared her nostrils, then stamped out of the office.

Abbot stared at me. I stared at Abbot. We did not say anything for close to a minute.

Finally Abbot said, "Apparently there has been a mistake."

"There certainly has," I replied indignantly.

Abbot stared at me again. But this time the stare was different. It was as if he were pondering his options. I considered leaving, but the matter of my misplaced socks was still unresolved.

"I'm still missing a pair of black socks. They are thick and made by O'Keefe."

Abbot did not respond to my comment. Rather, he continued to look at me. What he was contemplating, I didn't know. What he was contemplating, I didn't want to know. For no apparent reason, he sighed then said, "I think it only fair to tell you that Jacquanda is married."

If I hadn't been concerned about the way Abbot looked at me before, and I had been, then the look he gave me after making that statement would have set my flesh crawling with fear. Instead of wanting to have a drink with me, I got the distinct impression that he might want to poison me. The disgust and disdain in his eyes spoke volumes. Finally, I gleened the reason for his newfound dislike of me. "Hey, wait a minute," I began defensively, "I am not some sort of stalker."

"And how many times did you say you have been a guest of our hotel?"

"Several."

"I believe you said forty."

"This is my thirty-second time staying at this hotel. I'm certain that it will be my last."

"So on thirty-one previous occasions that you have stayed here, nothing like this has ever occurred."

"Not that I can recall."

"And yet, on the thirty-second time, you wind up with the bra of one of my assistant managers."

"I didn't wind up with her bra. The bra was misplaced in my laundry bag."

"So you say."

"Listen, I don't like what you're implying."

"But you must admit that it is quite a coincidence."

There was an accusatorial edge to Abbot's comments that both irritated and concerned me.

"Look, I'm going back to my room now. If you find my socks, have someone other than you, return them to me."

"Until you leave, Mr. Hughes, I am going to keep my eyes on you."

I was afraid that Abbot just might do that. The thought that he might be around any corner, or on any elevator spooked me. I scurried back to my room, pulled out a daily reflections book from the nightstand, and turned on the radio to a classical music station.

Not quite ten minutes had elapsed when I heard a knock on the door.

I opened the door—it was none other than Jacquanda. Her hair had been curled tight in a bun, now it was long and free flowing. There was glitter above her eyes, and the delicate scent of perfume clung to her body. She looked at me, and I looked at her. But Jacquanda's eyes stopped and visually inspected parts of my body that I did not want inspected.

"I understand," Jacquanda said, smiling in a way that I thought not possible some thirty minutes ago.

Jacquanda may have understood, but I did not understand. More importantly, I did not want to understand. What I wanted was simply to get my missing socks, and go to bed—poor choice of words, I should have said, go to sleep.

Jacquanda heard the music—something from Bach, Brahms, or Beethoven, I wasn't sure.

But Jacquanda knew—she knew far too much in fact. "I love a man who listens to Bach," she said, her voice, sultry, passionate, and suggestive.

I switched radio stations—to a classic country station.

Her eyes were the eyes of a woman who would not take no for an answer. She moved within an arms-length of me. "I love a man who listens to Roy Acuff." Her crimson hot breath singed my eyebrows.

In another half minute, I would have been in her clutches. Fate intervened however. There was yet another knock on the door.

"Mr. Hughes. Mr. Hughes. I know that you are in there."

I recognized the voice—it was Daniel Abbot—in the nick of time.

Preferring that Abbot not know about Jacquanda's presence, I motioned for her to duck into the bathroom. She smiled coyly, then complied.

I opened the door just wide enough to make eye contact with Abbot. "Did you finally find my socks?"

"Actually no."

"Well, Mr. Abbot it's been a long day. I intend to grab a few hours sleep. So what do you want?"

Abbot's facial expression changed once more. Now he appeared contrite and remorseful. "Perhaps if I could step into your room, I could say what I have to, then leave you alone."

"After all that has happened today? You have got to be kidding! There's no way that I am going to let you set one foot in my room."

"Well, yes, I suppose that is understandable. I guess under the circumstances, you might have misconstrued or misunderstood some of my actions or comments."

"Oh, I understood all right. I should report you to your superior."

"And that is precisely why I have come up here. I would respectfully ask that you not mention our earlier conversation to any one."

Actually, I had no intention of reporting Abbot to his superior. It would be difficult if not impossible to retell the events of the day without raising suspicions about my own peccadilloes. But I wouldn't tell Abbot just yet. I'd make him sweat overnight. "I'll have to think about it, Abbot," I returned, closing the door in his face.

Jacquanda stepped into the bedroom. I noticed that the top two buttons of her blouse were unbuttoned.

"I am glad that he's gone. He almost spoiled the moment."

There was no moment, no hour, no time to be in the same room with a woman of substantial stature, and unfulfilled fantasies. "You have to leave now."

"I know where your socks are."

"You do."

"I certainly do." She laughed a laugh of a woman ready for amore. Jacquanda stood on the opposite side of the bed from me. She laughed again, and said, "You see, it's a little game that I play. When I see someone is interested in me, I place a piece of my clothing in their laundry, then after they report it missing, I return it."

"All right, if you would just give my socks, then I will forget everything else."

"Well, you'll have to find them. They're somewhere on my body."

I cringed. I didn't want to contemplate where my socks could be on her body. "Stop playing games, Jacquanda, and give me my socks."

"I love a big strong man who is also forceful."

Well if Jacquanda wasn't going to leave, then I would. Moving toward the door, she stopped me.

"All right, all right," she began. "Jacquanda was just having a little fun. If you want your socks, you can have your socks." Jacquanda sat on the edge of the bed. I shuddered at the thought of her removing my socks from—well I couldn't imagine. To my surprise, Jacquanda flipped off her shoes, then removed my socks. I shuddered anyway. Jaquanda wore size fifteen triple E shoes which translated into extra large, extra wide socks. I on the other hand wore size ten double A shoes which meant my socks were stretched in ways they were not meant to stretch. Adding insult to injury, there was a hint a lilac pressed into the heal of my socks. So, my socks were returned, but I never wore them again.

As for Jacquanda., she rolled her tongue around her lips. "But next time, Jacquanda will get what she wants." Smiling, I noticed for the first time, two gold molars on either side of Jacquanda's mouth. Before Jacquanda left, she turned back the bed, and placed her phone number and a bar of chocolate on my pillow.

There was never a next time, for I never returned to the Pilmoor Hotel, and I never contacted Jacquanda. Oh, and one final thing, I never used the guest laundry services of another hotel I visited. I chose not to tempt fate anymore.

Hotels 2

It was supposed to be a special weekend—a father-daughter week-end—just me and Millicent. A weekend full of fun and frolic. And so far it had been a blast. First, we dropped by the ice cream shop and treated ourselves to double thick and creamy strawberry sundaes. Then we stopped at the mall, so I could buy Millicent a purse she regarded as the *neatest purse on the planet.* Then we drove two hours to the Arena, and purchased courtside seats, so that we could watch our favorite team the Cricketts win in overtime. Tomorrow, it would be an all-day visit to the amusement park, followed by a special dinner at an exclusive restaurant.

But that's another story. Up through the basketball game, it had been a great weekend—a memorable one. Daddy could do no wrong. Daddy was the best daddy in the world—no, make that the galaxy, no, no, make that the universe. Daddy knew just what to do. Then we parked at The Cameron Inn. I should have known better. Something about the name just didn't sound right. Besides there were potholes in the parking lot, and a basketball hoop without a net. I got the feeling that a person would have to be pretty desperate to shoot a game of hoops at The Cameron Inn. The travel guide said it was a three-star accommodation. As soon as we walked to the reg-istration desk, I knew that The Cameron Inn might be two-stars, but never three. Nevertheless, all we required were two beds, and some clean towels—so, I figured that The Cameron Inn would be okay for one night. As I found out, Millicent's desires differed from mine in several key respects.

Up to that point, Millicent had been extremely talkative, and animated. At the game, she booed and hissed at the referees, and asked if they needed trifocals. That was my daughter. In some respects, she understood the finer points of basketball better than me. But when we reached The Cameron Inn, everything changed—and not for the better either.

Millicent lingered in the car. Actually, the truth of it is she refused to step foot in the pot-holed parking lot. After ten minutes of coaxing—to no avail, I carried Millicent, and her rolling garment bag into the hotel. In the lobby of the hotel, Millicent tried not to touch any of the furniture. I believe she wanted to hose down each item, and then disinfect the entire common area. Still, I think she thought that the lobby was not reflective of the rest of the motel. Boy was she wrong.

Millicent entered the hotel room. Immediately, I could tell that it did not meet her exacting standards. There were two single beds with standard issue linen. There were two chairs with well-worn brown fabric.

She pursed her lips as if she had sipped a teaspoonful of vinegar. Millicent's eyes drooped, but she managed a forced smile.

Sensing Millicent's disappointment, I remarked, "It's just for tonight."

Millicent visually surveyed the room, then asked, "Where's the mini-bar, daddy?"

"There isn't a mini-bar, sweetheart."

Millicent giggled. "No really, daddy. Where is the mini-bar?"

Millicent's eyes twinkled with that little girl innocence. She thought that this was a joke that daddy was playing on her. She just knew that in a moment or two, that daddy would say 'Surprise', and take her to another, better room—a room that she was more accustomed to, and contained the little pleasures that she expected, and assumed (at least until that night) were standard in all hotel rooms across the country.

It never occurred to me that a mini-bar would be at the top of Millicent's hotel room necessities. But when I thought about it for a minute or so, I realized that I shouldn't have been surprised by Millicent's reaction. Normally, when the family traveled, we stayed at a multi-suite hotel, or one with separate sleeping and living quarters. And yes, I suspect that there had been a mini-bar in each previous hotel room. However, a mini-bar had never been an indispensable part of my hotel stay. And in fact, I had no particular desire to pay ten dollars for an ounce of cashews, or three dollars for six ounces of carbonated soda. Such concepts and concerns were foreign for Millicent though. She knew what she wanted, and was undeterred and unfazed by my comment that there was no mini-bar in the hotel room. *Daddy must be wrong, she thought.* Maybe the mini-bar was underneath the bed. With that she raised each bed apron, and ran her hand down the entire length of exposed underside of the bed. She found two inches of dust, but no mini-bar.

Millicent conducted a tour of our cramped quarters. She opened the closet door and found no mini-bar. She opened the bathroom, and found, a sink and toilet, but no mini-bar. She opened the armoire, and found a television, but no mini-bar.

"Daddy, there's no mini-bar," Millicent sadly remarked, finally accepting my initial observation.

"Look, dear. We're only going to be here for one night. We don't need a mini-bar for one night."

"You know, daddy, Cindy from school mentioned that she had been in a hotel room without a mini-bar—and without a concierge—but I didn't believe her. I mean how can someone build a hotel room without the necessities."

"I assure you that neither a mini-bar, nor a concierge is a necessity."

"To me they are."

As I stated earlier, I suppose I had no one but myself to blame for Millicent's warped perception of reality. Under the circumstances, I was determined to expand her horizons. "You don't need a mini-bar, Millicent."

"But I might get hungry late tonight. What are we going to do for snacks? And in the morning, what if I want some juice? Where will I get some juice?"

"I'll tell you what, dear. We can go to the convenience store and get some juice, and soda, and pretzels, and other snacks. How does that sound?"

"We wouldn't have to do that if we had a mini-bar in this room. If we had a mini-bar, then we could just open it anytime of the night, and get what we want."

"But we don't have a mini-bar. So, are you ready to go to the convenience store?"

"Didn't grandpops say that only a crazy person would go to a convenience store at night? I mean isn't grandpops always talking about how Johnny Jackson got shot six times, thirty eight-years ago, when he went to the convenience store to get a two-cent piece of candy."

"Your grandfather talks about many things, dear."

"Well, I don't think we should go to the convenience store. It's dangerous."

"I'll give you ten dollars, if you go, and promise not to tell grandpops."

"I'd still prefer a mini-bar. But grandpops also says that anytime you offer money, take it. So, it's a deal daddy. We simply won't mention tonight to grandpops."

We drove to the nearest Lime and Green Store. Millicent darted down every aisle and found goody after goody, and treat after treat.

The total bill for the different snacks amounted to over thirty dollars. Including the ten dollars that I paid Millicent, I figured that I would have come out cheaper if we had found a room with a mini-bar.

When we got back to the room, Millicent dumped her treasure trove into her rolling garment bag. She worried about contracting a communicable disease from coming into contact with the bedsheets. I assured Millicent that she should suppress such fears. I am pretty sure that Millicent had been told by her mother not to trust me when it came to matters of personal health. After all, I was foremost and always, just a man. So Millicent covered a chair with my jacket and sat. I shrugged my shoulders, and watched cable while Millicent immersed herself in the snacks. "May I have some cashews, daddy?"

"Sure, sure," I replied, not really paying attention to Millicent.

When Millicent finished the eight-ounce bag of whole cashews, she asked, "May I have a grape soda, daddy?"

By that time, I was drifting in and out of sleep. "What?" I asked, prying one eye open.

"May I have a grape soda?"

"Sure, sure," I replied before my head hit the pillow.

When Millicent finished twenty ounces of grape soda, she asked, "May I have some chocolate crème cookies, daddy?"

Trying to wake up to catch one of the sports shows, I took a quick peek at Millicent. She had spilled grape soda on both her T-shirt, and my jacket. There were bits of cashews on the floor. Nevertheless, I said, "Sure, sure."

Over the next twenty minutes, Millicent ate half the twenty-ounce bag of chocolate crème cookies.

Millicent asked me something else. I mumbled, "Sure, sure."

It was almost midnight, and I had been in deep sleep for half an hour. Millicent had sampled almost all the snacks that we had bought. Finally, Millicent let out a pitiful moan. Instead of responding to my daughter's anguish, I rolled over.

Millicent tapped my shoulder. "I don't feel well, daddy."

I wiped a bit of drool on my shirtsleeve. The corners of Millicent's mouth were covered with cookie pieces. Other than that, her face appeared almost bleached. Millicent rubbed her stomach.

"It's my stomach, daddy. I think you let me eat too much."

Millicent had indulged her sweet tooth, and junk food cravings. The carpet was strewn with pretzels, and candy bar wrappers, and potato chips.

What kind of parent would let their child eat snacks all night? A parent who snored and drooled for several hours, that's who.

"Daddy, I don't really feel well."

At some point during the moaning, I woke up. At some point during the moaning, I realized that I was in trouble. Marcia would never let me hear the end of it. At some point during the moaning, I figured that Malcolm would attempt to use this incident to his benefit. At some point during the moaning, I realized that I had better take Millicent back to the convenience store and get some medicine for her upset stomach. A second trip to the convenience store cost me another twenty-five dollars—five for the medicine, and twenty to Millicent. My daughter might have been sick, but she was not comatose. She recognized the opportunity and seized it. She even stated that for some other undisclosed amount, she might be persuaded to not mention to mommy what had happened tonight. I declined, since the offer did not include not telling Malcolm.

The medicine worked. Around three, Millicent fell asleep in my arms. I thought about placing Millicent in one of the beds—then thought maybe she had suffered enough. So I stayed up for the rest of the night and cradled Millicent in my arms. And you know what—she was safe in my arms. And that's a great feeling for a parent to experience.

Kids and Stuffed Animals

Anyone who has raised a child knows quite well that the child becomes emotionally, and sometimes, physically attached to at least one stuffed animal during the first few years of life. I suppose that one of a parent's worst nightmares is for a child to lose a treasured toy or keepsake. In my daughter Millicent's case, it was her prized stuffed animal known affectionately as "birdy"."

Normally, I would give Millicent a small cup of water, read her a story, and tuck her into bed by seven-thirty. But that routine was disrupted on the particular evening in question. I called Millicent to come to bed. Millicent stuck her head into the bedroom, as if looking for something, then waddled down the hall. A minute later, she returned to the bedroom. Her face expressed a jittery desperation.

"What's wrong?" I asked.

"Where's birdy?" she asked.

I figured Millicent had misplaced birdy, just like she had on countless occasions before. It was probably beneath the bed. I checked. No birdy there. Oh, what was I thinking, Millicent must have left birdy in her toy chest. I checked. Whoa, no birdy there either. Sometimes, birdy was stuffed in between the pillow covers. I checked. No birdy.

Millicent's eyes widened. "Birdy," she whimpered. "Where's birdy?"

I looked high and low in the house and could find no birdy.

With each passing moment, Millicent's cries grew a bit louder. "Birdy left me. Why did birdy leave me, daddy? Why?"

I could neither answer that question, nor come up with an acceptable or believable response that was suitable to a four-year-old.

My daughter Millicent was inconsolable. She thought that her birdy might have flown away, never to be seen again. Throughout the night I heard the sobs and crying of a little girl devastated over the loss of her most precious possession.

The next day, Marcia and I searched every room, every closet, every cabinet, every box, and every crawl space in the house. Further, we looked underneath every bed, sofa, and chair. The two of us upturned every sofa cushion, and recliner. We recovered, a stuffed alligator, three stuffed bears, thirty-seven cents, a year-old can of peanuts, and a winning lottery ticket worth five-fifty. But nowhere, did Marcia or I find Millicent's stuffed birdy.

The third night was the worst. Millicent refused to eat dinner—her favorite dish—bow tie pasta with butter sauce. She wouldn't watch television, or read a book, or play with any of her dolls, or any other toys. There was a forlorn, almost haggard look on Millicent's face—much too sad and depressing for a four-year-old. Millicent confined herself to one corner of her bedroom. There she rocked with no purpose. As parents, it pained both me and Marcia.

"Birdy," she cried.

"We'll find birdy," I tried to reassure Millicent.

She gazed at me, though her eyes were hidden by diamond-shaped, milky tears. "Birdy's gone," she said, in a tone of complete anguish and despair.

Try as I might to reassure Millicent, that birdy had to be somewhere in the vicinity, I could not console her. Marcia rocked Millicent, and told her everything would be all right. Millicent wanted so badly to believe that everything would indeed be all right. But at that moment, her world had unraveled, and she was uncertain about the future.

Millicent sobbed and cried for hours. She emptied an entire box of tissue that night, drying her eyes, and blowing her nose. Even when Millicent finally drifted asleep, she whimpered. It was a traumatic night for all concerned.

The next morning, Millicent barely ate her breakfast. It was as though she had lost her purpose in life. On the way to pre-school, she asked me, "Will I ever have another spiffy-doodle day, daddy?"

If I hadn't understood the gravity of the situation before, Millicent's probing question alerted me to her very sad state. For Millicent, a spiffy-doodle day was a day of sunshine wrapped in cotton candy and drizzled in honey. It was a fantabuloso day, without worries or problems. Simply put, a spiffy-doodle day was picture perfect in every way imaginable. And as a sweet child, every day should be a spiffy-doodle day. So when Millicent, at age four, wondered if she would ever encounter another spiffy-doodle, I was quite concerned.

The next day, Marcia and I continued our search for birdy. Not one square inch of the house, cars, the garage, the attic, or our offices at work was overlooked. Birdy was nowhere to be found. During my lunchbreak, I contacted every toy store in town, and a couple mail-order toy houses. Not one of them had birdy. More depressing, several of the toy stores thought that birdy was not even manufactured anymore.

I remembered that I had a few photographs of Millicent with birdy, and at least one with birdy alone. Perhaps, if I enlarged the photo, some craftsperson could create an exact duplicate of birdy. Stewart, from cubicle 6B at work advised that I not take that approach, since I would in all likelihood be in violation of several intellectual property, and copyright laws. He had a better idea—why not contact the manufacturer directly and see if I could purchase The Nighttime Birdy from the source. It was certainly worth a try. So right after work, I contacted the Blankship Toy Company of Owensboro, Kentucky.

A woman with a slight southern drawl answered the phone on the seventh ring. "Blankship Toy Company—Where children's happiness is our number one concern. I am Patty Sue. How may I direct your call?"

"I want to purchase a toy—a stuffed animal, actually."

"Do you know the name of the person that you want to talk to, or in the alternative, the name of the department or division in Blankship Toy Company—a wholly-owned subsidiary of Smootens Corporation—the world's six hundred seventh largest conglomerate —that you would like further access to?"

"No, actually, I thought that you might direct me to the correct department."

"Sir, first of all let me state that my job duties do not cover or permit me to make an independent connection to a department. You must provide me with that information. But even if I did have such authority, I would have to decline. Blankship Toy Company—rated as the number one toy company for Moogles six years in a row has fifty-eight separate divisions, and six thousand and two employees. So I must ask you for either a name or a department or division."

"All right, all right. Give me your stuffed animal department."

"I am sorry, but we do not have a stuffed animal department."

"I see."

"But we do have a stuffed animal division. Would you like access to that division?"

"Yes."

Patty Sue connected me to the stuffed animal division.

A man with a mechanized-sounding voice answered.

"This is Paul Revenuewonca speaking. I am manager for the stuffed animal division of the Blankship Toy Company—America's favorite way to play. And how might I help you?"

"I am looking for one of your stuffed animals. I believe that it is called, birdy."

"Birdy?"

"Yes, birdy."

"We at Blankship Toy Company—a nominee for visionary company of the decade do not manufacture a stuffed animal called Birdy."

I provided Mr. Revenuewonca with a detailed description of the stuffed animal that Millicent and I knew as Birdy.

Immediately, Mr. Revenuewonca replied, "Oh, you are referring to Bingo Bongo Bird."

Quite frankly, I preferred Birdy. But if the stuffed animal's proper name was Bingo Bongo Bird, then so be it. I cleared my throat, then said, "All right. I was wondering if you still manufacture the Bingo Bongo Bird?"

"I'm afraid that we haven't produced the Bingo Bongo Bird in four years. It sold relatively well, but not up to the standards of the Blankship Toy Company—America's most dynamic toy company."

My heart sank, but I asked a follow-up question. "By any chance did Blankship Toy Company keep any of the Bingo Bongo Birds for posterity sakes?"

"Well Blankship Toy Company—producing great toys for great kids—does maintain a toy museum that contains samples of every toy manufactured by our company. But those toys are not for sale."

"I'm sure that on occasion, exceptions have been made."

"Not to my knowledge."

I plead my case to Mr. Revenuewonca, but to no avail. I could not purchase birdy at any price.

I returned home without birdy. My options were dwindling by the minute. I considered canvassing the second hand stores and garage sales. It was a longshot. But it was worth a try.

Marcia greeted me with a kiss. Something was different about her demeanor. Then it hit me—Marcia was smiling. I had not seen Marcia smile in the last few days. I immediately felt better for when Marcia smiled, my spirits were boosted.

"What? Did we win the lottery?"

"Better than that."

I was about to ask what could be better than winning the lottery, when Marcia's mother, Edna entered the living room with missing toy number one—Birdy.

"I was rummaging through the guest closet this morning, and found birdy. Millicent must have left birdy at the house on her last sleepover."

"But I am sure that Millicent brought birdy—" I stopped in midsentence. I realized that at that moment it made no difference what had happened to birdy over the last week. What mattered was that birdy had been found, and that Millicent would sleep well again—for the first time in two weeks.

"Hello, Millicent," I said hugging her. Millicent was limp as a rag doll. "Guess what?"

"What?" Millicent said in a sad, pitiful tone.

"Grammy found birdy."

Edna handed Millicent birdy. Millicent smiled briefly, then narrowed her eyes and frowned. "Bad birdy," Millicent said. She placed birdy at the foot of the bed.

"Why isn't she sleeping with birdy? I mean she didn't sleep for days when she thought that birdy was lost. Now that birdy has been found, she doesn't want to sleep with birdy. Why not?"

"I think Millicent is punishing birdy," Edna whispered. "She wants to make sure that birdy never leaves her again. I'm sure that by tomorrow all will be fine."

For the first night in a week, Millicent smiled and cooed as she slept.

I tip-toed up to Millicent and kissed her on the forehead. "Night dear. Pleasant dreams."

I was certain she would have the best of dreams. And I was certain that birdy would never leave without permission again.

At that moment, all the frustration of the past week melted, and I experienced an inner peace that only a parent can truly enjoy and appreciate. I smiled, kissed Millicent again, then left. It truly had been a spiffy-doodle day.

Kids and Preschool

It is natural for parents to want the best for their children—to make sure that their kids have more and better opportunities than they had. My first wife and I were no different. We wanted the crème of the crème for our son, Malcolm.

So it was no surprise that we wanted Malcolm to attend the most exclusive pre-school in town. For me, the most exclusive school was Shannon's Center of Knowledge. Marcia had other ideas though. If Malcolm could not attend Miss Pringle's, then she toyed with the idea of keeping Malcolm out for a year or two until he could attend.

While most people called the pre-school Miss Pringle's or The Academy, the official name of my son's first learning institution was Miss Pringle's Fine Academy for the Educational Development of Pre-school Children. It was *the pre-school* in the metropolitan area. Every parent with money and/or stature wanted their child to attend. But even celebrity status did not guarantee placement for a future star.

Miss Pringle informed me that there was a waiting list of over five hundred children. Those on the outside looking in included the son of a movie star, the daughter of a United States Senator, and the twin girls of the inventor of the P51 Gaming System. Even the Mayor's daughter had not been admitted for the fall semester. Miss Pringle said that I was welcomed to apply, but that there was virtually no chance of Malcolm being admitted for the fall semester.

As I said, we wanted the best for Malcolm. But after touring Miss Pringles, I had to admit that I was actually relieved. The Academy raised snobbery to new levels. I could not envision that The Academy was the proper environment to rear our child. As I observed the children interact with other children, and with the teachers, I thought that the curriculum was too unstructured. Now I am not suggesting that four-year old children should be required to learn quantum physics in a pre-grade school environment. However, in light of the outrageous tuition that the Academy charged, I did expect more emphasis on the children mastering basic concepts such as ABC's, and numbers through one hundred. Instead, The Academy stressed individuality, and the beauty and integrity of self-expression.

Marcia stated that she would not take 'no' for an answer. Malcolm was going to be a Miss Pringle's kid, one way or another. She immediately arranged another interview with Miss Pringle. Marcia mentioned to Miss Pringle that they belonged to the same sorority. Apparently, that was the magic word, because Miss Pringle added Malcolm to the fall list of accepted students.

Afterward, Miss Pringle asked us to share with her our thoughts on child-rearing. Marcia expressed views that were different from her customary practice. To put it another way, Marcia sounded like a Miss Pringle advocate, when in fact, her views of child-rearing were almost identical to mine. I suspected that Marcia fed Miss Pringle that self-serving pablum solely to solidify her relationship with Miss Pringle. It worked, for Miss Pringle smiled as Marcia allowed me to talk. I however, engaged in no pretense or deception. I expressed my child-rearing rules in no uncertain terms. Marcia kicked my shoe in an effort to get me to tone down my rhetoric. But I was unfazed.

Miss Pringle told me that my impressions and views on child-rearing were wrong, radical, and quite disturbing. She noted that it was fortunate that I was turning over Malcolm's development to the staff of The Academy. To put it bluntly, she intimated that I had perhaps inflicted irreversible damage on my son, and there wasn't a moment to spare.

For the first few weeks, I paid tuition, and kept my mouth shut. I tried very hard to give Miss Pringle's Academy the benefit of the doubt. But nothing that I witnessed at the Academy re-assured me that we had made the right decision to send Malcolm to the school.

In particular, for me, one incident captured the essence of the Academy's shortcomings. I decided to join Malcolm for lunch. My son was especially pleased that his dad, his *best fwiend,* was spending some quality time together. Malcolm and I ate at a special table for parents and children. The other children, typically ate inside at their tables. While they were encouraged to spend the first five minutes quietly eating and savoring the events and activities of the morning, there was no rule demanding quiet time. But on that particular day, one of the children, a boy named Timmy, seemed to be in a particularly energetic mood.

"What's going on?" Timmy cried out as he climbed on the table. "Why is everybody so quiet? This ain't no funeral! Come on, let's have some chatter, some conversation." At that point, Timmy stomped his feet on the table. The sheer force of his feet pounding on the table caused lunch boxes, and drink cartons to topple over.

"Where are your teachers?" I asked Malcolm, convinced that they should take charge and restore order.

"They're eating lunch," Malcolm replied matter-of-factly.

"Shouldn't a couple of them be in here supervising the children?"

"That's not the Miss Pringles way," Malcolm replied as he finished his ham sandwich.

Timmy not satisfied with the ruckus he had already caused, continued to agitate his lunchtime brigade. "Say Sam," he said loudly, "are you going to eat those potato chips? I've got pretzels. I'm not into pretzels today. So do you want to trade?" With that Timmy tossed his pretzels to Sam, who in turn flipped his chips to Timmy.

I was appalled by the actions of master Timmy. But some of the other children applauded his aggressive behavior. A couple of the children even joined Timmy on the table, and began waving soda bottles, and assorted bags of snacks. "Who are we?" they shouted in unison. "We're the kings of the hill." Upon hearing that there could possibly be equals in master Timmy's kingdom, Timmy took immediate and swift action. He knocked the pretenders and intruders off the table. Timmy realized that there could be only one king—and that one king was none other than Timmy, himself.

Nothing that the child had done, upset Miss Pringle or the other teachers. In fact the only comment that they made concerned Timmy's use of the word *ain't*. They informed Timmy that wherever possible he should avoid using words that were classified as slang words. Timmy asked what was a slang word. Without hesitation, Miss Pringle recited the dictionary's definition of *ain't*. The definition she uttered was difficult for an adult, much less a child, to understand.

Timmy was not impressed, and continued to lead the revolt. An hour later, with potato chips, pretzels, and peanuts strewn over the room, and in the children's hair, Timmy tired and took a nap.

"He was just expressing himself," Miss Pringle observed.

"Picasso expressed himself," I shot back. "Timmy was out of control."

Miss Pringle chided me. "Mr. Hughes, I instruct my teachers not to use such negative terminology when speaking about the children. I will ask you to observe the same admonition. It is neither constructive nor fair to refer to any child as being *out of control*."

But it was factual to refer to a child as being *out of control,* especially as it related to master Timmy.

Anyway, on Wednesday mornings The Academy held Paper Plate Breakfasts. During these informal get-togethers, a nationally recognized child-rearing expert would share impressions and advice with the impressionable parents. Over a ten-week period, I attended four of the breakfasts. I attended the conferences more out of a desire to confront and challenge the so-called expert as opposed to seeking tips and embracing the expert's child-rearing philosophy. In a nutshell, the common theme dispensed by the child-rearing expert was that children needed their individual space, and that parents should never, ever, at no time, to infinity plus, intrude upon their child's individual space.

Without question, I considered each guest speaker as certifiably crazy, and incompetent to offer opinions on raising squash much less children. Consequently, I could have simply dismissed their comments as third-rate fiction. But I watched some of the other parents, both mothers and fathers taking copious notes and buying into the *expert's* tall tales.

Finally, during the tenth session, I had had enough. The speaker was a particularly offensive gentleman by the name of Brendan J. Bucknell the Fifth. After listening to him, I wanted to either down a fifth, or invoke the fifth. Bucknell said many outlandish things during his child-rearing session, but the one that caused me to confront him, was his observation that parents should never punish their children. He added that punishing children stifled their creativity and caused them to grow-up maladjusted and psychotic.

By punishing children, I took him to mean that a parent should not spank or strike a child. That approach was quite frankly against my value system. My parents, my father in particular, believed spanking cured all children's ills and abhorent proclivities. On periodic occasions during the year he gave me and my brother a "preventive" spanking designed to make us think twice before we did wrong. At other times during the year, he gave us a "make-up" spanking which effectively cleared the slate on punishable actions that we had done over a matter of weeks, but had not been caught. I must say, that spanking had a profound effect on me. While, I did not necessarily subscribe to "preventive" spankings, and "make-up spankings", I certainly saw a proper justification for them in certain circumstances.

At any rate, I had had enough of Bucknell, so I challenged his fundamental proposition on child-rearing. "So," I said in an arrogant tone, "You do not believe that parents should punish their children by spanking?"

The parents gasped in union. The horror and outrage stamped across their faces, and etched in their eyes, spoke volumes. *Was I crazy? What the hell was I thinking? Do you think we have time to lynch him?* Miss Pringle, appeared ready to faint. If she could have expelled me immediately, I'm sure she would have.

But if you saw Bucknell in person, you might mistake him for no one in particular. He was that nondescript. He appeared to be somewhere between forty and sixty, with a receding hair-line, a touch of gray, and quite ordinary facial features. Actually, Bucknell was more amused than outraged by my question. He smiled smugly, then said, "I am sorry that you misunderstood what I believed was a rather elementary proposition. When I said that children should not punish their children, I was including any form of punishment."

"That makes no sense," I said in a tone tinged with utter disdain and contempt.

Bucknell pulled a pipe from his shirt pocket, and tamped a bit of tobacco into it, though he made no attempt to light it. The other parents held their breath in collective anticipation. Bucknell peered over his reading glasses. After what seemed an eternity, he said, "And your name might be?"

"Hughes, Michael Devin Hughes."

"Tell me, Mr. Hughes. How many books on child-rearing have you written?"

"None."

"I see," Bucknell said, turning to the other parents, and shrugging his shoulders as if to say, *What do you expect from an amateur?*

"Tell me, Mr. Bucknell. How many children have you raised?"

"With seven self-help books on surviving grade school through high school, seven books I might add that have been translated into thirty-seven languages, and sixteen dialects, it is safe to say that I have raised millions of children. More importantly, I have raised the awareness of parents worldwide on the pitfalls of child-rearing. I have stressed the importance of children expressing themselves. It is a philosophy that is gaining acceptance throughout the civilized world, though there are still nagging pockets of resistance."

No doubt, the last comment was directed at me. Perhaps I imagined it, but I was almost certain that the other parents collectively murmured '*Amen*' in praise of his last remark.

Though it was an uphill battle, I was determined to expose the flawed thinking of Brendan J. Bucknell the Fifth. "All right," I began defiantly. "Let me ask how you would discipline a child in the following situation."

Miss Pringle jumped to her feet. "Mr. Hughes, I have had just about all that I intend to take from you."

Bucknell held out his hand in an attempt to both stop Miss Pringle, and calm her. The gesture accomplished both objectives. Miss Pringle sat down. Bucknell turned back toward me and said, "Mr. Hughes, I believe that you were in the middle of posing a hypothetical to me."

"I certainly was."

"Then by all means, proceed. I am all ears."

It was at that point that I noticed his ears and thought they resembled crinkled potato chips—but that was another story. I chuckled to myself, for I knew that he would have to abandon his lax discipline message once he heard my hypothetical. I felt confident that in just a few seconds, that smug smile, that confident smirk would be replaced with a contrite frown. When all eyes in the room gravitated towards me, I set forth my hypothetical. "Suppose that you decide to go the Art Museum to see an exhibit by one of the masters. Because you don't have a babysitter, and it's the last day of the exhibit, you have to take your five-year old son with you. But Junior tells you in no uncertain terms that he doesn't want to go. All the way to the Art Museum, your son throws the worst temper tantrum of his life. He kicks and screams and whines, and throws things. By the time he reaches the Art Museum, he is incorrigible. So much so, that as soon as he sees the highlight of the exhibit, he lunges past the security guards and manages to damage the prize painting before being restrained. Under the circumstances, what discipline would be appropriate?"

"What master was it?"

"What?"

"You said that the child ruined the painting of a master. What master was it?"

"Is that really important?"

"It might be."

"Why?"

"Because quite frankly, there are masters, and then there are impostors. And we must be careful when we impart titles on those who are not worthy of such titles."

It took every bit of will power that I possessed to keep me from calling Bucknell an impostor, and a half-baked child psychologist.

"All right, all right. The painting was by Bontonni."

"Before or after his first suicide attempt?"

Exasperated by the irrelevancy of the questions, the smugness of Bucknell, and the overall lack of support that I was receiving from the other parents, I snapped, "It doesn't make any difference whether it was before or after Bontonni's first suicide attempt. The only question that I posed was how would you discipline the offending child?"

Before Bucknell could answer, Miss Pringle jumped in, and said, "You needn't be subjected to anymore of this bullying, Brendan. I am sure that I am not alone when I say that I would like to apologize for the ill-mannered, and uniformed comments of Mr. Hughes."

Again, Bucknell laughed in a manner to suggest that none of us was his intellectual equal. "That's all right Sylvia. You need not be defensive on behalf of Mr. Hughes. All right, how would you have handled the hypothetical, Mr. Hughes just presented?"

There was perhaps a two second pause, then Sylvia Pringle said, "I would hug my child, say it was all right to damage the master's painting, and then give my child more space, so as not to stifle my child's creativity, and passion for living."

"I see," Bucknell said, with his eyes slightly arched. "And how would the other members of the group handle the hypothetical posed by Mr. Hughes?"

The other parents agreed with Sylvia's approach.

Bucknell flashed an arrogant smile. "I am gratified to say, that Sylvia, and the rest of you—save for Mr. Hughes—would have reacted properly to the hypothetical presented by Mr. Hughes. Nurturing the child, allowing the child to express him or herself is critical in early child rearing. And believe it or not, nurturing and permitting creativity becomes even more important as the child enters adolescence and puberty. It is the bedrock of sound, fundamental emotional growth. In fact, there is a similar hypothetical noted in my book, *Don't Stifle Creativity*. In the book's hypothetical, a teenager angered by unwarranted discipline by a parent, chooses to exact revenge by smashing the front window in a mint condition Edsel. Rather than grounding the teen, or requiring the teen to pay for the damage, I state that the proper course of action is to buy models of cars for the teen to smash. By re-directing the rage, the teen will confront his or her destructive forces, channel those energies into activities, and become a vibrant link in society."

If eyes were daggers, then my body would have been riddled with over fifty stab wounds. Indeed, all the parents thought that I was abrasive, and an unfit parent.

Bucknell sensed that the parents were about to tar and feather me, so he attempted to diffuse the tense situation. "By most parent's body language, I detect deep-seated hostility and resentment towards Mr. Hughes. While such emotions may have positive consequences in some circumstances, I suggest to you that this is not one of those circumstances."

In spite of Bucknell's comments, I was ostracized by the others for the rest of brown-bag lunch. Bucknell spouted a number of theories on child rearing—though none contemplated discipline, self-restraint, or placing limits on a child's activities.

After what seemed an eternity, Bucknell wrapped up his talk. "Remember what I have said," Bucknell offered, "and you will raise expressive, well-adjusted children, who will become productive members of society. Though I have another engagement across town, I will stay for a little while to answer any specific questions that you might have."

A handful of parents, congratulated Bucknell on his eye-opening insights. They would be better and wiser parents because of his advice. Some asked Bucknell to autograph their copy of his latest book. He obliged, and noted that his next book—*Don't Overreact!*—would be stocked in bookstores nationwide in the next three months.

I considered confronting Bucknell one more time, then changed my mind. It was entirely possible that Bucknell was a fraud, and did not believe one word of the drivel that he spouted to impressionable new parents. Or perhaps, he was a true believer in his misguided approach to discipline. I decided that it did not really matter, for Bucknell had thousands upon thousands of followers, and I realized that common sense or countless examples would not change his views on child-rearing. I prepared to leave.

Unexpectantly, Bucknell extended his hand. "I want to thank you, Mr. Hughes."

"For what?" I asked, astonished that he could sincerely extend any thanks in my direction.

"For galvanizing the other parents toward my philosophy."

"I'm not sure if I follow you."

"Wherever I speak, there is always one parent like you. Someone who simply does not believe in my sage advice. So that parent, like you today, challenges me, and because I am prepared for such a verbal confrontation, I always prevail. Not only that, but the confrontation solidifies my reputation with the other parents, and is a gold mine for selling my books, tapes, and other assorted merchandise. So, I am sure you did not intend for this to happen. But you have helped me quite a bit. And for that, I just wanted to say, thanks."

"Then it's not an act? You really believe that kids should not be punished?"

"I confess, Mr. Hughes. I am a product of my environment. I was never punished, and look at me as an adult—normal with no latent hostilities or repressed urges. The point is that agression breeds agression. As a child-rearing tool, punishment and other physical activity has no place in our society."

"Your parents never spanked you, or pinched you, and boxed your ears when you disobeyed them?"

"That's just the point. I had no rules, so I never disobeyed them. As a result, I flourished creatively. Just look at me, Mr. Hughes, and tell me what you see."

I suspected that Bucknell wanted me to acknowledge that he was a sterling testimony to his philosophy. But the fact of the matter was that I thought Bucknell's philosophy was wrong and convoluted. Setting boundaries for conduct, enforcing discipline, and if need be, a love tap to the rear on occasion was essential child-rearing as far as I was concerned. I stared at Bucknell with a forlorn look, and said, "I see a man who hasn't a clue on how to raise a loaf of bread or children."

"Good-bye, Mr. Hughes. I wish you well."

Strange, but at that moment, I almost felt sorry for Bucknell—but the operative word was *almost*.

On the way out, Bucknell stopped to wash his hands in the restroom. As he exited, little Timmy confronted him.

Timmy squinted, and asked in a most unpleasant voice, "Hey, what are you doing in *my* bathroom?"

"Excuse me," Bucknell returned, mildly annoyed by Timmy's aggressive behavior.

"You heard me. What are you doing in my bathroom?"

"I am sorry to have to inform you young man that the bathroom is not your bathroom, but rather the school's."

"Then you must not know that I am king of the school."

Bucknell laughed lightly. "Well king, would you please move?"

"Move? Hey, you ain't my father."

Bucknell attempted to go around, master Timmy. But the precocious tyke would have none of it, and promptly and swiftly kicked Bucknell in the shins.

The famed child-rearing specialist winced in pain, and hopped on one foot.

Hearing the commotion, Miss Pringle entered the common area. "What is going on, out here," she asked, casting a stern stare in my direction.

Bucknell's response was sharp and unpleasant. "Your student—that one there. He kicked me for no reason."

Helpful parent that I was, I added, "I witnessed everything. Timmy was simply expressing himself. I am certain that he should be rewarded for his actions.

Rewarding Timmy was not what Bucknell had in mind. But Miss Pringle re-inforced the notion that Timmy's creativity should not be stifled. So, instead of being spanked or given an afternoon-long time-out, Timmy was sent outside to play. Timmy smiled and left for his next conquest.

Timmy never knew it, but for his next five birthdays, I sent him five gallons of vanilla ice cream, and a birthday card that simply said, *Thanks.*

Birthday Parties

When it came to birthday parties, Marcia and I had rather simple rules—she would accompany Millicent to all of her parties, and I would take Malcolm to his birthday parties. On the Saturday in question, I drove Malcolm to Samantha Lovejoy's seventh birthday party. Samantha was not Malcolm's classmate, but rather a member of his afternoon tennis class. At his elementary school, I was accustomed to birthday parties being held at movie theaters, and bowling alleys, and skating rinks. Malcolm informed me however, that Samantha was having her party at the Children's Museum.

Looking back on that day, I should have realized that something was not quite right as soon as I drove into the Children's Museum parking lot. It was Saturday afternoon, typically the most crowded day at the museum. Yet, in a five hundred car lot, there were only ten cars parked. And if the ten cars were not a tip-off to an exclusive event, then the parking attendant clad in a tuxedo should have been. Nevertheless, as my second wife often said, I wasn't too bright.

Anyway, Malcolm had been invited to Samantha Lovejoy's birthday party. Apparently, Samantha liked Malcolm, though he was completely oblivious to her affection. It was that affection I suspect, that was the only reason Malcolm had been invited to the party.

Malcolm and I entered the Museum and were immediately greeted by a magician. He introduced himself as The Great Muldini. After the introductions were over, he draped a bedroom sheet over

Malcolm and recited a poem. There was a flash, and The Great Muldini lifted the sheet. To my surprise, Malcolm was gone.

"Not to worry," the magician assured. "Your son has been transported to the third floor, along with the other children. You can meet him there, or enjoy the Museum for a while, before you are re-united with him."

I had not visited the Museum in some time, so I chose to stroll by the various exhibits. I passed one father and two mothers who were also enjoying the historical artifacts, and interactive sites.

After sampling the culture on the first floor, I took the elevator to the second. Stepping off the elevator, I noticed the gathering spot for the parents—a long and lavish buffet table.

Perhaps it was just me, but I thought the thirty-foot buffet was a tad bit much. There was pizza, hot dogs, hamburgers, and filet mignon. And then there was the ice cream cart with seventy-one flavors. I mean how much of a demand could there be for kiwi raspberry ice cream? I asked that question and promptly learned that kiwi raspberry was Samantha's favorite.

Samantha's mother greeted me. "And you must be Malcolm's father. I can see the family resemblance."

I wasn't sure if the observation was a compliment or not. Nevertheless, I smiled, and replied, "Thanks. And thank you for inviting Malcolm to Samantha's birthday party."

"Well the one person that Samantha wanted to make sure that we invited was Malcolm. She's quite smitten by him, you know."

"That's what I hear."

"So how long have you been members of the club?"

By club, I suspected that Samantha's mother was referring to the Halton-Murray Golf and Tennis Club where Samantha and Malcolm took tennis lessons. Halton-Murray was the most exclusive and expensive country club in the state. Its application fee was more than some people make in wages in a lifetime. The club was a favorite of old wealth, politicians, musicians, and athletes. Since I was none of the above, I did not qualify for membership at Halton-Murray. However, the club did offer an afternoon tennis program for children, which was not dependent on membership in Halton-Murray. That was our association to Halton-Murray.

"We're new to the club," I bluffed.

"Well be sure to sample Chef Maynard's blueberry pancakes on Sunday mornings. They are to die for."

Samantha's mother was not the first person to rave about Chef Maynard's culinary creations. Supposedly Halton-Murray had enticed Chef Maynard to take a leave of absence from his signature Paris restaurant, *Beau Food*. Since the restaurant was open to all on the weekends, perhaps there was a chance that I would get to sample his wares. First however, I would have to save one full paycheck, in order to pay for the average meal. Good food was by no means cheap.

One of the mothers inquired of Samantha's mom, "Did Samantha receive an invitation to Jane's birthday party?"

"Yes."

"Did you see where the party's going to be?"

Samantha's mom placed her hand over her mouth, and laughed lightly as though she were at a tea party. "Yes, at the bowling alley."

"It's sad that her parents showed a complete lack of imagination in party preparation."

Lack of imagination in party preparation? I could tell that they were social vultures looking for their next feast, and I certainly appeared vulnerable.

At that moment Samantha's mother turned to me, and asked the obvious question. "So Michael, what will be the theme of Malcolm's birthday party?"

Theme? There wasn't going to be any theme to Malcolm's birthday party. He was going to have balloons, cake, ice cream, and cheap party bags. I figured that the party wouldn't cost me more than fifty dollars top. In comparison, it appeared that Samantha's candles alone cost more than fifty dollars.

My conscience told me to come clean with the ladies and confess that Malcolm was going to have a plain, inexpensive, and uneventful birthday party. My vain side told me that I would be a fool to admit to the truth, and that I should lie for as long as possible. My vain side won easily.

I admit that I was intimidated by the sheer size of Samantha's birthday party. Instead of answering honestly and telling Samantha's mother that Malcolm's next birthday party was going to be held at the nearest bowling alley, I succumbed to the surroundings. As I sipped on champagne, I replied, "I'm still working on the details of his birthday party. I was thinking that I might go with a carnival theme."

"A carnival theme?" Samantha's mother repeated.

I did not know what to make of her response. Had my answer confirmed her suspicion that I was an uncouth slob without an original bone in my body? Or had my answer pleasantly surprised her and revealed that I was both creative and a big spender? Not sure, I followed my vain side that said lie until caught, then lie some more. "Yes, you know, perhaps with a small midway."

"Carnival? Midway? Why it's ingenous. And you know what?"

I had a feeling that I did not want to know the answer, but I asked anyway. "What?"

"My husband's firm represents a giant conglomerate that owns a carnival. I believe that it is Trapezoid Shows Unlimited. Call me next week, and I can give you the phone number, and the E-mail address."

"Thanks." It did not take a thermo nuclear physicist to see that I was out of my element. I should have walked away and viewed the museum exhibits alone. But like any regular joe, I was attracted to the sheer power and wealth that these parents represented. So I followed two of the mothers back to the buffet.

There I was at the buffet with a couple of the other parents. A gentleman dressed in tuxedo prepared a plate for me that consisted of a hamburger with mustard, pickle, and ketchup, french fries, and a cola. I chatted with Terry's father. He was the CEO of a multinational conglomerate. Though our professional paths were completely different, we bonded over sports. He loved college basketball, as I did. We supported different teams, but appreciated the efforts of gifted athletes, both men and women. Anyway, Terry's father had to leave after receiving an urgent page.

I conversed a bit with a couple of other mothers. They talked about the best boutiques in San Francisco, and Paris. I listened mostly, offering an occasional comment about Marcia's favorite shopping areas. But I realized that they were including me in their conversation only out of polite pity. A few more mothers gathered, and the discussion shifted from shopping to skiing. I had skied once in my life, in the Poconos of Pennsylvania. While the Poconos received better than expected reviews as a destination for newlyweds, not one of the mothers mentioned the Poconos as a preferred ski destination. One mother who briefly discussed her latest trip to some ski resort out west was greeted by yawns or feigned interest. Apparently, skiing at domestic resorts was for the moment out of style. Switzerland and Japan were the hottest ski destinations. Anyway, after fifteen minutes or so, the mothers tired of their game of one-upmanship, and drifted apart.

I took advantage of the break by returning to the buffet line for a third time.

"I'm sorry, I don't recall your name."

"It's Michael."

"But of course." Samantha's mother turned back to Anjolie's mother and said, "Well, Michael was just telling us that he's planning a carnival theme for his son's birthday party."

"A carnival theme?"

"Yes, a carnival theme."

"Really?"

There was a certain edge and bite in Anjolie's mother's remarks that I did not appreciate. More importantly, she did not seem impressed by my pronouncement. Perhaps she saw me for the phony and liar that I was. Perhaps the carnival theme was yesterday's news. Perhaps I should have undergone analysis for allowing my vanity, and competitive juices to affect my better judgment.

Anjolie's mother gave me the once over, the second over, the third over. Each time she raised and lowered her eyes, staring at every square inch of my body.

"Frederick, we must talk."

I raised my eyebrows. "The name is Michael."

"Really? You don't look like a Michael. A Frederick perhaps, but not a Michael."

"Trust me, it's Michael."

"Oh well, I suppose that's your problem. But I digress. The fact of the matter is that your son cannot have a birthday party with a carnival theme."

It was my turn to give Anjolie's mother the once over. "What do you mean my son cannot have a birthday party with a carnival theme?"

"My daughter Anjolie is having a birthday party with a carnival theme. Obviously, she must have innocently told your son, who told you, and you decided to steal my original idea."

"Steal your idea? That's preposterous."

"Really? Well, you look like the type of person who would have your son's birthday party at a miniature golf course."

While that observation was right on point, I indignantly replied, "I've been planning a carnival theme birthday party for my son for almost a year. If anyone stole the idea it would have been you and your daughter."

"You have been planning the birthday party?" She either burped or laughed lightly. I could not tell which. "You really are a novice, aren't you? You don't plan a birthday party with a carnival theme. You have a birthday party planner do that. You co-ordinate the actions of the birthday party planner. Anyway, if you had been planning a birthday party with a carnival theme, then you would know that it takes over a year to properly co-ordinate. Why securing the proper permits for the midway rides sometimes takes almost a year by itself. And I am not even factoring in the time to file the necessary paperwork for the Chinese acrobats, and French jugglers."

Chinese acrobats? French jugglers? I was about ready to say that Malcolm could have his birthday party at the nearby Funky Burgers. But there was something in Anjolie mother's demeanor that prevented me from acquiescing just yet. "The only birthday planner I trust is me. The preparations are proceeding exceedingly well. I can't go into all the details right now. But I am positive that Anjolie and the other children will be thrilled by the carnival theme."

Anjolie's mother was still skeptical. "Okay, tell me how much land have you secured for the party?"

"I'm still negotiating that aspect."

"You need at least fifty acres to do justice to that type of party. Our estate has one hundred acres. So if you can't secure—"

"I will have the necessary land."

I could tell that Anjolie's mother did not believe me. To her, I was both a low-class liar and a nuisance. With each detail of the carnival-themed party that she revealed, it became more apparent that I could not afford the sawdust for the midway, much less one midway ride. She was annoyed by my lying. She was peturbed by my reckless ways. Indeed, Anjolie had grown tired of my charade. "All right, how much will it take to get you to drop the carnival theme for your son's next birthday party?"

"You don't have enough money."

Anjolie's mother laughed. It was a laugh that I have never forgotten. It was a laugh of person who was clearly amused by the utterly preposterous comment of a commoner. Anjolie's mother raised her eyebrows, and cocked her head. I sensed that she had played this game before, and was quite good at it. She cleared her throat in order to make the grand announcement. "My husband spends more on toilet tissue, then you spent on your house. My husband makes more in one day, then you would make in fifteen lifetimes. My husband makes more in a year than the gross national product in thirty of the world's countries. Now how much will it cost?"

In spite of the fact that Anjolie's mother insulted me twice in under a minute, it was her last comment that grabbed my attention. *Makes more than thirty of the world's countries.* That statement impressed me. From that moment forward, I saw Anjolie's mother in a different light.

"Let's face brass tacks, Michael, shall we? My daughter Anjolie is going to have a birthday party with a carnival theme come hell or high water. Now perhaps you can mortgage your house, and pawn the gold in your mouth, and eat peanut butter sandwiches for the rest of your life in order to afford the party. But I guarantee you I will do whatever it takes to make sure that Anjolie's party is first, larger, and more extravagant. That, in turn, will render your son's similarly-themed party immaterial. Tell me, is that what you want?"

"You would do that, just to ruin my son's party? Is a carnival theme that important to you?"

"The answer to the first question is—in a heartbeat. The answer to the second question is—yes. Now, I'll ask again. How much is it going to take to get you to drop the carnival theme for your son's birthday party?"

Two things suddenly dawned on me. The first revelation was that Malcolm had never requested a fancy or terribly expensive birthday party. I suspected that Anjolie had not asked for such an exotically-themed birthday party either. It was the parents of each child that were carrying a happy occasion to ridiculous lengths. I got caught up in the moment of trying to impress parents of my son's class-mates—parents that I didn't know, and probably would not associate with socially, if I did know them (with Terry's dad being the possible exception).

As important as the first revelation was, it was the second revelation that provided greater insight into the human soul—namely that I would be crazy if I didn't let Anjolie's mother buy me out for an outlandish sum.

Over the next several minutes, Anjolie's mother and I dickered over the amount of the buy-out and terms associated with the buy-out. Ultimately, I agreed to forego throwing a carnival-themed party for either Malcolm or Millicent for four years. Moreover, if I chose to sponsor a party for any of my children, other than a party at a theater, bowling alley, or fast food restaurant, I would have to receive prior approval from Anjolie's mother. For effectively relinquishing rights to throw an extravagant birthday party (something until that day, I had never even considered), I received a sum of money that was obscene by most standards. Under terms of the birthday party settlement agreement, I am not allowed to reveal the exact sum. However, let me just say that the amount I deposited in the bank was enough to pay for a year of college at an Ivy League School.

For the rest of the afternoon, I ambled around the museum. I marveled at the interactive attractions. There were no lines and no fees. Everything was free. Just the way I liked it.

The party was supposed to end at five pm. I discovered however, that these type of themed birthday parties continue until the last child leaves with a parent.

"Don't forget your goodie bag, Malcolm," Samantha's mom said.

What Samantha called a goodie bag was actually a hand-stitched and embroidered limited edition Doshwe rolling garment bag. By itself, the garment bag cost five hundred dollars. "Here, Malcolm. Thank you for coming to my party. I sure hope you had a good time."

Malcolm unzipped surveyed the contents of the goodie bag. "What? Oh yeah, I had a good time. Thanks for inviting me."

"See you Monday at tennis." Samantha batted her eyelashes and threw my son a kiss. No doubt, she was infatuated with Malcolm. But like any boy under the age of eight, Malcolm would have rather kissed a frog, warts and all, than to have any mushy contact with a girl.

"Okay," he said, barely acknowledging her existence.

We walked towards the front door. "Wait, Michael!" Samantha's mother called out. "We have a goodie bag for the parents as well."

"Really?" Samantha's mother presented me with a larger garment bag. The larger version was seven hundred dollars at least. "It was indeed a pleasure meeting you. I hope that we can get together again in the near future."

Once inside the car, I glanced inside the "goodie bag", and noticed that among its contents were a bottle of Dom Perignon, a bar of pure gold, and a cashmere sweater. Malcolm informed me that his "goodie bag" contained a pair of the hottest most expensive tennis shoes around (the Lance-em-ups), a personal DVD player, the latest video game system, a year's gift certificate for four to several Florida theme parks, and a personal organizer. At seven, I wondered what Malcolm would have to organize. In the end analysis who cared. What mattered was that Malcolm enjoyed the party, and I made the right move by being bought out by Anjolie's mother. The goodie bag gifts alone would have caused bankruptcy.

I admit that it would be nice to have rich friends that could lavish with me gifts and good times on a frequent basis. But the fact of the matter was that Samantha's infatuation with Malcolm would not last forever—or even probably past the next week. So, in a real sense, I doubted that I would be receiving invitations to the mansion. Nevertheless, beyond the vanity, and deceit, and one-upmanship, I longed for Malcolm to remain on the A-list for birthday parties.

Malcolm played with a Zeus Pocket Player, a sophisticated video game device that had not been officially introduced for sale yet. Like I said, Samantha's mother knew how to throw a birthday party.

"How was the birthday party, son?"

"It was okay."

Okay—that was high praise indeed from Malcolm. We drove home.

Movies

Ah, a weekend with Malcolm. Next week school would start in earnest, and Malcolm's routine would be much different. He would be studying, preparing reports for school, and playing in his weekend tennis league. But on the last weekend of mindless freedom, it would be fun time for me and my son to just kick back and spend some quality time together. He probably would ask to go to the water park, or the mega-arcade, or perhaps the miniature golf complex. Yes, I was sure that it would be something outdoors, and fun.

As a special treat, I bought gooey cinnamon rolls and hot glazed doughnuts for breakfast.

Malcolm grabbed two doughnuts and a cinnamon roll. With cheeks stuffed, he said in a muffled voice, "Thanks, pops." He poured a glass of milk.

"So what would you like to do today, son?"

"I want to go to the movies, pops. I want to see The Bantalears—Movie #4—The Rescue."

"The Bantalears? You mean those bear-like creatures with the hypnotic eyes. Pick another movie. I sat through the first three movies and watched some of the most non-sensical plots imaginable. There's no way that I'm going to go sit in a crowded theater with hundreds of screaming kids and watch those furry smudgepots battle characters who are evil and are devoid of morals."

"You promised, pops."

"I did?"

"Yeah, you said, if The Bantalers were still at the movies the Saturday before Labor Day, you would take me. Well, it's still playing at the Uptown 23."

"Are you sure?"

"I checked this morning's paper, and called the theater hotline. The Bantalears are being shown at the Uptown 23 at noon, two, four, six, and eight. I thought that if we caught the noon show, that would give us enough time to play a few games at the mega-arcade."

From my perspective, megaplex theaters should be banned if they were going to carry movies past their prime. I mean there was a time before megaplexes that you had to rush and see a movie in a couple of weeks, or be forced to wait until it was shown on television years later. But with the advent of megaplexes, and discount theaters, and videos, and DVDs, and video on demand, and cable movie networks, it appeared that movies no matter how awful, despised, or woeful from a box office standpoint were guaranteed immortality. I realized that it would be futile to suggest another movie, so I grudgingly agreed to take Malcolm to the noon showing of The Bantalears.

"Thanks, pops." Malcolm said, as he finished his milk. "We're going to have a great time at the movies."

"Yeah, a great time," I replied, trying to get mentally up for yet another Bantalears movie.

We arrived at the Uptown 23 at a quarter to noon. There were roughly a dozen people in front of us. Not one of them purchased tickets for The Bantalears. Maybe the theater was already sold out, and we would have no choice but to go to another movie.

I crossed my fingers as I said, "One child and one adult ticket to see The Bantalears."

The ticket attendant raised her eyebrows. It appeared that she wanted to say something about our choice of movie. I smiled. Certainly she was going to tell us that there were no available seats for the movie. But I was wrong, for after the pronounced pause, she said, "That will be six dollars."

I slipped a ten under the glass partition.

She slid the change and tickets back. The attendant noted, "Theater twenty-three."

We stopped at concession stand number one to buy the fundamental movie snacks—popcorn and soda. I paid for the refreshments, then we proceeded to our designated theater.

"Say pops, do you remember The Bantalears #3—The Mission?"

"Yes."

"It was a great movie, wasn't it?"

I couldn't remember anything about The Bantalears #3, or any of the earlier Bantalears movies. But I could never forget the crowds, especially for the first movie. With unprecedented promotion, publicity, and hype, The Bantalears #1, was the most eagerly anticipated movie of that long hot summer. Advance word of the movie dictated that it play in at least six theaters of the movie complex.

By the time, we purchased tickets, the line snaked around the far corner of the movie complex, and down a service alley. At least seven hundred kids and parents waited impatiently for the theater to open. Every kid knew The Bantalears theme song, and they sang it at every chance during the movie, which seemed like every five minutes. Not content with singing the song at the movie, Malcolm sang it every hour on the hour for one solid day, until I finally forbade the song from being sung, hummed, or mentioned in the house. By then however, it was too late, for that drippy melody had been permanently etched in the recesses of my memory.

But I digress. Theater number twenty-three was located in a tiny alcove, separated from the other movie screens. It appeared that theater number twenty-three had been an afterthought—a place to view movies that were one step from being released in video or DVD format. The movie was so far removed from any of the concession stands, that Malcolm had munched a quarter of his popcorn by the time we reached theater twenty-three.

We entered theater number twenty-three. Instead of being over-whelmed by the sight of hundreds of children chanting and stamp-ing for the start of The Bantalears #4—The Rescue, I was greeted by the sound of theater background music.

"Where do you want to sit, pops?" Malcolm asked, his voice echo-ing off the walls.

I scanned the theater, and quickly counted the open seats. There were one hundred fifty-seven stadium seats in theater twenty-three—and all one hundred fifty-seven of them were empty. Five minutes before the start time of the movie, and there were no other patrons.

"Isn't this great, pops? We've got the whole theater to ourselves."

In over forty years of watching movies at theaters, I could not once remember a theater being so empty, so quiet, and quite frankly, so clean. There were no candy wrappers, or crumpled cups of soda, or trails of mashed popcorn on the floor of the theater. It was as if theater twenty-three had not been used in quite some time.

The dual questions that I immediately pondered were—one—was the movie theater empty because all the children in town had already seen The Bantalears movie, or two—was the theater empty because The Bantalears movie was so bad, even by children's movie stan-dards, that after the opening weekend, no one dared venture to see the movie. I briefly considered asking for a refund. But Malcolm's unabashed contented expression dashed that thought.

Since I did not express any preference for seats, Malcolm chose two seats in the middle of the top row. "Great seats, huh, pops? I mean, did we luck out, or what? We got the whole theater to our-selves. This is great. I hope it stays that way."

Malcolm's wish was granted because no one else entered theater twenty-three. No child, no teenage couple, no adult—I repeat—no one else stepped into theater twenty-three to watch The Bantalears #4—The Rescue.

Around the fourth or fifth preview—a cartoon about an arma-
dillo with supernatural powers, I dozed off. I am not sure how long I
slept, but it was long enough to drool, and let out one rim-rocking
snore. Malcolm nudged me, and whispered, "The movie is about to
start, pops. I know that you don't want to miss a minute of the
action."

I thought to myself, *If there is a minute of action total in this movie,
then that would be the surprise.* Not wishing to ruin Malcolm's fun
however, I replied, "Thanks, son."

Malcolm whispered again, "You want some popcorn, pops?"

"You needn't whisper, Malcolm. We're the only ones here. So
enjoy yourself."

"Oh, yeah," Malcolm said in a much louder voice. "Isn't this great,
pops? There's no girls, and no one else to bother us. It's just the
guys." Malcolm squeezed my shoulder.

I had to admit that in an odd sort of way, it was nice to have the
movie theater all to ourselves. We didn't have to watch what we did
or said. It was just two guys at the movies, and having some fun.

With the previews over, it was now time for the main feature.
Most people watch movies quietly, so as not to miss any of the
action. Malcolm was not the typical movie-goer, however. No, Malcolm was what I called a participatory movie-goer. Every scene provided Malcolm with another opportunity to interact with the
characters on the screen. When one of the Bantalears was about to be
clubbed, Malcolm yelled, "What's wrong? Are you blind? Evil King
Mactomacto is about to knock you out. Turn around before its too
late!" Of course, the Bantalear neither heard nor heeded Malcolm's
warning, and was promptly knocked out. Not only was one Bantalear knocked out, but all four Bantalears were clubbed on the head,
and tied up.

When Malcolm was not speaking to the movie's characters, he was
bombarding me with questions. Some pertained to the movie we
were watching—most did not. Among the questions he asked me

were—Why were hot dogs called hot dogs?—What was my favorite Bantalear movie?—Who invented crayons?—and Which Bantalear was my favorite? To each question, I answered, "I don't know." Rather than stop asking me questions, Malcolm bombarded me with more.

"You're going to miss one of the more important scenes in the movie, son."

"Okay, pops. You can tell me why babies aren't born with teeth later."

No one would ever confuse The Bantalears with great cinema. There was absolutely no chance that the film would win or even be nominated for an award in any movie classification or category. Not even the title song would rate a nomination. But The Bantalears did work on one level—it was marginally entertaining with a plot that was both implausible and uplifting. In the end, the characters prevailed over the forces of evil.

The movie ended, but we lingered, while a concession clerk checked for discarded drink cups and popcorn boxes. There were none, for we had already disposed of our trash in the proper receptacles. As the end credits rolled, we counted over two hundred animation artists. Malcolm was impressed, and I was amazed that that many adults could be associated with the movie.

As soon as we left the theater, Malcolm asked, "Can we buy the video, pops?"

Ordinarily, I would expect that the video would be available four to six months after release. However, with the latest Bantalears movie, I suspected that the video would be hitting the retail stores within a couple of weeks. In the scope of things, Malcolm's request was modest. "Sure, son. We can buy the video."

Based on the rather stark ticket sales, it was entirely possible that Malcolm would be one of a select few who would purchase the video. And based on past viewing practices it was likely that Malcolm would watch the movie at least a dozen times in the first week that he had the video.

"I love you pops. You are my best friend."

I hoped that when Malcolm became an adult he would still consider me his best friend. For the moment though, I was his best friend, and I didn't think things could get much better.

As we walked out of the Uptown 23 Theaters, Malcolm asked, "Pops, will you take me to see next the Bantalears movie when it comes out next summer."

"Sure, son. That's what best friends do."

Bad Dreams

Some people have good dreams, others bad dreams. Yet others have dreams that they cannot remember. But of course, bad dreams are worse. And to a little girl, not much taller than a tennis racket, bad dreams are beyond description.

On the night in question, I was sleeping blissfully. I had just been elected President, and I was busy taking congratulatory calls from the world's leaders. Then, in my dream, I heard a tiny voice call out, *Daddy!*

"What?" I mumbled.

"Millicent called for you," Marcia answered.

So the tiny voice had been real, as opposed to imagined. I rolled over and searched for my bedroom shoes.

"Daddy! Daddy! Daddy!" Millicent yelled out with all her little girl might.

I ran to her room and opened the door. With her night light providing just enough illumination, I could see Millicent wrapped up in her sheets. On either side was one of her stuffed animals. I suspected that they were supposed to protect her until I arrived.

"Daddy, daddy, I had a bad, very bad dream."

"What was the dream about?"

"Oh, daddy, it was awful. I was lost in the woods, and I was trying to get back home. And I was calling out for you and mommy, but you couldn't hear me. And the only thing could hear me was the big bad woofin bear."

"The big bad woofin bear?"

"Yeah."

This was not Millicent's first encounter with the big bad woofin bear. It was the current recurring nightmare. He was over eight feet tall, with scraggly black hair, and large brown teeth with sharp gold tips. Big bad woofin bear was not nice, and his nostrils flared when he growled.

"Everything is going to be okay. Everything is going to be all right."

"Are you sure, daddy?"

"Of course, I'm sure"

"But what if the big bad woofin bear comes back?"

"He won't, I promise."

"But what if he does, daddy?"

"Then I will beat the big bad woofin bear so bad, that it will never want to come back to our house or your bedroom."

"Really, daddy?"

"Would daddy, lie?"

"No, daddy never lies," Millicent said, as she squeezed my hand.

I kissed Millicent's forehead, then returned to my bedroom.

Marcia rolled over, and asked, "Did Millicent have another bad dream?"

"Yeah, I had to battle big bad woofin bear."

"Again?"

"Yeah, but I got rid of him once and for all this time," I responded.

Marcia yawned. "That's what you said last time, and the time before that."

"Well he's gone for good." I nudged Marcia. "When you were a little girl, what types of bad dreams did you have?"

"I can only remember two, and in both I was lost at sea."

As bad dreams go, Marcia's were boring.

I drifted back to sleep. It was just before two. Soon I was dreaming about spiders, cowboys, and chocolate pudding. Somehow, they all made sense in the dream, though I do not recall now. At any rate, my dream was interrupted by the frantic voice of Millicent. Glancing at the radio-clock, I noticed that it was seven minutes after two. Well ten minutes of sleep was better than nothing.

"Daddy, daddy!" Millicent cried out. "Come here quick!"

I stepped back into Millicent's room, only to find her clutching her pillow, and shivering, as though she had confronted some monster. I clutched Millicent, and rocked her gently. "What's wrong, my dear?"

"I had another bad dream, daddy."

"Well, it couldn't have been the big bad woofin bear."

"Oh no, daddy. It wasn't the big bad woofin bear, daddy. He wouldn't dare come back, after you told him not to."

"Then what was your bad dream about?"

"It was the gigantic smelly yellow bird, daddy. And he was chasing me all around the house. I told him to stop chasing me—that that was not a nice thing to do. But he wouldn't listen to me—So I called you."

I shook my fist into the air, and scowled. "Listen gigantic smelly yellow bird. You leave my daughter Millicent alone. Leave this house immediately, and never come back. If you do, then you will have to fight me, and I assure you that it will be your last fight."

We listened for a minute or two and heard nothing but the ticking of Millicent's clock.

"He's gone, dear," I observed. "You'll have no more bad dreams about him."

Millicent's eyes darted around the room, making sure that there was no trace of the gigantic smelly yellow bird. "Thank you, daddy."

"You're welcome." Again, I kissed Millicent's forehead. "Now, I want you to have pleasant dreams—dreams about roses and carnations and cool summer evenings watching lightning bugs flicker as night approaches. Do you think you can dream about beautiful and pleasant things, dear?"

"I'll try."

In ten minutes, Millicent had drifted back to sleep. There was a faint smile on her face, as she rolled near a stuffed animal.

I slipped back into bed.

"Another bad dream?" Marcia asked.

"Yes. She dreamed about gigantic smelly yellow bird this time."

Marcia asked another question, but I did not answer, for I was already asleep, and dreaming. My dream was pleasant and beautiful—one of roses and carnations on a cool summer evening with lightning bugs flickering in the distance—suddenly the beautiful dream turned ominous—the roses and carnations grew legs and stormed out of the garden. With beady eyes, and thorny arms, they searched for me. I tried to hide, but lightning bugs led the roses and carnations to my secret refuge. I was trapped and just about to become an evening feast for flowers when I was saved by the voice of my daughter.

"Daddy, daddy! I need you now. Please come quick."

For the third time in one night, I rushed to Millicent's room. This time, she had turned on her desk lamp.

"It wasn't big bad woofin bear, daddy. And it wasn't gigantic smelly yellow bird. This time it was huge and heavy orange elephant."

"Well you know that it was a dream, right?"

"It seemed so real daddy. The elephant tried to grab me with his trunk. I escaped, but barely."

As I comforted Millicent, Malcolm, wearing Bantalear pajamas, trudged into her bedroom. Rubbing his eyes, Malcolm seemed a bit peturbed that dreams about his favorite cartoon characters had been interrupted. "Hey pops. I keep hearing Millicent calling for you. What's wrong?"

"Millicent is having bad dreams."

As the younger brother, Malcolm enjoyed any opportunity to embarrass, irritate, or belittle his sister.

"Hey pops. Don't pay attention to Millicent. She's faking the nightmares. She just wants some attention."

"I'm not faking, daddy," Millicent responded defensively.

"Sure you are Millicent. Just like every other time."

"And just how would you know, son?"

"Because, every time Millicent has bad dreams she claims that they are about big bad woofin bears, and gigantic smelly yellow birds, and huge and heavy orange elephants. And everybody knows that there are no such creatures. So she's got to be faking."

"And you're sure about that?"

"Sure, I'm sure. I mean none of us has actually seen a big bad woofin bear, have we?"

I did not answer.

"I have," Millicent said.

"I rest my case." Malcolm paused then added, "Now if you were talking about The Mummy, or The Creature from the Black Lagoon, or even Count Dracula, then that would be a different story—for those monsters are real. And she could have a bad dream about them."

"I've got news for you, son. The Mummy, The Creature from the Black Lagoon, and Count Dracula are not real either."

"Yes, they are pops."

"No, they are not."

"Yes, they are. I've seen them on TV."

"Just because something's on TV does not mean that it's real."

"Oh, I know some things on TV are not real, like the weather reports. But The Mummy—I mean they even have stories about The Mummy on cable—they showed his tomb and everything—that's as real as it can get."

I returned to the matter at hand, which was comforting Millicent. "Are you going to be okay, sweetheart?"

"Yes, daddy. I am not scarred at all anymore." Millicent cast a disapproving glance towards Malcolm. "And when Malcolm wakes up later tonight, I'll help him—especially since he thinks that The Mummy is real."

"Hey it is real."

Before they got into an argument, I intervened. "Stop it, both of you."

Malcolm made a series of menacing faces towards Millicent.

"Daddy!" Millicent cried. "Make Malcolm stop. He's twisting his face real spooky like. It's scaring me."

"Stop making faces, son."

"Sure thing, pops."

Because of Malcolm's early morning stunt, it took another fifteen minutes to calm Millicent's fears and anxiety. In time, she drifted off to sleep.

I checked on Malcolm. He was asleep, but curled up in a ball. That typically meant that my son was having a bad dream. All that talk about movie monsters probably had unsettled my youngest.

As my second eye closed, I heard the shuffle of little feet in slippers sliding closer to the door. A round head poked into the bedroom.

"Malcolm, is that you?" I asked groggily.

"Hey, pops," Malcolm said as he tugged on my pajamas, "I'm pretty sure that I saw the Creature From the Black Lagoon hiding in one the closets upstairs."

"I told you that there is no such creature."

"I know that you're saying that, pops, because you want me to be brave. And that's just fine and dandy. But the fact of the matter is that I'm a little kid who is afraid of the Creature From the Black Lagoon. So can I get in bed with you and mommy?"

I was about to say "no", when Marcia said, "Sure son."

Malcolm breathed a sigh of relief, then scooted under the covers between Marcia and me.

Less than a minute later, Millicent stepped into the bedroom. Afraid of shadows and hallway monsters, Millicent seldom ventured outside her room at night, preferring to call me, when needed. That she had confronted her fears, and zipped down the corridor, lit only by a nightlight, was significant.

"Millicent, what's wrong?" Marcia asked.

Spying her brother snuggled in mommy and daddy's bed, Millicent ignored Marcia's question, and instead asked, "Say what are you doing in here?"

"I was checking on mommy and daddy. I wanted to make sure that they were okay."

"You came in here because you're scared."

"I'm not scared. There's nothing to be scared of—right, pops?"

"Right," I mumbled.

"What's wrong?" Marcia asked once more.

"I heard squishy squealy mouse."

"You're letting your imagination get the best of you," Malcolm remarked, as he propped his head on Marcia's shoulder.

"Look who's talking. Maybe I should call The Mummy, and see if he wants to have you for dinner—literally."

"That's not funny—not funny at all. Pops make Millicent stop talking that way."

"All right, Millicent."

"I'm sorry, daddy."

"Would you like to sleep in our bed tonight, sweetheart?" Marcia asked.

Millicent nodded, and squeezed between Malcolm and Marcia. Millicent sighed contently, then said, "Night, Malcolm, daddy, mommy."

Marcia kissed her on the forehead. In minutes, they were both cooing.

So Millicent, and Marcia slept quite comfortably. I tried. But my buddy, my pal Malcolm nudged me for the rest of the night. "You all right, pops?" he asked me on numerous occasions. "Because I am all right. I am safe and sound in this bed with you, mommy, and Millicent. There are no creatures or monsters in this bedroom with us."

"Go to sleep, son," I urged Malcolm. "Nothing is going to happen."

Malcolm tossed and turned, and squirmed and rolled, and wiggled his toes and cracked his knuckles, and did everything that a child that could not sleep would do. When I finally drifted off to sleep, Malcolm nudged—actually poked me in the side and said, "Wake up, pops! Wake up! You're snoring like you're all alone. But you're not. There are some of us that are trying to go to sleep. So, wake up, and stop snoring, pops!"

Finally, just before daybreak, Malcolm fell asleep. With one hand behind his head, he smacked his lips, and emitted odd sounds as he slept.

Bad Grades

Simply put, grades C or below in our household were unacceptable, without extenuating circumstances. Being out of school for a few days with a cold was not a sufficient excuse or reason for bringing a C home on a report card. In order to justify a C, the loss of enough blood to require a transfusion, and a hospital stay of at least a week would be necessary.

Each day, when we picked the kids up from school, either Marcia or I would ask about their daily grades. Normally, they told us, and we would move on to other subjects. But not on that day—that day was different.

"How was school today?" I asked, not expecting any earth shattering news.

Millicent proceeded to give me a ten minute re-cap on her day's activities. In her words, it had been backwater cool. I am not exactly sure what that meant, but I guessed that was the current slang for a nearly perfect day. Millicent was all smiles.

Malcolm on the other hand was an oh so sad boy. If his head had been any lower, he could have licked breadcrumbs from the kitchen floor.

I asked, "What's wrong, son?"

"Well, I sort of had a problem on one test this week, dad."

"What test?"

"State capitals."

"So what was your grade?"

"I didn't fail the test, dad."

"What was your grade?"

"In fact, considering the complexity of the test material, I would say that I did quite well."

"What was your grade?"

"In fact there were some kids that failed the test."

"I am not interested in the other kids, only you. What was your grade?"

Instead of telling me his grade, Malcolm handed me the test paper. It was not a sea of red ink. But it was far more than I expected. On a test of state capitals, Malcolm's score was seventy—a C minus. I stared at the grade. I turned it sideways, and upside down. The grade did not improve. I stared at Malcolm. He fidgeted in his seat. He realized that unhappy days were just a few seconds away. Malcolm avoided eye contact with me.

For some kids a C minus is a perfectly acceptable grade. But not for Malcolm. What frustrated me more was the fact that I knew Malcolm could do much better than C work. After all, Malcolm could get to the forty-fifth level of some video game. He could recite from memory the current and past year's batting averages for virtually every major league baseball player. Yet for some inexplicable reason, he could not multiply six times seven.

"Let me ask you, son. Is a C minus an acceptable grade in our household?"

"Under special circumstances it is, dad."

"Tell me, son. Were there any special circumstances that would justify the grade that you received?"

"Well—"

"Well what?"

"Well, you snored, dad—really loud—so loud in fact, that I could not get a good night's sleep. I was probably too tired to take the test. That's probably why I made the C minus. Wouldn't you consider that a special circumstance?"

It was true that I snored, and on occasion I disrupted the sleeping habits of the other family members. But my snoring had nothing to do with Malcolm's grade.

"My snoring does not constitute a special circumstance."

"Oh," Malcolm replied just above a whisper.

Malcolm stared at me, hoping for a miracle—hoping that I would be kind and not punish him for his unacceptable grade. But I would not oblige Malcolm.

I cleared my throat, then said, "Effective immediately, you are not permitted to play video games, or computer games. You may use the computer for school work, but only if supervised by either me or your mother. You may not watch television. You may not talk to any one of your friends on the phone, unless it is to get a homework assignment, or the phone call is to discuss a homework assignment. In either case, I will be monitoring all of your incoming and outgoing telephone calls. You may not use the cell phone except in the case of an emergency in which the threat of bodily injury is imminent. You may not play with any hand-held electronic games. You may not watch any video movies or DVD movies. You may not use a palm assistant, or any other electronic device unless it is in connection with schoolwork or homework. In short, you may not use, play with, or view anything electronic or video until further notified."

"Dad, there's got to be an alternative—some middle ground—maybe if you just take away my computer games for a few days. I'm sure that will teach me a lesson."

"Look at me son, I am not smiling. This is serious. You have had chances before. You always told me that you would do better. But this grade was totally preventable and unnecessary if you had just studied."

"But I did study," he said, sensing the extreme gravity of the punishment.

"Oh, I'm sure that you did study. Unfortunately, you studied how to get to the fifth vector of Planet Chazbow, as opposed to studying for your geography test."

"I tried, dad. Honest. But the test was hard, really hard."

"It was a test on state capitals, son. You listed Notre Dame as the capital of Indiana. It's not even a town. It's a university."

"You referred to Notre Dame as a capital."

"I referred to it as the capital of college football, not the capital of the state of Indiana."

"Well, it should be the capital of Indiana."

"And you wrote down that Jersey City is the capital of New Jersey."

"That's what Bobby O'Shea said."

"You're not helping yourself, son. That's the same Bobby O'Shea who says he's personal friends with Puxatawney Phil the groundhog. And need I remind you, that Bobby O'Shea has been in the fifth grade for five years. He's the only kid in your class with a driver's license, and a voter registration card."

"He says he's been diagnosed with a learning disability."

"It's not that he has a learning disability. It's that he has a disability when it comes to learning. He's downright lazy."

"Well—"

"You even missed the capital for our home state."

"I got confused."

"Well you finally made an accurate observation."

"Dad, do you know the capitals of all the states?"

"I don't know the capitals of all fifty states, son. But you know what?"

"What?"

"I am not in school anymore. I don't have to know the capitals of all fifty states. And I am not going to take a test on them. Like you have."

"So, it's okay if you don't know the state capitals. But I've got to know them now, so I can forget them later. It sounds like a double standard to me."

Every parent has heard the double standard argument on occasion. A child assumes that the parent-child relationship is somehow a functioning democracy—complete with justice and fair rules. And if a parent strays from decency and equal treatment, then the parent has committed (gasp and horror of horrors) a grievous sin against the child. It sounds exactly like an argument that would be raised by a child who had spent time at Miss Pringles Academy. I should have taken Malcolm to a hypnotist and erased any trace of that misbegotten year. Nevertheless, Malcolm, and every other like-minded child missed the central point—that being, that the parent-child relationship is not a democracy, but rather a benevolent dictatorship.

"There is no double standard, son. There is only one standard—and that standard dictates that you make A's and B's on your tests and grades."

"So you admit that you don't know the capitals of the states."

To prove a point, I accepted Malcolm's challenge. "Okay son. Go ahead, try to stump me with a state capital."

"What's the capital of Illinois?"

"Springfield."

Malcolm was surprised, but figured it was just a lucky guess. He picked another state. "What's the capital of Kansas?"

"Topeka."

"The capital of Maine?"

"Portland."

"The capital of South Dakota?"

"Pierre."

"The capital of North Dakota?"

"Bismarck."

Malcolm was both amazed and horrified by knowledge. My son wasn't aware that I won every state capital challenge when I was in grade school. Of course, in the scope of things, my mastery of state capitals was nothing out of the ordinary or spectacular. But for Malcolm, it was as though I were some artificially intelligent creature from another universe. He could not believe his dad's skill—could not accept it. With increasing rapidity, he asked me to note the capital of each state. In less than three minutes, I prevailed.

"What do you have to say now, son?"

"My life is over," he sadly exhaled.

I studied Malcolm's face. I never recalled having seen Malcolm as hurt as he was at that precise moment. His face expressed no hope, and he was genuinely hurt—almost as if he were in a suicidal daze. It was as though his best friend had just lowered the ultimate boom on him.

At that moment, I suppose I should have shown some compassion. I should have hugged my son, and said it was going to be all right. I should have told my son that his life was not over, and that the punishment was only temporary. I should have done all of that; but I didn't. My fatherly instincts told me that this was the time to re-inforce to Malcolm that there were drastic and negative consequences for bad grades.

"If you equate video games, and computer games, and television, and video movies as being the sum and substance of your existence, then I guess that yes, your life is over."

Malcolm sighed again, and the second sigh was more melancholy and sad than the first one. For one brief second, I was about to believe that Malcolm's life was indeed over.

"I'm never going to have fun again," Malcolm moaned.

I suppressed the urge to laugh.

Malcolm spent the next thirty minutes placing all things video and computer into a rather large plastic container. He gazed at me with pleading eyes. He believed that I still had the power to reduce his punishment. But it was too late, and I had no desire or inclination to alter the punishment. This would be a painful, but hopefully not too long, learning experience for Malcolm.

For the next several evenings, Malcolm re-established, admittedly reluctantly, an emphasis with his school studies. He was both disciplined and focused. Marcia and I were extremely pleased with his new outlook on studies. In fact, after Malcolm finished his studies, he read something other than a comic book. My prayers had been answered.

Happily for Malcolm, he took my stern words to heart. After two weeks, Malcolm had regained his video game playing privileges. After another week, Malcolm regained his computer privileges.

"Are you happy, pops?'

"Yes, I am, son. But I am happy because you have re-established your priorities."

"I don't understand, I thought the better grades would make you happy."

"Look, son, don't get me wrong, I am happy that you have made all A's on your course work for the past couple of weeks. But understand that you should be equally happy about making good grades. Because ultimately, good grades will help you, not me or your mother or sister, get a good job. And good grades are a reflection of knowledge, and knowledge is something that no one can take from you."

Finally, Malcolm understood. He smiled.

I gave Malcolm two thumbs up. Malcolm reciprocated. We hugged and the nightmare was finally over.

Later that evening, I watched Malcolm elude monsters, dragons, death rays, and other obstacles, while reaching Level 23 of *Escape from the Cave of Zonn*. There was something different about Malcolm's demeanor. Perhaps it was that he didn't seem so obsessed playing the game. Perhaps it was my attitude about him playing video games that had changed.

"Do you want to play, pops?"

I was surprised, yet heartened by Malcolm's offer. Disciplining him was tough and hard. But not requiring Malcolm to re-establish his priorities would have been relinquishing my duty as a parent. At any rate, it appeared that father and son had survived a rough spot, on an otherwise smooth sea. I took control of the video game. "Thanks, son."

"You're welcome, pops."

We played for a couple of hours. As Malcolm would say, he creamed me. I was no match for him. Yet, on that night, it was not about who won or lost. No, that night was far more special. For on that night, father and son re-connected. We became more sensitive to the other's feelings.

At the end of the video game session, Malcolm flashed two thumbs up in my direction. I returned with two thumbs up of my own. It was a great way to end an evening. Few evenings in life would ever be better than that one. And that was my reward for a bad grade.

Men's Reading Club

On the sixth month anniversary of The Men's Reading Club, I realized that I had learned quite a bit about every member of the club—every member, that is, except for Coogan. In fact what was most disturbing was that I did not even know Coogan's first name. So after the sixth meeting, after we had trashed some French novel that no one could read, much less had read, after Coogan had left, I asked the other club members if they knew Coogan's name.

Winters said he thought it was Jackie, although, he might be confusing Coogan with the actor.

"No, no, it's not Jackie," Roger Bracey replied. "Coogan doesn't have a first name."

"That's ridiculous," I returned. Everybody has a first name.

"Not Coogan," Bracey said dryly.

I could not accept or entertain the possibility that Coogan did not have a first name. Of course he had a first name. His parents certainly had to have given him a first name, and that first name would be listed on Coogan's birth certificate. Retrieving a copy of Coogan's birth certificate, should be a piece of cake. All I needed was his birthdate, place of birth, and parents' names.

I asked the group if they could supply me with any of the information. Instead of answers, I received blank stares.

Discreetly, behind the scenes even, I had asked a number of Coogan's closest associates if they knew his first name. To my complete surprise, all replied, "No."

"You mean no one knows what Coogan's first name is?"

They nodded in unison.

As bizarre as I thought it was for none of Coogan's closest friends and associates to know his first name, it was absolutely unthinkable to even briefly consider that Coogan might not have a first name at all.

At the following month's meeting, I apologized to Coogan for not knowing his first name. I added, "So what is your first name?"

"I don't have a first name."

"But everyone has to have a first name," I stated matter-of-factly to Coogan.

"Why?" Coogan asked matter-of-factly.

I wasn't exactly sure why, but there had to be a reason. After all, it just seemed un-American not to have a given first name.

"All right, what's your first initial?"

"Is it really important?"

"It is to me."

"Why is it important to you, when it isn't important to me."

"Because everyone has a first initial."

"Will it make you happy, if I tell you my first initial?"

"Absolutely."

"Then I will tell you. It's 'C'."

"So your initials are 'C' 'C'?"

"No."

"But you said, that your first initial is 'C'."

"And it is. It just so happens that my first initial is also my last initial. In this case, 'C' stands for *Coogan*."

"I refuse to believe that you don't have a first name. Since you don't want to reveal your first name, it must be an embarrassing name—like a girls' name, or it's a profane name that you can't mention in public, or it's a foreign name that's unpronounceable in English."

"You're wrong on all accounts. I simply don't have a first name."

"I intend to find out your first name."

"You're wasting your time, Hughes. I have no first name."

I couldn't understand why Coogan wouldn't reveal his first name to his friends and associates. There had to be a reason—probably an embarrassing one—why Coogan wouldn't share his first name with anyone.

What bothered me most was that no one else seemed to care that Coogan was not forthcoming with his first name. Well maybe everyone else could be nonchalant about Coogan's deception. But not me. I was determined, obsessed some would say to discover Coogan's first name.

Every attempt however, was unsuccessful—led to another brick wall. With each failure, my level of frustration inched higher.

A couple of days later, I ran into Coogan, and his daughter Destiny at the neighborhood supermarket. I struck up a conversation with Coogan, and talked about the usual stuff—you know—football, politics, first names. Coogan laughed, repeated that he had no first name, then moved onto another subject. A few minutes later, he asked me if I would watch Destiny for a minute or so, while he retrieved a can of peas from aisle seven.

I replied, "Certainly." I smiled. I couldn't believe my good fortune. I was alone with Coogan's six-and-a-half year-old daughter. Without question she knew her father's first name. My prayers were about to be answered. After all those weeks of wracking my brain, my question would be answered from the mouth of a child. It was so simple, I should have thought of this much sooner. I smiled at Destiny, and said, "Your father told me that you are a very bright girl."

"Yes, I am," she returned with all the confidence that a six year-old could muster.

"Well, let me see just how smart you are."

"Okay."

"Tell me, Destiny. Does your father have a first name?"

Destiny smiled at me impishly and said, "Of course he has a first name."

"Okay, then tell me what it is."

"Silly," she replied, "It's daddy."

Indeed I was silly. I had been reduced to asking a six-year-old the name of her father. I was starting to descend into an *Apocoloypse Now* abyss, from which I wasn't sure if I would return sane. And yet at that moment, I did not care about my sanity. What mattered to me was finding out Coogan's first name.

Coogan returned. "Thanks, Hughes. I hope that Destiny was no problem for you?"

"No problem at all. We had a splendid time talking."

"Yeah, daddy. Mr. Hughes asked me questions about you daddy."

"Really. And what questions, did Mr. Hughes ask you, dear?"

"He asked me what was your first name?"

Coogan did not seem upset by my intrusion into his privacy. In fact he seemed amused and content. Smiling, he asked, "And what you tell him?"

"I told him that your first name was daddy, daddy."

Coogan laughed at the futility of my actions.

I left, more determined than ever to uncover Coogan's first name.

A few nights later, I parked my car a half block from Coogan's house. I waited silently in the dark. I ducked from eyesight when a car drove by, or a jogger ran past the car. I waited—passing the time by drinking caffeinated cola and listening to a novel on tape. An hour passed—two hours—two hours and forty-five minutes. Sometime after eleven, Coogan rolled a green garbage can to the front curb.

It was midnight. I slipped into the house with a slightly torn black trashbag. It was Coogan's. I had swiped it from his curb, after he turned out his front lights. Inside the trashbag was molded cheese, and a T-bone, no meat, just the bone, and empty cartons of orange juice. Nestled in the middle of half-eaten fruit was a treasure trove of personal information about Coogan. Certainly, one of the bill stubs or magazine notices, would reveal Coogan's first name. I was alone in the kitchen with floodlights casting an eerie glow on me and the mountain of paperwork I had stacked on the dinner table.

Marcia joined me. She was convinced I was ready for a secluded place with rubber walls, and shoes without laces.

"Why don't you give it up," Marcia asked, worried about my deepening obsession.

"Give up?!" I returned with a wild-eyed glare.

I was undettered, for I was obsessed with finding out Coogan's first name. I was absolutely, positively convinced that Coogan had a first name. I suppose some trivia purist would claim that Coogan's last name amounted to a first name, since it was his only name. But there had to be a real first name—otherwise how could he have received a Social Security number, or a credit card, or even a voter registration card. Without a first name, he would be virtually indistinguishable from millions of other Coogans worldwide.

I retrieved his phone bill. Drizzled with spaghetti sauce, the bill yielded no results because it was in his wife's name. Sifting through other mail, resulted in no breakthroughs. Every bill, magazine, circular, and piece of junk mail was in his wife's name or addressed to occupant.

"You are in bad shape, Michael Devin Hughes."

Marcia only called me by my full name when I was in major league trouble, or when I was obsessed.

"Did you ask, Betty, his wife?"

"Yes. She says Coogan doesn't have a first name."

"That is simply impossible. What kind of parents would not give their child a first name?"

"Are his parents alive?"

"I believe both his parents are still alive."

"Then why don't you call his parents, and ask them. You should have considered that option weeks ago."

I slapped my forehead in disgust. Marcia's suggestion was both simply brilliant, and brilliantly simple. I recalled from one of my earlier conversations with Coogan that his parents lived in Bronxdale, Pennsylvania, which was about thirty miles south of Erie. That next morning I booked my flight on line. In less than thirty-six hours, I would be a heartbeat away from finally discovering Coogan's first name. I hadn't been this excited since my first wedding night.

Marcia said that I should have called Coogan's parents before I boarded the plane. "Just to make sure that they would be there," she offered. But I wanted the element of surprise. If I had called ahead of time, Coogan's parents could have contacted their son and they could have concocted a story, devoid of facts and the truth.

Coogan's parents house was a majestic two-story wooden structure. It had a wrap-around porch, with a swing out front. The lawn and garden were immaculate.

I rapped on the door a half-dozen times.

Both Coogan's mother and father greeted me at the front door.

Coogan's parents were not exactly as I had envisioned them. For one thing, they appeared a bit older than I imagined. Both parents were blondes, while Coogan's hair was jet black. Of course, someone could have dyed their hair, but I didn't think so. But the most striking difference, was that neither parent stood taller than five-foot-five, while Coogan was at least six-foot-six. I studied their facial features, and could find little family resemblance, except that both Coogan and his father had rather pronounced noses.

Coogan's father ushered me into the front parlor.

"Thank you for seeing me."

"No trouble at all. Any friend of our son is a friend of ours. What can we do for you?"

I was about to answer, when his mother asked, "Would you like some lemonade? If I do say so, it's pretty tasty."

"It's better than that, dear." His father cast his eyes toward me and said, "You know, mother's lemonade has won first place at the county fair three years running."

"In that case, I'll take a glass."

"Coming right up. By the way, do you want ice cubes, or shaved iced in you lemonade?"

"Shaved ice I guess."

Coogan's mother handed me a tall glass of lemonade. I sipped a bit, and had to admit, that it was the best lemonade I had ever tasted.

"So I guess we got sidetracked by the lemonade," Coogan's father said, as he rocked in an antique rocking chair. "Anyway, you were about to ask a question. What was it?"

"Well, it's a rather simple question, though, for some reason, it has been especially difficult to find out."

Coogan's father finished his lemonade. "Go ahead and ask."

"Your son says that he doesn't have a first name. But that seemed impossible to me. Nevertheless, I checked a number of sources, and could not find any record of your son's first name. So after several weeks of work, I thought I would come to the two people who would know above all the first name of their oldest son."

Coogan's father cracked a piece of lemonade ice. He rubbed his clean-shaven jaw. "You mean to tell me that you traveled all this way just to find out Coogan's first name?"

"In a manner of speaking. Like I said, I have tried all conventional sources—close friends, high school sweethearts, his personal barber, even his parish priest. Either they don't recall Coogan giving them his first name, or they say that Coogan does not have a first name. It's like there's one big conspiracy. I mean the answers are too well rehearsed."

"Well there's a real good reason why our son hasn't given you his first name," Coogan's mother noted.

"And that would be?"

"Coogan does not have a first name."

"I don't understand. You are his parents. Why wouldn't you give him a first name?"

"Well, actually we could not agree on a first name for our son."

"Yes, but still—"

"Actually, there were extenuating circumstances."

I could not imagine any set of circumstances that would permit newborn Coogan to leave the hospital without a first name.

"Coogan was adopted."

All right, that was one circumstance that I had not contemplated. But that fact would only account for the difference in physical characteristics between Coogan and his parents. The adoption agency would either have listed a first name for Coogan, or his parents would have been required to give him one at the time the adoption became official.

Coogan's father said the child of a neighbor gave up Coogan before naming him. I was suspicious, but gave Coogan's parents the benefit of the doubt.

"So you never gave Coogan a first name?"

"Actually," began Coogan's mother, "father and I could never agree on a first name for our little bundle of joy. Father wanted to name our son, Abraham, after our great president. I wanted to name our child Theodore, after my maternal grandfather. We thought about using both names. But in the end we just chose not to name our son. So, Coogan remained without a first name from birth."

"But surely, you would have been required to give him a first name for identification and Social Security purposes."

"You would think so, wouldn't you? But we found out otherwise. Legally, you don't have to have a first name."

Coogan's mother's explanation seemed a bit too convenient for my tastes. Yet, there was no apparent reason not to believe her.

We chatted for another hour. I drank four more glasses of lemonade. Coogan's parents were genuinely nice. But when I left I was no closer to solving the mystery of Coogan's first name. Maybe everyone was right—maybe Coogan didn't have a first name. I sighed—said good-bye, and headed back to the airport.

As I drove the rental car back to the agency, my cell phone rang. I figured it was Marcia, eager to receive a full de-briefing about my long and expensive journey.

"Hello."

"Michael Hughes?"

It was not Marcia. The voice on the other end was unfamiliar.

"Yes."

"I hear that you are trying to find out the first name of the oldest son of Colton and Meghan Coogan."

"How did you get my cell phone number?"

"That's not important."

"Who the hell are you?"

"That's not important either. The question is, are you still trying to find out the first name of the oldest son of Colton and Meghan Coogan?"

"Yes."

"I know his first name."

"You do?"

"Yes."

"Well, what is it?"

"I can't tell you. Your phone is not secure."

"Secure? Look is this some prank?"

"I assure you this no prank. You are returning to the airport, correct?"

"Yes."

"I will meet you at the coffee shop in the airport."

"Wait! What's your name?"

"As I have said, my name is not important."

"Well at least tell me how I will recognize you."

"You need not recognize me. I will recognize you."

"But how?"

There was no answer—only the sound of a disconnected phone. Immediately I discounted the mystery phone call. Somehow, Coogan must have found out about my trip. He must have arranged this elaborate ruse. There could be no other explanation. In fact, I would bet my brother's car that when I arrived at the airport, I would find Coogan revealing himself as the mysterious caller.

I would have lost the bet, and my brother's car, for fifteen minutes later, I met the mystery man at the airport coffee shop. He was an everyman dressed in everyday clothes—if I were paid a million dollars I could not recall what he wore that day. He may have worn a moustache, but quite frankly I don't remember any distinguishing marks or recognizable traits.

I stood to shake the man's hand.

He refused the gesture, and said in a deep, guttural voice, "Sit down."

"I still don't know your name."

"Don't worry about my name. It's Coogan's first name that is of interest to you, correct?"

"Yes."

"Then listen very carefully. All records of Coogan's first name have been erased because for the last several years, Coogan has been part of the Federal Witness Protection Program."

"Is this some kind of joke? If Coogan's records had been erased, then I wouldn't have been able to visit his parents."

"He doesn't have any parents—not any more at least."

"You are aware that I just left his parent's house."

"You met federal agents who portray Coogan's parents."

That statement would explain the lack of physical resemblance between Coogan and his so-called parents. Yet, if the thought that Coogan had no first name was hard to accept, then the thought that Coogan was part of the Federal Witness Protection Program was beyond comprehension. The man was expressionless. Yet, he had to be lying.

"None of this makes any sense. If Coogan was in the Federal Witness Protection Program, why on earth would you tell me?"

"It's simple. You've been asking too many questions. It may already be too late for Coogan. But if not, then I'd like you to back off for his safety."

Obviously, Coogan had prepared for my so-called unannounced visit. As I considered how he learned of my trip, I guessed Marcia must have told his wife, who in turn told Coogan. Well since Coogan spared no expense on this entire set-up, I figured the least I could do was go along with the gag. Feigning concern, I asked, "What could Coogan have done, to warrant him being placed in Witness Protection Program?"

The man did not blink, or flex a muscle, as he replied in a deep monotone, "Well I could tell you, but then I would have to place you in the Program as well."

The thought of receiving an entirely new identity courtesy of Uncle Sam did not set well with me. "I don't need to know that badly."

"That's advisable."

"And you realize that you are not to reveal any of this conversation to anyone, including, and especially your wife or children."

"I understand," I replied attempting to sound sincere.

The mystery man left without another word. I boarded the plane, certain that what I had witnessed was an elaborate scheme on the part of Coogan. But somewhere over Baton Rouge doubt seeped into my mind. Suppose the mystery man had been telling the truth? By airphone, I contacted Marcia and asked if she had inadvertently told Coogan's wife about my trip. Marcia assured me that she had not. After reviewing all pertinent facts, I reached the conclusion that Coogan was not Coogan, but someone else with an outrageous past, and a curious present.

At my next opportunity I would confront Coogan.

A week later, I ran into Coogan at the supermarket. Normally, he smiled when we met. On that day, it was different. I mean he smiled, but there was something about the smile that was different. He motioned me to aisle six—inspect sprays, and barbeque supplies. "I heard that you went to my hometown to discover my first name."

"Yeah, but it was another dead end."

"Well, my parents said that they didn't think that you believed them."

"Look, I didn't mean to doubt your parents. It's just that—"

Coogan interrupted. "I even heard that you talked to Sam Waterstone."

"Who?"

"Oh yeah. I forgot that he wouldn't have told you his name." Coogan quickly described the man from the airport. "I suppose that he told you that I was in the Witness Protection Program."

I did not answer.

"It's okay, Sam has always been one grand kidder."

"He didn't sound like he was kidding to me."

"Come on, Hughes. You don't honestly believe that I am some individual with an identity crisis, and a connection to the Witness Protection Program? That's too bizarre for words. Sam Waterstone was one of my high school classmates. Ever since we were in school, he's been a prankster. Saying that I am part of the Witness Protection Program is just another one of his pranks. And you fell for it. Well, I guess I shouldn't be surprised. He has always been quite convincing."

"So there's absolutely no truth to his story as it relates to you?"

"Not a word."

"And you really don't have a first name?"

"No."

For the first time in the entire encounter, there was a pause, a brief hesitation before Coogan answered. Had I finally worn Coogan down?

"Listen Coogan, if it's a secret—"

"I made my parents promise that they would never tell a living soul the name that was jotted down on the note that was left in my crib."

"So you do have a first name?"

Coogan swallowed hard enough for me to see his adam's apple. "Yes," he replied. He cast his eyes away from me, then added, "It's Claymore."

"Claymore?"

"Don't say it too loud. Someone might hear you." Coogan stared deep into my eyes, as he lightly held each shoulder. "Now you understand why I don't go by my first name. And I hope you understand why I don't want anyone else to know that my first name is Claymore."

I had never seen Coogan so emotionally shaken. And given the circumstances of the conversation, there was no particular reason for him to lie. In fact, if my parents had named me Claymore, I am sure I would have either dropped or changed my name upon reaching eighteen. And yet there were nagging questions that remained—chief among them was that telling his parents not to use his first name did not explain why there was no record of his first name—on any official document. The absence of any recordation of a first name, strangely supported Coogan's parents' account that they simply failed to provide their adopted son with a first name. Nevertheless, I was prepared to give Coogan the benefit of the doubt.

"All right, Coogan."

"Then I can count on you to keep this little secret between us."

"Yes."

I left Coogan and returned to my shopping. Stopping in the next aisle, I couldn't decide which brand of sugar to buy. To my surprise, I heard Coogan talking to someone. Curious, I peeked around the corner and noticed that he was carrying on a conversation with someone on his cellular phone. Since his back was facing me, he did not realized that I had returned. I heard Coogan say, "Yes, yes, I recounted plausible explanation Z-1." A few seconds later he said, "He suspects nothing." And finally he observed, "Mission accomplished."

Garage Sales

I never thought too much about garage sales until my neighbor K. C. told me that he had pocketed fifteen hundred dollars during the last neighborhood sale. I found that figure all the more astonishing since I had seen the trinkets and cast-offs that had accumulated in his garage. It was all junk. In fact, KC's odd assortment of broken gadgets, mismatched clothes, useless utensils, and abominable artwork was several steps below junk. It was reject junk. It was so bad, that I thought he would have had to pay someone a couple hundred dollars in order to remove that trash heap. Yet, for some inexplicable reason, the masses gravitated toward his garage, and scooped up all the unmentionables and odd ends. Now the next neighborhood garage sale was less than a week away, and K.C. was sorting and cataloging yet another heap of junk for eventual disposal.

"What do you think of it?" K.C. asked, as he handed me an object that defied description.

"What is it?" I returned.

"I haven't the foggiest idea what it is. I believe that I bought it during a trip to Hawaii. But that's all that I remember."

"What does it do?"

"Beats the hell out of me."

"And yet you still intend to sell it?"

"Absolutely. And the beauty of it is that someone will buy it."

"That's hard to believe."

"Well believe it. For the right price, people will buy anything." K.C. sorted through some mismatched tennis shoes. See if you can find the mate to this shoe."

Underneath a stack of shoes and clothes, I found the particular match for the man's tennis shoe. There was almost no tread left, and the white canvas on top had been stained by grass and dirt.

"Thanks," K.C. said. Turning toward me, he asked, "You ever think about selling your accumulated housewares and clothing at a garage sale?"

"Can't say that I have."

"Well, it might just pay for a new large screen television. That's what I bought with the money from the last sale."

"I don't know. I mean I don't have anything as, well, as unusual as you."

"If you've got clothes that you don't wear, then you've got some merchandise for a garage sale."

"You really think so?"

"What do you have to lose? And after all, I've seen your garage, and there are definitely some items that you could sell."

K.C. and I seldom agreed on anything. However, perhaps he had a point concerning the garage sale. Certainly if he could rake in over a thousand dollars on cheap jewelry, fake furs, and chipped plates, then I could make twice that much with a superior brand of merchandise.

Yes, that would be my contribution to society, quality merchandise for the neighborhood garage sale. After all, who wouldn't want to buy a once-used designer dress, or a slightly irregular, but never worn tennis outfit from Bertomi? And come to think of it, I had an old laptop computer, that still had more capacity than most desktop models I had seen. I smiled, for I realized that I had stumbled onto the mother lode. To think that the discarded clothes and other items in my garage were a veritable gold mine and money machine all rolled into one. By dusk on Saturday, I would be able to take a bath in cash. Yes, I could envision the possibilities. They were all good. My smile grew wider.

Over the next few days, I separated, sorted, and classified several boxes of forgotten goods. K.C. cautioned me against throwing away even items that seemingly should have been destroyed by fire.

That Saturday, I awoke at six-thirty. By seven, I was in the final stages of neatly placing the sale items on coffee tables and assorted shelves. The morning air was cool and crisp, and pastel blue painted the sky.

As an extra touch, I roasted my special brand of coffee for the shoppers to sample. At eight-thirty, I noticed an enthusiastic crowd gobbling up everything in sight at KC's. At my house, the steam from the coffee rose with no one to savor the delightful aroma. Were it not for crickets and squirrels, I would have been all alone. Maybe it was a temporary condition. Yeah, that had to be the case. Soon my garage would be swamped. Thirty minutes later, only two kids had checked out the goods.

"Got any video games?" a child, sucking a lollipop asked.

"No," I replied.

"Too bad," the other kid returned. "Video games are garage sales magnets."

They left. No one else stopped by until K.C. strolled over to check on how things were going. "I couldn't help but notice, Hughes, that you haven't had too many visitors."

"Go ahead and gloat."

"I'm not gloating, Hughes. I am stating a fact. Your traffic count has been below average. So tell me what do have as your hook?"

"Hook?"

"Yes—one item, either merchandise or refreshment that guarantees steady customer traffic."

"Well I got some foreign language DVDs."

"That's not exactly what I had in mind. You know, sometimes if you have fresh pound cake, or doughnuts, and steaming hot coffee, that will attract potential customers."

"I fresh brewed some coffee, but no one has sampled my java."

"What brand is it?"

"It's an Italian roast."

"You got a domestic brand—something easy to pronounce?"

"Not really."

"You got any video games or vinyl records?"

"No."

"Too bad. Video games and vinyl records act as garage sales magnets."

"So I have heard."

"I always manage to have a couple of dozen on hand. Normally, they are the first items to be sold."

"Okay, so maybe I don't have domestic coffee, or video games or vinyl records. But I still don't see why people haven't bought any of my junk." I lamented.

"Your merchandise is too expensive," K. C. replied, shrugging his shoulders.

"What do you mean it's too expensive?"

"People on the garage sale circuit are accustomed to paying no more than a dollar for most children's clothing. Look here. You've got one of Millicent's dresses priced at forty dollars. No one is going to pay that kind of money for an everyday dress."

"Everyday dress? I'll have you note that Millicent's dress is a one-of-a-kind designer creation from Saks Fifth Avenue. It costs five times what I am asking for it."

"No garage sale regular cares whether it's a designer dress or not. They are simply not going to pay forty dollars for a little girl's dress."

"Well I just can't give away the dress."

"Then perhaps you should consider an invitation only sale for the Palm Beach set."

"Don't get sarcastic with me."

"Face it, Hughes. Nobody is going to buy your stuff at your prices."

"Well, I refuse to lower the prices. I must maintain my dignity."

"Tell me about your dignity after the sale," K. C. said as he returned to his driveway to greet another customer.

I simmered while K.C. continued to sell item after item from his garage. I didn't recall that he had as much odds and ends in his garage, as he was selling. It seemed as though he had secured other people's junk, just to sell at the garage sale.

People trickled by my garage. They sorted through the clothes and other goods. Each potential customer continued to lowball what they were willing to pay for the merchandise.

About fifteen minutes later, a man dressed in a red check shirt, green plaid pants, and blue deck shoes that were spotted with chlorine or paint stopped by the garage. He examined the coffee maker, and the nine-inch color television. He picked up a couple sweaters from one of the tables. The old man inspected in silence. Finally, he pointed to my old reading lamp and said, "I'll give you fifty cents for it."

I paid at least thirty dollars for the lamp. It still worked. Offering me fifty cents for a functioning lamp was an insult. Yet, I remembered the recent words of K.C. that no one would pay over a couple of dollars for garage sale goods, no matter what the quality. I swallowed my pride and replied, "You can have it for two dollars."

"I'm not offering you two dollars. I'm offering you fifty cents. To be honest with you, I'm not sure if it's worth that much any way."

"Well, I'm not going to sell it to you for fifty cents. It's worth fifty times that amount and you know it."

"Tell me, sonny. Is this your first garage sale?"

"Yes, but that doesn't have anything to do—"

The elderly gentleman cut in, "Let me give you a little advice. If you want more than fifty cents for any of these items then take an ad out in the paper. Ask for any price that you think is fair. But if you're going to sell items at a garage sale, then don't ask for a fair price because a fair price isn't going to sell. Ask for a price that is designed to move merchandise. And believe me when I say that the lamp is worth fifty cents tops."

One part of me said to run the scoundrel out of the garage on a rail, while another part of me said, take the money and run, while yet another part of me said to admit defeat and close shop now. I chose none of the above, and repeated to the man that two dollars was my one and only offer for the reading lamp.

"Suit yourself." The man left without buying anything.

An hour or so later K.C. returned. "Hey Hughes, did you ever sell anything?"

"No," I returned sadly. "Someone almost bought my answering machine—but they had spent all their money buying junk at your house."

"You don't say."

K.C. inspected the reading lamp that the old man had earlier examined. "Did Mr. Carlyle offer you fifty cents for this lamp?"

"You mean the old man in the lime green pants?"

"Yeah, that's him."

"Yes. He offered me fifty cents for the lamp. I rejected the lowball price."

"You should have taken the money."

"It was worth at least twenty. But the cheapskate wouldn't even pay two dollars for the lamp."

"Mr. Carlyle is a very wealthy eccentric. He could buy everything we own a thousand times over. He scouts garage sales for an occasional work of art or lost item of value. But mostly he just buys junk, tons of absolutely worthless junk. He never pays more than fifty cents for the ordinary pieces. But he will buy all of that you have. If you have two hundred buttons, he will buy the whole lot for fifty cents per button."

"What?"

"If you had just gone along with him, he would have bought everything from you. As I recall, you had over two thousand items for sale."

"I-I didn't realize."

"You let your pride affect your business sense.

Painful as it was, I had to admit that K.C.'s observation and analysis was correct. My stubborn pride had ruined any chance for a successful garage sale.

K.C.'s next question stabbed me just above the heart. He rubbed his forehead, and asked, "So you didn't sell anything?"

"No, I didn't. Go ahead, rub it in. I deserve it."

"Hey, I would never do that. By the way, do you still have your dignity?"

"What?"

"Earlier, you said you wouldn't reduce you prices because you intended to maintain your dignity."

"I guess I didn't," I replied dejectedly.

"No, I didn't think that you would."

"You should have taken the money from Mr. Carlyle."

"But I didn't. Look I know I am a failure. Why don't you just leave now?"

K. C. whipped out a wad of dollar bills from each side pocket of his pants. He licked his fingertips, then proceeded to count out thirty dollars. "Here," K. C. began, "Take it. I'll buy the answering machine, and that sack of children's clothes."

Had it come to this? My neighbor participating in a mercy buy for my benefit. It just didn't seem right. In fact, I should have been insulted. But people without dignity—without one single sale in a garage sale simply had no right to feel insulted or angry, or even peturbed. No, a person without dignity—like myself, had to face the cold, hard fact that thirty dollars for two hundred fifty dollars worth of merchandise was as good as it was going to get. And yet, a person without dignity—like myself, still could not suffer the further humiliation of taking money from my smug and classless neighbor.

K. C. just smiled, and continued to hold the thirty dollar bills in his left hand. "It's the best offer your are going to get. Hell, it's the only offer you are going to get."

"I can't do it," I said, turning away from the money.

"There's an old saying that says a stubborn man will die of thirst rather than drink water from the well. Stop being stubborn, Hughes, and take the money. If you never participate in another garage sale, at least you can say you made some pocket change."

I couldn't bring myself to take the money from K. C.. But in my heart, I knew he was right. My dignity was a distant memory. Yet, my stubborn side prevented me from accepting his offer. I pondered the options for a few more seconds, and determined there were no more options. So, I half-heartedly said, "Just leave the money on the table, and take whatever you want."

K.C. placed the money on the table.

I left the money on the table.

Much later, Malcolm returned from an afternoon at the movies with his friends. Like any child, he naturally gravitated to the table with the thirty dollars on it.

"Is that all you made on the garage sale, dad?"

"I'm afraid so."

Malcolm scanned the items that remained on the table and the pile of discarded clothes. He noticed that one of his T-shirts was missing.

"You sold my Dirt Hex T-shirt?"

"K.C. must have picked it by mistake."

"It was my favorite T-shirt, pops."

"You haven't worn that smelly-stained T-shirt in years."

"I know, but it was still my favorite."

"Whatever you say, son."

Ten seconds later, Malcolm turned to a more pressing subject. "Hey, pops. Me and the guys were thinking about going to Funky Burgers. Is that okay?"

"Yeah, I guess."

"Well, I sort of need some cash."

"Take the money on the table, son."

Malcolm stuffed the bills in his pocket, and left before I changed my mind.

The next day I dumped the clothes and other items into the trunk of my car. I delivered them to the nearest branch of Needy Neighbors.

A few weeks later I learned that the items I donated sold as a unit to some eccentric for a little over a thousand dollars. Supposedly, he was particularly impressed by the designer children's dresses and suits.

I sighed and mumbled, "It figures."

As of this date, I have not participated in any further garage sales. And if I maintain my senses, I won't in the future.

Laundromats

Anyway, there was a period of about six months after I split from Marcia when I lived in the Conquistador Apartments. Let me assure you that I lived there for one reason only, it was cheap. The complex catered to newly divorced and/or separated husbands.

On my first day at the Conquistador, I met Bob Hammersmith a fifty-something who had just left his wife of thirty-three years. Bob was not a happy soul. He blamed his wife for everything from the cancellation of *Gilligan's Island* to the 1906 San Francisco Earthquake. Bob was a gentleman who needed many things, including a new outlook on women. But the trials and travails of Bob Hammersmith was another story—actually several stories.

This story is not about Bob Hammersmith, but rather about laundromats. As I mentioned, the Conquistador was cheap and primarily because there were no appliances in the apartments except for a war surplus refrigerator. Therefore the residents were left with two choices—either go down to the basement and use the washer and dryers in the so-called laundry room, or trudge your dirty clothes down to the corner and use the laundry facilities of the Maplewood Laundry.

For the first week at the Conquistador, I washed clothes in the basement laundry room. The washers might as well have been scissors for they sliced and cut holes in over half of my clothes. I mentioned it to the on-duty supervisor, and he told me that the problem would be remedied immediately. When it wasn't, and I was down to a few pair of damage-free socks and underwear, I decided to try the Maplewood Laundry.

Brightly lit, and lined with yellow tile walls, the Maplewood Laundry was a gathering place for the neighborhood.

I scanned the laundry until I found an empty washer.

A short and chubby man with three-day stubble on his face greeted me as I placed two weeks of white socks and t-shirts in one of the washers. "You're new around here, aren't you?"

"Yeah, I just moved into the Conquistador Apartments."

"The Conquistador, eh? I should have guessed. You look like someone who's been taken to the cleaners by your ex-wife."

And he looked like a whale beached on South Padre Island, out of place and conspicuous.

"Well I'm Humphrey T. Petty, the second shift manager at the Maplewood Laundry. I am not sure what other laundries you been to, but the Maplewood is a respectable place that caters to families with single mothers. So we have a list of rules and regulations that are to be strictly observed."

Humphrey T. Petty ran down a long list of rules. For most of them, I listened then forgot. Only two rules caught my attention. Rule fifteen stated that running around the laundromat was forbidden. Apparently, the laundromat's insurance did not cover injuries from running or sliding on soap or water spills. And the last rule, which as Humphrey so eloquently noted—

"And no damn profanity will be tolerated."

As you have seen throughout this book, this was an instance in which it would have been far better for me to keep my mouth shut. But as you well know, I didn't. I found the foul-mouthed ironic hypocrisy of his statement far too tempting to just simply ignore. I shot back, "Do you realize that you just broke one of your rules by cursing?"

"Hell, what did I say?"

"You said 'damn.'"

He gave me the once-over and determined that I was a bit too big for my britches. He blew a smoke ring toward me. "I see you're gonna be a trouble-maker. You one of them college-educated smart asses aren't you?"

"Look, all I'm saying is that if there is a prohibition against profanity, then you shouldn't use it either."

"You're starting to piss me off."

I dropped my discussion with the laundromat supervisor. I had made my point, but it zipped over his head like a mosquito in heat. So, I turned my attention to more mundane matters like washing a month's load worth of clothes.

My neighbors had told me never to buy the detergent at the laundromat, unless I had no other options. They also suggested that whatever washing powder I buy, it should be both cheap, and a lot. In keeping with that advice, I purchased twenty pounds of a detergent called *Clothes Clean* from a close-out store. The detergent, plus fabric softener, bleach, and dryer sheets cost less than ten dollars. According to my neighbors, I had enough washing supplies for well over a month.

Humprhey T. Petty was none too pleased that I had brought my own washing supplies. To him, I was an importer—someone not willing to pay three dollars for a thimble-sized sample of detergent or clothes softener. He sneered in my direction as he walked around the laundry. Certainly he was contemplating adding a rule sixteen—All washing supplies must be purchased at The Maplewood Laundry. A couple of the regulars talked to him, though he mostly made sure that people were not overloading the washers.

I poured almost a pound of *Clothes Clean* into each of the washers, and saw not one bit of suds. After five minutes, I checked again and noticed that the water was dirty, but there were still no suds. I added more detergent. Nothing but brown water. Maybe it was the washer as opposed to the detergent. This was going to be one long night, I thought. I sat down and began reading a magazine that was about a year old. My sixth sense told me that I was not alone. I turned, and saw two large brown eyes peeping over the cigar-holed sofa.

"Whatcha doin man?" a small child asked.

"I'm washing some clothes," I returned.

"Whya washin clothes, man?"

"Because they're dirty."

"Whenya goin to finish, man?

"I don't really know. What's your name?"

"My mommy, told me that I should never tell a stranger my name, man." She scampered across the laudromat, to a woman I suspected was her mother.

I couldn't argue with her mother's warning. I returned to my magazine. The lead article was about some exploratory expedition that was lost in the Amazon for two months. Though a couple pages were missing, I got the gist of the story—being lost in an unchartered land is no picnic.

A minute or so later, the little girl peered over the sofa again. "My name is Penny."

"I thought your mother said you shouldn't tell a stranger your name."

Penny watched me intently. She shadowed me from the washer to the dryer to the folding table.

"My mom said it was okay to talk to you. She said, you looked okay, even if you were just a man."

"I see."

One of the washers buzzed, signalling that the washing cycle on my whites had finished.

A heavy set woman, smoking an unfiltered cigarette, opened the washer, and proceeded to dump the clothes on a corner folding table.

"Hey, I was just about to take those clothes out of the washer."

The woman, wearing a black T-shirt that was stretched beyond the dictates of good taste, inhaled the cigarette in one long draw. Her lungs seemed to capture half the smoke from the cigarette. She sneered, "You're too slow. I'd be ready for a pine box by the time you were ready to remove your clothes from the washer. I've got five loads to finish. And my husband is back at the apartment drinking a case of beer and waiting for dinner. So I got no time to waste."

The way the woman pronounced *husband* struck me as unnatural. Flaring her nostrils as she said *hooooooooosband*, it was as if she had inhaled all the air around her.

The manager emerged from his cage. "What's wrong Susie? This man hasslin you?"

"Nothing that I can't handle. He's a slow slob. You know the type."

I took exception to being called a *slow slob*. Well maybe I was a slob, but I wasn't slow, at least not when it came to washing clothes.

"I told you I didn't want any damn trouble, didn't I?"

"There's no trouble, just a minor misunderstanding."

"You know, I can ban you for life from this laundromat."

Like that would be a tragedy that would emotionally scar me for life. After all, there were only sixty-two other laundromats in town. Nevertheless, I suspected that for tonight at least, I better act humble. "I'm sorry," I said contritely. "It won't happen again."

"Make sure that it doesn't," he returned in a surly tone before going back to his cramped cubicle.

Penny observed, "He's not a nice man, is he man?"

"No, he's not."

"Can I watcha fold clothes, man?"

"I guess so, if it's okay with your mother."

"Oh it's all right with her, man. She's got six loads washin now, and two in the dryer. We're going to be here for a while."

I started to fold my jeans and overalls.

"My mom, doesn't fold clothes like that, man. She says only boneheads fold clothes like that."

"I'm not a bonehead, Penny."

"I didn't say you were, man. That's what my mom says. She talks a lot about boneheads, and weasels, and lizards. But she's not talking about animals really. She's actually talking about men, man."

"Tell me, Penny. Is your mother single?"

"Divorced. My dad said he couldn't take it no more."

I can see why, I mumbled to myself.

"Can I help you fold clothes, man?"

She batted her eyebrows. How could I resist such an offer? I handed Penny three pairs of my socks. Penny proceeded to tie them in a knot, rather than rolling them, or folding them. "That's how you fold clothes, man."

"I see." I handed Penny six more pairs of socks.

She folded them as well. "You sure have a lot of clothes, man.

"I'm divorced too, Penny. For some reason, divorced people seem to have lots of clothes."

"I guess you're right, man. Sometimes, I stay with my daddy, and that's all he does—wash clothes. We seem to spend all the time in the laundromat. That's why I know so much about them because I stay in them a lot."

It did not seem fair that Penny should have to spend all her free time in a laundromat. But I guessed it couldn't be helped.

With each load of clothes, Penny helped me a bit more. Occasionally, her mother would walk over and make small talk.

Finally, after close to three hours we both finished washing and drying clothes. I said goodnight to Penny, then I headed to my car.

"I hope to see you again, man." Penny said, as I placed the last tub of clothes into my car.

Over the next six months, I saw Penny every Tuesday evening between six-fifteen and eight-thirty. She taught me how to fold a dress shirt, so that it would not wrinkle in a garment bag. I taught Penny simple magic and card tricks.

One Tuesday, neither Penny nor her mother showed up at the laundromat. I was both sad and concerned that they were not there. For the next month they were no-shows. Finally, I found out from one of the other mothers that Penny and her mom had moved to Louisville—a promotion and a substantial raise.

Penny sent me a Christmas card. On the outside was Santa with his sleigh on the roof of some house. Inside, there was a simple note—*Hope you have a merry Christmas, man!*

I smiled. Some things never changed. For that, I was truly happy.

The Fight

We grunted as we passed each other in the kitchen. Marcia poured a cup of coffee; I buttered a couple slices of toast.

It was the third morning after *The Fight*. Not just any nickel and dime fight, mind you. It had been a classic—one of those that could have raked in the bucks on pay-per-view. No blows were administered. None were needed. For a well-timed and placed verbal volley could inflict as much damage as a jab to the mid-section.

The Fight was *bk—before kids.* In retrospect, it was a good thing that the kids had not witnessed daddy speaking in a language that only he understood. Of course before marriage, our parents, relatives and friends had advised us against arguing in front of the children. They had also advised us not to go to bed mad at one another. Excellent advice, though in practice such a goal is much harder to achieve. Throughout our first few years of marriage, Marcia and I had been successful in patching up our differences before going to bed. In fact, the make-up kiss often signaled that the best was yet to come. But that had been before *The Fight*. For *The Fight* had changed everything.

Marcia was the queen of the raised eyebrows. When she arched them in that oh-so-special and terrifying way, it reminded me of a cat's back arched and ready to pounce on its prey.

"So are you going to apologize?" Marcia asked, casting an icy glare in my direction.

I did not answer. Marcia may have been the queen of the raised eyebrows. But I was the master of the non-response. Ultimately, such a tactic never worked, and Marcia made sure I spoke to any and all matters that she wanted addressed. But I felt that the non-response provided me with a perceived, morale-boosting victory—no matter how short, and in the final analysis, immaterial.

In a measurably raised voice, Marcia asked again, "So are you going to apologize?"

My silence drove Marcia to the edge. Her eyebrows arched so high that they nearly met in the middle of her forehead. As the old saying went, if looks could kill, I would be twenty feet under, entombed in granite.

"Don't make me have to come over there," Marcia said, her voice taking on a strange tonal quality.

I was angry, but not foolhardy. It was now time to answer Marcia. "Apologize for what?" I returned, irritated and agitated.

Marcia's nostrils flared. She could not believe that I would ask such a question. "You know perfectly well what you should apologize for."

Actually, I could neither remember what events had preceded and/or caused The Fight three nights ago, nor could I remember what actions or comments I made or did not make that required me to apologize. It was entirely possible that The Fight started over money. On some level, most of our fights were caused in part over differences in spending and saving. Or The Fight could have been caused by me incorrectly answering one of those test questions that Marcia periodically asked to judge just what kind of husband I would be in a hypothetical situation. I seldom answered correctly, and almost always suffered the consequences for my incorrect answers. I suppose The Fight could have even been precipitated by a relatively minor disagreement like whether one should scramble eggs with a fork or spoon.

Three days later however, I could not remember, for all the money in the world, what caused The Fight. So the real question was should I stand firm and offer no apology, or cut my losses and offer a general apology, and pray that Marcia did not ask follow-up questions that would require me to remember specific parts of The Fight. I chose the latter option.

With my head slightly bowed, and in a contrite tone I said, "I apologize. I'm sorry that I could not control my temper. Please forgive me."

To say that Marcia was not impressed or swayed by my apology was an understatement. In fact, her eyebrows arched another quarter of an inch. She stopped directly in front of me. Marcia's sweet hot breath singed the stubble on my face. With her eyes fixed firmly on my pupils, she said, "You don't even remember what you did to cause The Fight, do you?"

My eyes widened. I tried to convey the belief that I was shocked by her question.

Marcia was not fooled, however. "I can't believe it," Marcia said, shaking her head. "We have the worst fight of our marriage. A fight that caused us not to speak to one another for three days. A fight in which you said some terrible things to me, and about me. And yet, you cannot even remember what you did to cause The Fight. You have sunk to a new low."

In each of the previous four months I had sunk to new lows. But at least in those fights, I remembered something about the events and/or causes leading up to the fight. For this fight—The Fight, I was still drawing a blank.

Two hours, and one hundred seventy icy stares later, I finally remembered what caused The Fight. In retrospect, I was actually ashamed that such a matter had triggered such a disproportionate response and adverse reaction.

"I'm sorry." Two words. Simple and to the point. Yet, on that occasion, as opposed to earlier, those two words were sincere and from the heart. Marcia sensed the change in my attitude.

We kissed. Mind you, it was no ordinary kiss. It was a make-up kiss. And for the first kiss, after The Fight, it was no ordinary make-up kiss. It was long, and tender, and passionate, and plain, old tingly, with bells, whistles, and firecrackers. It was the kind of kiss that curled my toes, and knocked Marcia's shoes off. It reminded me of our first kiss ever. But this kiss, this special make-up kiss, was far better. It was a make-up kiss for the record books.

"Let's not promise never to have any more fights," Marcia said, when our lips unlocked.

Of course we had our share of fights after The Fight. And sadly, after one fight we simply chose to separate. To this day, I'm not sure why. Because deep in my heart and soul, I never stopped loving Marcia. But after our last fight, we didn't have a make-up kiss. If only I had remembered the make-up kiss after The Fight, then perhaps, just perhaps we'd still be married.

My First Ex-Wife and Plants

I am positive that plants and flowers all over the world have distributed my ex-wife Marcia's photograph. Underneath the photo I would imagine that there is a large caption in bold print stating that Marcia Hughes has been responsible for the untimely demise of countless plants, flowers, and shrubs.

Marcia had many sterling qualities. But growing plants and flowers was not one of them. Oh don't get me wrong. Marcia tried. She bought every gardening and landscaping magazine available. She attended workshops at the local community college, and tapped into every gardening advice column offered over the Internet. But try as she might, Marcia simply could not grow a flower, or a plant, or a bush, or a shrub, or a tree, or any living thing that required soil to survive.

I am sure that plants shuddered when Mavis entered a nursery. Perfectly healthy looking plants all of a sudden withered and lost leaves. Bright red roses wilted in front of people's eyes. And evergreens were not evergreen anymore. For all practical purposes, allowing Marcia to tend plants was a massacre on Ivy Lane.

Perhaps things would have been different if I had shown the slightest interest in plants, flowers, and shrubs. Marcia stated that I was not supportive enough of her hobby. In fact, she accused me of contributing to the plethora of problems exhibited by her not so healthy, not so green plants. On more than one occasion, she shared with me her suspicions that I was secretly adding large dosages of salt to the plants and shrubs' daily diet. On each occasion, I denied such a mean-spirited practice.

Well it was spring. And as with each spring, Marcia was bitten by the fresh flower bug. She was determined to grow flowers, and tend to plants, and shrubs, and even ornamental trees. She had drawn sketches of a grand garden that she intended me to build. The garden would have an irrigation system, and the flowers and plants would be spaced apart at the proper intervals.

Marcia carefully drafted and printed out a list of the necessary supplies. Three pages of soil nutrients, and spades, and new, must-have garden gadgets. "This year will be different," Marcia triumphantly observed.

For as long as I could remember, Marcia had purchased all her plants and gardening supplies at Pinnacle Nursery. That year should have been no different.

But it was different. When we arrived, a young man greeted us.

"I'm so sorry Mrs. Hughes, but we cannot sell you plants anymore."

"Excuse me," Marcia said, sure that the clerk must have misspoke.

"My boss, that would be Mr. Jeffords. He said that we can't sell you anymore plants."

"That's ridiculous. I've bought plants, shrubs, and flowers from this nursery for better than ten years. I am one of your best customers."

"I realize that ma'am. But I've been given strict orders. If I sell you anything, I'll lose my job."

I laughed silently. I was sure that if plants could vote, they would have selected Paul Jeffords, nurseryman of the year.

"Well, I will just ask Mr. Jeffords about this insane directive."

So Marcia marched to Paul Jeffords' office. Jeffords reminded me of a bowling ball with arms and legs. "Mr. Jeffords, remember me? I'm Marcia Hughes."

He avoided eye contact with her. "Of course I remember you, Mrs. Hughes."

Marcia introduced me to Jeffords. He fidgeted in his seat, as though he had to rush to the bathroom.

"Now, now, Mrs. Hughes, you know I really like you personally. But—"

"But what?"

"Well ma'am—"

"Yes."

"Forgive me for saying this."

"Go ahead."

"You've been blacklisted by the Tri-County Nursery and Florist Board, an association I might add that includes every store that sells plants and flowers in the greater metropolitan region."

"That's impossible."

"I wish it were, Mrs. Hughes. But I'm afraid that this situation has taken a life of its own, and is actually more serious than the original blacklisting."

"What could be more serious than every nursery and florist in the metro area banning me from purchasing flowers, shrubs, and plants?"

"Well, your name, address, phone number and social security number have been posted on the Internet along with a photo of you that has been crossed out. That information is followed by an International Alert that warns all nursery owners and florists not to sell any living thing, or any utensils to you. In all my years in this business, you are the first person I've run across who received a Quadruple X rating."

"There's got to be a mistake."

"Oh, I'm afraid there's no mistake, Mrs. Hughes. As I've just said, obtaining such a dubious distinction is quite difficult to achieve. But in your case, well—" his voice trailed off.

"Well, what?"

"Well, may I be perfectly blunt?"

"Go ahead."

"Well, Mrs. Hughes, never in my entire life have I met someone so ill-equipped to raise flowers, plants, shrubs, basically anything that needs soil. Of course, you have tried. And the members of the Tri-County Nursery and Florist Board have tried. But the indiscriminate and disproportionate loss of seemingly healthy, robust plant life continues. And so at some point, you have got to say, enough is enough. At some point, the members of the Tri-County Nursery and Florist Board have to protect the interests of the roses, and the evergreens, and the ivy, and even the crabgrass. The plants in this region are innocent, Mrs. Hughes. They deserve a better fate, than the one they would receive with you."

"That's neither true, nor fair."

"Mrs. Hughes, I know that you mean well. But the fact of the matter is that you cannot handle the responsibility of tending to plants and bushes. And since you can't, there is simply no way to entrust you with any more living flowers or shrubs, or trees, or bushes. I am sorry that there cannot be another alternative. But really there cannot. You pose too much of a risk to the plant kingdom. I suggest that you consider a different hobby, perhaps needlepoint, or pottery."

"Say something, Michael," Marcia pleaded.

What could I say? Everything that Paul Jeffords had said was true. Marcia meant well, but she was a menace to plants. And I could not, in good conscience, participate in the charade any longer. Still, Marcia was my wife, and I tried to be supportive, as I explored other options. I asked Mr. Jeffords if I was barred from buying plants. He informed me that the ban extended to all living relatives—as far down as eighth cousins third removed—to any immediate neighbors, and to any known friends of Marcia's.

The Tri-County Nursery and Florist Board was determined not to allow some known acquaintance of Marcia's perform an end-run around their carefully constructed policy. I asked if the ban against buying plants could be removed at some point. Mr. Jeffords informed me that Marcia could apply for re-instatement of her plant buying privileges after one year. Thereafter the Tri-County Nursery and Florist Board would consider whether to lift the ban. However, Mr. Jeffords expressed doubt that the ban would be removed until he retired. At the time of the conversation, Mr. Jeffords was forty-one years old. Therefore, it appeared that the ban amounted to a lifetime sentence for Marcia. I explored a couple other options, but Mr. Jeffords quickly, and decisively rejected them. Though he was sorry that the action had been taken, he was firm in his conviction that the right action had been taken. At that point, I realized that he was not going to change his mind, or his ban. I informed Marcia that it was time to leave.

So we left the Pinnacle Nursery without a flower, or plant, or shrub, or bulb, or seedling, or even a pack of seeds.

After a week of sulking, Marcia decided that if she couldn't purchase real plants and flowers, artificial ones would suffice. She drove to the nearest arts and crafts store and bought almost five hundred dollars worth of artificial greenery. There were plants, and shrubs, and flowers, and even a plastic evergreen tree. Marcia carefully arranged the potted menagerie in the living and family rooms. It was as though we were living deep in artificial replica of the Amazon. At any minute, I was expecting a plastic cobra to slither from one of the fake bushes.

Marcia sprayed the living room with some flowery scent that supposedly created a real flower and plant allusion. But the spray fooled no one, and the plastic flowers looked as lifeless on day one, as they did on day thirteen. Even worse, Marcia could not even properly maintain the artificial stand-ins. In less than two weeks, there was dust and cobwebs clinging from the plants. In three weeks, the artificial leaves drooped to the floor.

Early one morning, a week or so later, Marcia asked me, "So what do you think about the artificial plants? Of course they are not real. But I believe there is a nice and genuine quality to them."

"What plants?" I asked innocently.

Marcia stopped suddenly. She noticed that inches from the front door, an artificial evergreen tree stood. It was as if it too were trying to flee the premises, before its plastic leaves, and rubber straw fell to the floor and were lost forever. To the side of the evergreen was a note. Scribbled in red crayon it read, HELP ME! FOR THE LOVE OF ROSES AND OTHER LIVERS OF THE SOIL! SAVE ME FROM CERTAIN DOOM! WHISK ME FROM THIS HOUSE OF DOOM! AND SET ME FREE!

Neither the prank nor the note amused Marcia.

I actually thought that the flower escape gag was one of my all-time best pranks. Marcia did not share my sentiment. While I suppressed the urge to laugh, Marcia contemplated her revenge.

Indeed she had the last laugh. A few weeks later, I awoke, only to discover the extent of my wife's revenge. As I attempted to roll out of bed and trudge to the bathroom, I realized that I could not move a muscle. My eyes surveyed my predicament and discovered that my bed had been transformed into one giant flower garden. Marcia had entombed me in a ton of potting soil. On either side of my body were real flowers. There were daffodils, and carnations, and ivy that circled just above my head. I could only imagine, that Marcia had spent a small fortune to have someone smuggle the garden supplies and flowers to her.

I tried to break free of my planted prison, but I was no match for hundreds of pounds of soil and dirt. "Marcia," I called out. "You made your point. The flowers are beautiful. You really do have a green thumb. But I need your assistance to get out of this literal flower bed."

There was no answer.

"Come on, Marcia. We've all got a real good laugh. And this is an excellent and creative payback for my prank with the plastic flowers. In fact, your prank is much, much better than mine. But enough is enough. I've got to get ready for work."

Still no answer.

"Marcia, you can't keep me in this flower cocoon forever. It's cruel and inhuman punishment."

Marcia drifted back into our bedroom. "You've never looked better," she replied in such an icy tone, that I wondered if my fate would be worse than that already exacted.

I laughed nervously. "I know I shouldn't have insulted your horticultural skills. And I know that I should have been more supportive of you when we were at the Nursery. Please forgive me. It was a crazy, thoughtless mistake."

"Yes, your prank was all of that."

"Can't you see that I am really sorry?"

"I see that you are entombed in potting soil."

"Marcia, I'm begging you."

"Maybe I should wait until molting season before I free you."

"I'm at your mercy," I pleaded.

Marcia left the bedroom.

As expected, I needed to scratch an itch. It was an itch on my left chest. It was the type of itch that could be relieved with a minimal amount of effort—all I had to do was scratch it. But of course, in my cocoon of dirt and soil, I could not scratch the itch or relieve the discomforting sensation. And unlike some itches, this one did not subside. This itch persisted. The itch almost drove me insane.

Marcia re-entered. She saw my distress and smiled—not a nice smile, mind you, but a possessed, this is the sweetest type of revenge smile.

I'm not sure if Marcia ever quite forgave me for my horticultural indiscretion.

An hour later, Marcia called K.C. and authorized him remove the soil and flowers.

"You never looked better, Hughes," K.C. remarked.

What's That

When you have four ex-wives and six kids of varying ages living with their mothers, it is a rare treat indeed to have a whole weekend to yourself. But that's what happened not too long ago. The kids were either at sleep-overs or sleep-outs, while three of my exes were soaking up sun and an herbal mudbath, and the fourth was trying to save baby turtles or the rainforest, or some other environmental cause.

I was going to watch a little basketball on TV. My recliner was in the proper position for either viewing or snoozing, whichever came first. Within arm's reach were the essentials, pretzels, popcorn, and soda. I was primed for a relaxing afternoon in front of the tube.

Just before tip-off, the front doorbell chimed. I squinted through the key hole, and saw the mishapen image of a person I suspected to be a salesperson. I opened the door. Indeed it was a smartly dressed, bright-eyed, slick-haired door-to-door solicitor.

"Afternoon sir. I hope that I did not disturb anything that was truly important."

"You shouldn't be here."

"If there is a better time, then I certainly can come back."

"I mean you shouldn't be here at all. The sign at the entrance to the subdivision clearly states that solicitation and door-to-door sales are forbidden."

"I'm not trying to solicit business."

"Then what do you want?"

"Today is your lucky day, Mr. Hughes."

"Why? Are you leaving?"

He laughed politely. "I like a man with a good sense of humor."

"I'm not laughing."

"But you do have a good sense of humor, don't you?"

"Why are you here?"

"Why am I here?" the man repeated, genuinely confused by my statement. After scratching his head for a few seconds, he answered, "Oh, I see. You think that I am some common, ordinary, run-of-the-mill door-to-door salesman. Well I am not."

"Then what are you?"

"I am the man who's going to change your life for the better."

"My life can't get any better. Now if you'll excuse me." I started to close the door. But to my surprise, he stopped the door with his right foot.

"Give me five minutes," he said with an air of confidence. "If I can't convince you in the next five minutes, then I'll leave and never come back."

"You've got four minutes and fifty-eight seconds left," I returned.

The salesman stepped inside, and removed a package from his briefcase. He pulled a pair of scissors from his inside suit pocket, and cut the top of the package. After placing the scissors in the briefcase, he pulled an orange object from the cellophane package. He carefully arranged the object on my coffee table.

"What's that?" I asked.

He replied, "That's that."

"That's what?"

"That."

"That?" I repeated.

"Yes, that."

"I repeat, what's that?"

"That's the key to your happiness—the key to everything good and pure—the key everlasting love and spiritual fulfillment."

"That?"

"Yes, that."

"How's that possible?"

"Because that's that."

I felt the first twinges of a migraine headache. I exhaled in pre-turbed exasperation.

The salesman saw the pain radiating from every inch of my face. He smiled, and continued his sales pitch. "I can sense you are a bit tense. It is all the more reason that you need that."

"Trust me when I say, I do not need that."

"And trust me when I say you are not the first person to say that. But, the fact of the matter is that that soothes, refreshes, energizes, and invigorates. Once you have that, you will realize how that significantly improves the quality of your life."

"My life is just fine without that."

"It will be better with that."

"I doubt that."

"Just hold that, and you will see what I mean." With that he extended that to me.

"I don't want to hold that."

"Give that a chance."

"Put that away," I demanded.

"Five seconds. I only ask for five seconds. Try that for five seconds, and you will understand the mystic power of that."

"I don't want that."

"Five seconds. That's all. That will change your life."

I stared at that, and I could have sworn that that stared back at me. Like a siren from the sea, that beckoned me to hold that. I succumbed to the alluring power of that. I held that. Nothing. I felt nothing holding that. Or so I thought. As I was about to hand that back to the salesman, I felt different—better, calmer, more alive. "Is that how that feels?" I asked.

"Yes, you're feeling the essence of that."

That, indeed, soothed my soul. And because of that, I contemplated complex thoughts.

"Didn't I tell you? That would change your life."

"I need that," I said, mesmerized by the orange cylinder.

"I knew that."

"How much is that?"

"That is only fifty dollars."

"That's all?"

"That's all."

"I would have paid twice as much for that."

"But that is for everyone."

I handed the salesman fifty dollars.

He handed me a brand new that.

I stopped him. "No," I said. "I don't want a wrapped that. I want that that."

"This that?"

"Yes, that that."

"Then you shall have that." He returned the open that to me.

K.C. dropped by a couple of days later. I was eager to show him that, and at the first opportunity I did. As he told me about his latest stock market conquest, I revealed that to him. "Behold that," I said with an air of confidence and superiority.

"What?"

"That."

"That's not that."

"What do you mean?"

"What you have is not that, but rather a fake."

"That can't be."

"Trust me. What you have is not that, but an it."

"I have an it as opposed to a that?"

"Yes."

"But I have a certificate of authenticity."

"That's a fake as well."

"And how do you know? How can you be so sure?"

"Because I have a genuine, and authenticated that."

"I don't believe that."

K.C. rushed home, then came back with what he said was that.

His that looked similar, though not identical, to my that.

I defended my that. "Perhaps it is you that have an it, and I have a that."

"That's not likely."

"Really?"

"I'm afraid so."

So, I tossed it in a wastebasket. What I thought was that, was simply an it that didn't change my life.

Oh well, that was my luck.

And that was that.

Chicken Foots Stew

My cousin, Cletus lived so deep in the country that it took a day and a half for high speed Internet service to reach him. My cousin Cletus was so country that he thought an automobile was a newfangled contraption. But as the folk in his neck of the woods used to say, Cletus was *good people*, and I genuinely liked him.

Once or twice a year he would breeze through on his way to a hollering contest, or a pig foot eating festival, or on occasion a more traditional event like a theme park or Country Festival. We'd catch up on old times, and compare notes on who had died, divorced, and had babies. Most of the conversations were strictly small talk. But they were about family, so there was a measure of importance to them.

Anyway, a couple of days after New Years a few years ago, Cletus and his wife Raylene visited me and my third wife Maureen. Their seven kids were back home with one of Raylene's relatives. Since we hadn't seen each other for such a long time, I figured that he and Raylene might want to spend sometime at our house catching up on old times. But as it turned out, Cletus and Raylene were on their way to Aunt Emma's house.

However, Maureen loved entertaining, and this occasion was no exception. "If you can't stay overnight," she said, "At least you and Raylene can stay for dinner."

Cletus was one never to pass up a free meal, so he quickly accepted.

In no time, Maureen whipped up two pans of fried chicken, real mashed potatoes, gravy, cornbread, green beans, iced tea, and for dessert peach cobbler. Of all my ex-wives, Maureen was, without a doubt, the best cook.

Cletus helped himself to thirds on everything. Raylene was just behind Cletus with thirds on everything but the peach cobbler. "Have to maintain my girlish figure," she said, patting her hourglass hips.

"That was a mighty fine dinner, Maureen," Cletus remarked as he picked his teeth with a chicken bone.

"I'm glad you enjoyed it, Cletus. Do you want anymore?"

"If I eat another bite, I just might pop just like a cork on a bottle of champagne."

"All right then." Maureen began clearing the kitchen table.

"Say Maureen, did you save the chicken foots?"

"Chicken foots?" she asked, thoroughly confused about his request.

"Yeah, did you save your chicken foots?"

"Chicken foots?" Maureen repeated.

"Yeah, I need a dozen chicken foots, for some chicken foots stew."

"Chicken feet stew," I replied.

"Chicken foots stew," he returned, smiling at my mistake.

"I'm sorry, Cletus. I didn't have any chicken foots."

"Yeah, cuz," I chimed in, "You caught us with no chicken foots. We threw out the last batch, just the other night."

Cletus did not grasp the obvious sarcastic nature of my comment. He replied, "Too bad, cousin. I was going to cook up one mean batch of chicken foots stew."

"I don't believe I've ever had chicken foots stew," Maureen remarked.

"Never had chicken foots stew?" Cletus couldn't believe his ears.

Maureen trying to be the good hostess asked the one question that I refused to ask, "How do you prepare chicken foots stew?"

Cletus smiled as though he had just won a hundred pounds of chitlins. "You really want to know how to fix a heaping mess of chicken foots stew?"

"I certainly do," Maureen replied.

A heaping mess indeed, I thought.

Cletus shared the recipe with Maureen. Now I share it with the world. Without further ado, here is the recipe for the world's famous chicken foots stew.

The Recipe—Make sure you clip the nail on each toe. Boil some seasoned water and drop about $1.60 worth of foots into a large pot. Cook until the foots are nice and tender, and then serve over hot gooey rice. Garnish with one foot spread wide on top of the dish from which you are serving.

Quite frankly I thought that would be the end of the story. But it wasn't. A couple of months later I was in a swanky restaurant in the Theatre District of Manhattan. Maureen and I scanned the menu. Nothing but the exorbitant prices grabbed me. After roughly five minutes, our waiter informed us of the daily specials. At the top of the list, he noted the chef's latest creation—Chicken Foots Stew.

"You mean, chicken feet stew?"

"How gauche," he said, sneering at me as though I were uncouth, and ill-informed. "It is Chicken Foots Stew."

"I see," I returned, rolling my eyes at the waiter. "The menu says that Chicken *Foots* Stew is market priced. And what would the price be tonight?"

"Of course you know, chicken foots stew is not for everyone."

"Just tell me how much is the stew."

"Tonight, it's thirty dollars."

I detected a distinct joy in the undercurrent of his voice. He figured that there was no way that I would pay thirty dollars for a dish that I could not even pronounce correctly. Well maybe I couldn't afford it—and maybe I didn't even want it—but by golly—I certainly wasn't going to let that smug waiter get the last laugh. I handed him the menu and said, "I'll have the chicken foots stew."

"Are you sure?"

"Absolutely."

"And will you be having wine with the chicken foots stew?"

"Wine?"

"But of course. May I suggest the Swani Nosson Madiera 1993?"

"Red wine with poultry?"

"To connoisseurs of chicken foots stew, red wine is the perfect complement. But if you would prefer a more bland white wine, such as a Bontonni Farms—"

"No, no, I'll have the Swani, whatever you said."

"As you wish."

I could have been irritated and upset with the waiter's condescending attitude towards me. But at that moment, I was more concerned and intrigued with how the restaurant got the recipe for Chicken Foots Stew. I realized that it wasn't a secret dish. In fact, it was considered a regional delicacy in Cletus' neck of the woods. However, I found it difficult to imagine that Cletus or anyone in his small town would have come in contact with anyone associated with this restaurant.

"And what will madame have?"

"I'll have the chicken foots stew as well—accompanied by the wine you recommended."

"An excellent choice. It will be a pleasure to serve you." The waiter placed particular emphasis on that last sentence. The clear implication was that serving me would be tedious and a chore.

I believe that the restaurant served Washington—that would be George—the first President—and everyone else in the restaurant, before we were served. With no help from Maureen, I nibbled down two baskets of Chicago hard rolls. Sometime before dawn, the waiter rolled out our entrée.

Maureen remarked on the wonderful aroma of the chicken foots stew. I could have sworn that the aroma of the dish was reminiscent of boiled day-old gym socks. But I was determined to down all of my chicken foots stew. I held my breath and took my first bite. To my complete surprise, the chicken foots stew was actually rather tasty. I took another, slightly bigger bite. I savored the nutty texture of the rice. The chicken foots stew did not require salt, pepper, or any other seasoning. I sipped the Swani Nosson Madiera 1993. I couldn't believe it. The waiter's recommendation was right on point. The wine was a perfect complement to the chicken foots stew. It was as though my tastebuds had been awakened from a year-long slumber.

Maureen savored the chicken foots stew as well. A talkative person by nature, she uttered not one word or sound, as she cleaned her plate with vigor and gusto.

On my next to last mouthful, I savored the gooey rice, then bit into something so hard, that I initially thought I had cracked two molars. I spit a hard-as-rock curved object into my linen napkin. After making sure that my teeth were still intact, I called for the waiter.

"More wine?" he asked drolly.

"No, no. Look—"

"Then might I suggest crème brulee with worchestier sauce for dessert."

"Hold your horses, pal. Look at what was hidden in the rice. It almost cracked four of my teeth."

"My aren't you lucky."

"Lucky?"

"Yes, it is not everyone who gets a chicken toenail in the chicken foots stew."

"A toenail!" I exclaimed.

"But of course," the waiter replied with his customary disdain.

"A toenail?! You're supposed to clip the toenails before you cook the chicken feet, er chicken foots and prepare the stew."

"Are you an awarding winning chef?"

"No."

"Have you ever prepared chicken foots stew?"

"No."

"Have you ever prepared any dish of any sort?"

"I have shished a kabob or two."

"A griller. I should have expected as much." The waiter jotted something on his order pad. Peering down with both contempt, and pity, he continued, "Master Executive Chef Jacques Noble is an award-winning culinary expert. He is an absolute genius. So I am quite sure that his preparation of chicken foots stew is correct."

I had grown tired of interacting with the waiter. "Check, please."

"You mean that you are going to eat chicken foots stew, but not eat dessert?"

"That's correct."

"It figures. You do not know how to appreciate a meal." The waiter handed me the check.

I returned it to him. "I take exception to that comment."

"The truth hurts, doesn't it?" the waiter replied, turning his head and nose upward.

"Look, I can enjoy a meal. We'll both have that crème brulee dish you mentioned."

"But of course," the waiter replied with his customary disdain.

Ordinarily I would have left no tip to such a rude, obnoxious, and condescending waiter. But I had to show him that I wasn't affected by his crass behavior—so I placed an extra fifty under my plate. That would show him, I thought.

As we left, I heard him say, "But of course."

Renting A Movie

The beauty of leaving kids with one parent, is that the absent parent can make promises on behalf of the parent that stays behind. On the weekend in question, I had the kids, and the responsibility to make good on any promises made by Marcia.

"Mom said we could rent a movie," Malcolm explained.

"And where's, mom?" I asked.

"In San Diego, daddy," Millicent replied.

"And if, mommy is in San Diego, then that means that she's not here, and therefore, has no authority for the time being."

"Mommy, said you might be difficult, daddy. But she said it was just an act. And who would know better than your dear, sweet, adorable daughter."

"Sorry kids, I hadn't planned on renting any movies. Maybe next time."

"But I want to see the *The Yellow Ant That Ate San Diego.*"

"And I want to see the Wagner sisters in *Missing in San Francisco.*"

I had not rented a movie in several years, and I didn't really want to rent two movies that night. But the kids were insistent that they wanted to see those movies, so I ultimately agreed to go to the video rental store.

For no particular reason, other than it being the closest movie rental store to my house, we chose the Big Big Brother Movie Store. The name sounded a bit too George Orwellian for me. As I discovered, the store's name and decor did indeed reflect a *1984* influence.

Inside the Big Big Brother Movie Store there were surveillance cameras throughout. No doubt the cameras were intended to discourage tape theft.

With over twenty thousand movies, it took nearly fifteen minutes to locate the desired movies. Both kids wanted to rent four other movies apiece. But on that point I remained firm and inflexible. I intended to rent two movies for two days. Nothing more.

Saturday represented a big movie rental day, so I waited in line for several minutes while two clerks handled a dozen customers in front of us. The man directly in front of us rented fifteen movies. Either he had a large family, or he was single with no social outlets. In either case, I could not envision any circumstance in which I would rent fifteen movies at one time. Finally, it was our turn.

"Do you have a Big Big Brother Movie Club Card?" Ron the checkout clerk asked.

"No," I returned.

"May I have your phone number?"

After giving Ron my phone number, he checked the Big Big Brother Movie Club database. "You don't have a movie club card?"

At that moment, I could tell that Ron was a bit slow on the uptick. "I already told you that, Ron," I replied. "All I want to do is rent a couple of movies for a couple of days. I intend to pay cash. Do I need a Big Big Brother Movie Club Card to do that?"

"Yes, you do."

I sighed. "What if I purchase the movies? Would I still need a Big Big Brother Movie Club Card?"

"Yes, you would."

I sighed again. "All right, where is the movie club application form?"

Ron, the checkout clerk ushered me a counter at the opposite end of the store. He handed me a Big Big Brother Movie Club Application Form. At the top of the form it read, *Thank you for applying for a Big Big Brother Movie Club Card. Please note, that the Big Big Brother*

Movie Club Card is Free Upon Approval. Every attempt is made to keep information supplied in the Application confidential. However, on occasion we share some of the information in order to enhance our ability to serve you. By applying for a Big Big Brother Movie Club Card, you are granting the Big Big Brother Movie Company permission to share information contained in your Application with selected vendors and officials. That was Red Flag number one.

Red Flag number two was the length of the application itself. There were over sixty questions spread over four pages. The application form appeared more detailed and comprehensive than some credit and tax forms. Question eighteen asked for three separate forms of identification. Question twenty-two asked for five references, of which only one could be a relative. Question thirty-nine asked to list every job for the past ten years. Question fifty-one asked for total annual income for the past five years. Question fifty-seven requested current bank account balances. And question sixty asked for a twenty-five word or less description on why I wanted to become a member of the Big Big Brother Movie Club.

Before I printed my name in the space designated for question one, Ron returned to the movie club application counter. "Have you finished filling out the application form?'

"As a matter of fact, Ron, I haven't gotten past item number one. Honestly, is all this information necessary."

"Yes."

"Are you telling me, that you really need to know my shoe size, and the name of my first high school sweetheart?"

"Those aren't questions on the application form."

"Well they might as well be, Ron—for the Big Big Brother Movie Club application form delves into some pretty personal areas. I mean question forty-four wants to know the names of all banks, savings institutions, and brokers I have associated with in the last ten years."

"If you feel uncomfortable about answering the question, then don't answer the question."

"And what if I don't answer a question on the Big Big Brother Movie Club application form, Ron? Will I still get my movie club card, and be able to pay cash for two movies that I only want for two days?"

"I don't know. I do not evaluate the information supplied on the application form."

"Then who does evaluate the information supplied, Ron?"

"That would be the manager, Mrs. Pasquale." Ron noticed that he was being summoned to the check-out counter. "Excuse me." Ron returned to assist movie club members.

I prepared to leave, for there was no way that I was going to provide answers for all the questions on the Big Big Brother Movie Club Card application form. Heading for the front door, I said, "Come on kids."

"Daddy, you can't leave, yet. You haven't rented my movie." Millicent batted her eyelashes, and gave me one of her, *Daddy I really want this* squeezes.

"I don't intend to rent from a store that requires so much information."

"But you promised, daddy. And you said, that we should never break a promise."

I also said, that fish would eventually drink all the water in the oceans, and no one ever believed that hogwash.

"What's wrong, pops? You don't have the money to rent the movies? If its money, I'm sure I can loan you what you need."

My son was all heart. The last time he loaned me money, he charged me thirty percent interest. Well at least it was all in the family. But of course, money was not the problem facing me at the moment. I simply did not want to complete a movie club rental application form that was more involved and detailed than most mortgage applications.

"Maybe you don't have to fill out the entire application form, pops."

"Then why would they include questions that they don't want answers?"

"I don't know."

Millicent added, "Well you should at least ask. Mommy always says that you should at least ask if you can skip over questions that you would prefer not to answer."

Rather than debate the issue with Malcolm and Millicent, I chose the path of least resistance, and confronted Mrs. Pasquale about the application form. "I find your form too expansive, in that it asks for detailed personal information that has no relation to renting a movie. I want to know if I have to answer all questions."

I expected Mrs. Pasquale to say *yes*. Instead though, she said, "All we really need is your name, address, home and work phone numbers. The rest of the information is optional."

"Then why do you ask the additional questions? It's an invasion of privacy."

"People who feel that certain questions invade their privacy simply decline to answer such questions. People who do not object answer the questions. There is no ulterior motive."

The logic was so frighteningly simplistic that it defied argument. Anyway, under the circumstances, I provided the only required information. Moreover, free from the offensive questions, I was now ready to rent the movies for Millicent and Malcolm. I walked to the check-out line, and handed Ron the movies. "I want to rent these movies for two days."

Ron replied in his typical monotone voice, "You can't rent a movie for two days. You can rent a movie for one, three, five, or seven days, but not two days."

"But on that sign above you, there is a listing for a two day rate."

"That rate is for our Golden Movie Club members."

"And what does it take to become a Golden Movie club member?"

"You have to fill out another application, and pay ten dollars."

I would have argued the point, but it was useless to argue with Ron. He was an employee with a singular mission—to punch a time-clock at the beginning and end of each workday. If he helped anyone in between, then that was a bonus. But Ron was just another soul in search of a paycheck.

I thought about going back to Mrs. Pasquale, but she had just left for her dinner break. So, in the end, I chose the seven-day rental because surprise, surprise, that rate was three dollars cheaper than the other rates.

That night I popped a pound of popcorn, and poured five sticks of butter on the giant tub of popped kernels. Millicent and Malcolm loved the movies and daddy/pops for one evening.

I was ten minutes late in returning the movies. I had to pay a ten dollar fine, and have my privileges in the *Big Big Brtother Movie Club* suspended for two weeks. It didn't matter. I never rented another movie. Once was quite enough.

Boys and My Daughter

I realized from the first moment that my daughter Millicent was born that I would at some point have to deal with boys coming to see her. Marcia always told me that that day would come sooner than I thought—sooner than I would want.

One evening after dinner, I commented on the growth and development of my sweet, innocent daughter. "What's happened to our Millicent? I mean I can still remember cradling her within minutes of her birth."

"Stop torturing yourself, Michael. Millicent is growing up."

My question had been rhetorical. But there was no question that Millicent was changing before my eyes. Overnight, Millicent blossomed. I mean one day she was wearing a ponytail, and now—well she was entering puberty.

As I rinsed scraps from the dinner dishes, there was a knock on the front door.

When I opened the front door, I was greeted by a teenager (around sixteen I suspected) with a lustful smile, and leacherous heart. He reaked of cheap, dime-store cologne, and sported a thin moustache, and chin whiskers. My eyes narrowed. I thought about slamming the door in his face. I didn't. In light of what happened though, I really should have.

"May I help you?"

"I'm looking for Millicent."

Millicent?! The boy with the cocked baseball cap, and pants three sizes too large could not have possibly asked to see my daughter Millicent. It had to be a mistake.

"I'm sorry, what did you say?"

"Millicent. I'm looking for Millicent. She lives here, doesn't she?"

"Excuse me," I returned. "What is your name, and how old are you?"

He smiled with an even more wicked smile than before. "Rafael. I'm eighteen."

Eighteen!!!! It was worse than I suspected. I recalled having that same type of smile when I was eighteen. I shuddered, for that memory of my adolescence provided me with no comfort. That smile conveyed an intent to do things with my daughter that I had no intention of Rafael doing.

"Say, are you like her old man?"

My inclination was to give Rafael a swift kick to his bottom and send him back to his car. But I resisted the impulse. I had to find out how he knew Millicent.

"Do you mind if I ask you a question?"

"What?"

"How did you meet, Millicent?"

"Well you see, I was hoping to meet her for the first time tonight."

First time!! Rafael had to be crazy or crazed if he thought there was any chance that I would let him meet my sweet daughter Millicent, tonight, or any night for that matter. Obviously though, there was a reason that Rafael wanted to meet Millicent. I decided to find out where he had seen or run across my daughter.

"If you've never met, Millicent," I began, "then how do you know about her?"

"I saw her at one of those cheerleading competitions. She was fantastic. I've never seen anyone so athletic. And her eyes, like those of an angel. Anyway, after the competition I did a little legwork and found out that the athletic girl with the angel eyes was named Millicent. With a little more investigation, I found out her address. And that is why I am here now—to meet Millicent."

"Well, if you had conducted any further inquiry you would have learned one additional critical fact."

Rafael thought I was about to share some intimate secret with him. In a way I was, though I am sure that it was not the type of information that he had originally contemplated. He scooched a bit closer, then asked, "And what don't I know about my angel eyes?"

Referring to Millicent as *angel eyes* caused my blood to boil at an even two hundred degrees Fahrenheit. I suppressed the urge to give Rafael two black eyes. I counted to sixteen before answering. "Are you aware that Millicent is twelve?" I asked as I rubbed the corners of my moustache.

"Twelve?"

"Yeah, just turned twelve two weeks ago."

He laughed, though I could not tell if he was embarrassed by my revelation. He rubbed his chin, then sucked air through the side of his mouth. "I guess, I made a mistake. It must be another Millicent that I'm looking for."

"I suspect so."

"Good-bye."

I closed the door then peeked through the curtains to make sure that Rafael and his car had left for good.

"Who was it daddy?"

"Someone who had the wrong address."

"Who was he looking for?"

"Someone much older—a woman."

Millicent moved closer to me. I peered into her eyes. At that very moment, I could think of no person move beautiful, loving, radiant, or innocent. I embraced my daughter, and gave her the biggest, warmest hug that a father could give his child.

Millicent returned the embrace, then asked, "Why the hug daddy?"

"Because I wish you would never grow up."

"For you, daddy, I never will grow up."

I hugged Millicent again. No further words were spoken. None were needed.

Lines 4—Sweepstakes

All I was supposed to get at the store was any brand of meat and mushroom spaghetti sauce. If the store didn't have any meat and mushroom sauce, then I could pick any brand, and any type of sauce. I would slip in and out of the store in ten minutes. With any luck, I wouldn't miss any action in the second half of the big game.

"Where are you going, daddy?"

"To the store, Millicent. I'll be back in a few minutes."

"May I go with you, daddy?"

I avoided eye contact because I was certain that Millicent was looking at me with her big sad eyes. If I saw them, for even one second, then I would give in and agree to take her to the store with me. But taking Millicent to the store would add at least ten minutes to my trip, and that would mean I would miss precious and exciting minutes of the second half of the big game. So I avoided eye contact.

As I grabbed my keys off a wooden rack, I headed for the front door. "Maybe another time, Millicent."

"But daddy, you said that the next time you went to the store, you would take me."

A father says many things, at any time, in order to placate children for the moment. At its best, the *next time* promise is a feeble attempt to delay the inevitable in the false hope that the child or children will somehow forget the *next time* promise. But children, my children especially, never forgot any *next time* promise I made. Millicent in particular could recall every *next time* promise that I had made since her birth. And she was relentless in reminding me until I settled the score. So realizing that *next time* was this time, I told Millicent, "Get your jacket, and come along."

Though only eight, Millicent was quite clothes conscious. She couldn't wear just any jacket to the grocery store. No, the jacket had to be color co-ordinated with the rest of her outfit. Millicent, spent five minutes accessorizing her wardrobe.

We approached the store's entrance. Millicent broke free from my grip, and sprinted toward the automatic door. Not watching for others, Millicent almost bowled over an elderly woman in a white shawl.

Both the woman and Millicent were startled by the collision.

"I'm sorry, daddy."

"Tell the lady that you are sorry."

Millicent walked back to the woman and apologized for her hasty actions. The lady with deep wrinkles and a broad smile forgave Millicent, and remarked that Millicent was quite pretty. She patted Millicent's forehead, reached into her handbag, retrieved a quarter, and placed it in the palm of Millicent's left hand.

Millicent skipped back to me, and chirped, "Look at what the nice lady gave me, daddy."

"Millicent, this time you were lucky. You could have injured yourself, or worse that woman. You need to be more careful, and pay attention to you surroundings. And most of all, you need to be considerate of others before you act."

"I understand," Millicent said in a contrite voice.

With Millicent, I was never sure if she was truly sincere and sorry for her deeds, or simply using me as a pawn in her life game of chess.

I hoped it was the former as I briskly entered the store, with child in hand, and walked with single-minded determination to aisle two. Spotting dozens of different spaghetti sauces, I plucked the store brand with meat from the middle shelf. My main task had taken less than one minute to complete. Now to address the junk food desires of my precious and precocious daughter.

"All right, Millicent. What do you want?"

"I want some chocolate covered raisins, and some super salty pretzels."

Like an obstacle course runner, I dashed around carts and avoided promotional displays. Quick as you could say *Let's Get Out of Here*, I found raisins on aisle five, and super salty pretzels on aisle ten. Time-wise, we were still looking good—less than three minutes had elapsed since we entered the store. Better yet, it appeared that we would be back at the house in less than twelve minutes.

With Millicent in tow, I considered it a minor miracle that we were already in the ten items and under check-out line. There were only two people in front of us. We should be on our way within a couple of minutes. With any luck, I would still see the last eight or nine minutes of the game. For one brief second I was content and happy. For one brief second that is.

Millicent snapped her fingers. "I forgot something daddy."

"What did you forget?"

"I forgot *Screaming Munchies*, daddy."

"And just what are *Screaming Munchies*?"

"It's just the most tasty cereal ever. We ran out of it a couple of days ago, daddy. Would you please get me some more?"

As I recalled, Millicent had said the same thing about *Sugar Magic Squares,* and *Tasty Corn Bars,* and *Yummy Wheat Shavings*. To me, it was simply the cool cereal of the week. But it was too late. "We're already in line, dear. Remind me next time."

"But I really want some *Screaming Munchies* today."

Only a child would even consider eating dry cereal in the middle of the afternoon. Regardless of what Millicent wanted, it was imperative that I remain firm. Otherwise, watching the climatic last minutes of the big game would be impossible. But Millicent would neither appreciate nor understand my desire to watch a sports contest. She had already been poisoned by her mother who called such epic struggles, *silly sports for guys*. In an instant it dawned on me that

Millicent would be far more understanding if I suggested that mommy was the reason we had to return home immediately. Yes, use Marcia as the scapegoat, so that I could watch the rest of my basketball game. Certainly, under those circumstances, Millicent would not hold a grudge against dear old mommy. I kissed Millicent's right hand "I'm sorry, sweetheart. We're next in line. And mommy really needs the spaghetti sauce, so that we can eat on time tonight. And we wouldn't want mommy to be late with dinner, would we? So I'm afraid, that I'll have to get you *Screaming Munchies* the next time I come to the store."

Maybe I had used Marcia as a convenient excuse one time too many. I'm not sure, but I guess it did not make any difference because Millicent did not buy my explanation. Rather, she offered her own assessment on the situation. "Daddy, you're really fast. They are on aisle sixteen. It will only take you a minute, and I'll hold your place in line. Please, daddy. Oh, you're the best daddy in the world."

The person in front of us had ten items exactly. The check-out clerk had to get a price check on an item that did not scan correctly. I sighed—for two reasons—the first was that the price check was adding precious seconds to the overall store experience—the second was that the momentary delay provided me with an opportunity to run to aisle sixteen and retrieve Millicent's *Screaming Munchies*. I should have resisted my child's pleas. But I couldn't. Her ever expressive eyes tugged at my heart. "All right, I'll be right back. Do not let anyone in front of you. And if our turn comes up before I get back, tell the check-out clerk that we're getting one additional item. Okay?"

"Okay, daddy." Without a care in this world, Millicent waited contentedly for my return.

I grabbed a box of *Screaming Munchies* from a promotional display and dashed back to the check-out line. Upon returning, I noticed an elderly woman was standing in front of Millicent. Noticing that the woman's sweater appeared familiar, I recognized that she was the same lady that Millicent had bumped into a few minutes earlier.

"I did like you told me to, daddy. I made up for my earlier actions, and let the nice lady get in front of us. She just had a couple of things." Millicent then flashed me her "daddy I've got you wrapped around my little finger smile".

Well the woman only had one item, a carton of eggs. How long could it take to process a woman with a single item? I soon found out.

The check-out clerk scanned the item, then said, "That will be eighty-five cents."

"What did you say?"

"Eighty-five cents."

"Eighty-what?"

"Eighty-five. That will be eighty-five cents."

"Eighty cents did you say?"

"No, I said, eighty-five—eighty-five cents."

Feeling that this verbal exchange could last several more minutes, I decided to resolve the confusion over the sale price by paying for her eggs. However, before I could pay, a contingent of store personnel approached our line. They were all smiles.

"And what is your name?" the store manager asked the elderly, white-haired lady.

"Emily Stephens," the woman replied cautiously.

"Well Emily Stephens, this is your lucky, lucky day."

"It is?"

"Yes. You are Peabody Stores four millionth customer."

"I am?"

"Yes. And as Peabody Stores four millionth customer, you are the winner of a host of prizes."

As the cameras flashed, and Emily Stephens stood there shaking hands with the store manager, and genuinely overwhelmed by her good fortune, I felt nauseous. After all, that should have been me accepting the accolades and prizes. If I hadn't gone for those blasted *Screaming Munchies*. If Millicent had not chosen today of all days to do a good deed for her elders. I wanted to knock Emily Stephens out of the way, and get what was rightfully mine. But I suspected that I already had gotten my just desserts.

Millicent's munching on *Screaming Munchies* punctuated an otherwise silent ride back home.

Marcia greeted us at the front door. "You just missed the most exciting conclusion to a basketball game ever. You know that I normally don't watch your silly men's games. But this game was different. I actually sat down and watched the last ten minutes. One of the announcers said that the lead changed twelve times in the last eight minutes. Nevertheless, the Scorpions held a four point lead with two seconds. And guess what happened?"

"The Twisters won."

"Yeah. Burns dribbled the ball, past half-court, flipped the ball to Morrison, the All-American guard, who took a thirty-five foot jump shot, that barely grazed nylon. Talk about a sweet jumper. Anyway, he was fouled on the shot. Three-tenths of a second remained in the game. Morrison intentionally misses the free-throw, and Burns tips the ball in at the buzzer. I'm sure that the game will be featured on tonight's sportscast."

"I'm glad that you enjoyed the game," I returned with a tinge of envy.

Millicent, eager to describe the events at the store said, "Guess what, mommy?"

"What sweetheart?"

"I let a little old lady in front of us at the store, and she won a trip to Paris."

"What?"

I recounted the events at the store. Instead of being saddened, Marcia smiled, and hugged Millicent with one of those special mother hugs. "I am so proud of you, dear."

In the end, I guess that said it all.

Mistaken Identities—Sweepstakes

For at least the last ten years, I have received, on average once a month, a circular or E-mail proclaiming that I just might be the latest winner in the largest sweepstakes conducted in American history. Most of the circulars inform me that I am not obligated to purchase anything in order to be eligible for the grand sweepstakes prize. In fact, Mrs. Dixie Darling, official contest supervisor guarantees that I have the exact same chance of winning, whether or not I order something. However, since I have to return the entry form, I might as well order magazines, or silverware, or a cappuchino maker from the sweepstakes sponsors. I choose never to accept the gracious offer of the company sponsoring the sweepstakes. Consequently, I never expect to win any grand prize money, consolation money, or any complimentary gift. About a year ago though, I experienced the ultimate in sweepstakes frustration.

It was a Saturday afternoon, and I had just answered fifteen down in the local newspaper's weekend crossword puzzle. I proceeded to seventeen across—a seven letter word for *rich, financially secure*. I pencilled in *wealthy*.

The phone rang. Expecting that it might be Marcia, I answered on the second ring. "Good afternoon."

"I would like to speak to Michael D. Hughes."

"You're speaking to him."

"Well, Mr. Hughes, it gives me great pleasure to inform you that you are the grand prize winner of Sweeptstakes 101J54P35 in The National Readers Conglomeration Sweeptstakes."

"Grand prize winner?"

"Yes."

"And exactly how much is the grand prize?"

"You mean you don't recall all the circulars that have been mailed to your address, detailing the amount of the grand prize for Sweepstakes 101J54P35."

"At the moment, it escapes me."

"Well, the grand prize for Sweeptstakes 101J54P35 is fifty million dollars."

I believe the young woman continued talking, although upon hearing fifty million dollars, my mind wandered to Easy Street, and the Land of Good Times. I could buy a boat, but a boat would not do for the fifty million dollar grand prize winner of The National Readers Conglomeration Sweeptstakes. No, I would require a yacht, ninety-six feet long, with three decks, a fifty-seat theater, a dining area large enough to seat one hundred of my closest friends, and an Olympic-sized pool. Or I could buy a house nestled in the mountains, but a mere house nestled in the mountains would not do, for a multi-millionaire. No, I would buy the mountain, and build a mansion right in the mountain itself. Or I could buy a plane, but a plane sounded so simple for a man of enormous personal wealth. No, I would buy a jet large enough to transport all one hundred eighty-eight of my high school classmates.

The possibilities were endless. Then I thought, what in the world was I thinking. I couldn't tell anyone—at least not until after the formal announcement.

"Mr. Hughes," the woman repeated.

I was still in a multi-million dollar daze. I thought the woman said something, but I wasn't sure.

"Mr. Hughes,' she repeated.

"Let me just verify some information for our computers."

"All right," I said, not believing my good fortune.

"You're phone number is Area Code 899-555-5565."

"That's correct."

"And your street address is 1612 Laughingbird Lane."

"Yes."

"And your full name is Michael Dambreau Hughes."

"Well, actually, it is Michael Devin Hughes."

There was a pronounced pause. "Your middle name is not Dambreau?"

"No. I'm sure that it's just a typo though. The address is correct, and I am Michael D. Hughes."

"But the 'D' does not stand for Dambreau."

"No, it does not. But as I said, it just must be a typographical error."

"This has never happened before."

All of a sudden, I did not like or appreciate the tone or direction of the conversation. "Is there a problem?" I asked, hoping that she would reassure me that everything was all right.

"I'm not sure. I am going to have to talk to my supervisor."

I tried to prevent the woman from talking to her supervisor, but to no avail. There were strict rules and procedures that had to be followed. From what I gathered, she suspected that my situation might be a violation of Rule 1.06(b—33.8)—Mistaken Identity. I asked what were the consequences of violating Rule 1.06(b—33.8)—Mistaken Identity.

"I have to talk to my supervisor," she repeated.

There was dead silence—there was no music—no programmed messages—no special offers to purchase magazines—nothing. If there was a mistake, it wasn't my fault—it was the The National Readers Conglomeration Sweeptstakes' fault. I couldn't see how they wouldn't be responsible for awarding me the full amount of the grand prize money. My thoughts turned back to how to spend the monetary windfall.

Finally another voice addressed me. "Mr. Hughes."

"Yes."

"I am Mr. Ralph Rhodes. I have been informed by Prize Award Executive, Debra McKinney that in connection with The National Readers' Conglomeration latest sweepstakes drawing 101J54P35, there is an apparent violation of Rule 1.06(b—33.8)—Mistaken Identity."

To be honest with you Mr. Rhodes, I am not aware that there has been any violation of any sweepstakes rules."

"I see." Mr. Rhodes paused a moment, then continued, "Mrs. McKinney tells me that you are Michael Devin Hughes, as opposed to Michael Dambreau Hughes."

"That's correct."

"Then that would be a violation of National Readers' Conglomeration Sweepstakes Rule 1.06(b—33.8), in that your full legal name differs from the name that was sent the winning entry."

"But as I was telling Mrs. McKinney, there must be a typographical error, because the rest of the information in your data base is correct."

"But you do admit that you are not Michael Dambreu Hughes."

"You know that I am not Michael Dambreau Hughes."

"Sir, I only know what you tell me. And today, for the first time, you tell me that you are not Michael Dambreau Hughes. And more importantly, before today, you chose not to inform us that the name listed on the front of the envelope was incorrect?"

"It never occurred to me to inform you that the name was incorrect, since I did not read the contest information. I simply returned the registration card, and other necessary information."

"And so you were willing to assume the name and identity of one Michael Dambreau Hughes?"

The conversation was drifting into an area that I believed would be ultimately unproductive, and potentially hazardous to my goal of becoming a multi-millionaire. I tried to clear-up any confusion, and redirect the conversation to its proper focus—namely me winning fifty million dollars.

"For the record, I did not assume any person's name. I simply returned a registration card with my correct address, and a correct first and last name, but an incorrect middle name. That however, should have no bearing on my winning the fifty million dollar sweepstakes."

Mr. Rhodes stopped my explanation and said, "I'm sorry. Would you please repeat your last sentence?"

"I said, 'The mix-up with my middle name should not have any bearing on my winning fifty million dollars."

"Let me correct you. You haven't won fifty million dollars. Michael Dambreau Hughes won fifty million dollars."

Exasperated, I replied, "Mr. Rhodes, this conversation is getting us nowhere."

"On the contrary, we have made progress. We have determined that you are not eligible for the fifty million dollar grand prize."

In my entire life, I do not believe that I have heard fifteen words that have hurt as much. It was as if Mr. Rhodes had poked a crimson-hot lance into my chest, and then twisted slowly for what seemed an eternity. *Not eligible for fifty million dollars.* My dreams of a radically altered lifestyle vanished. But fifty million dollars was worth pursuing further. In fact, it was worth engaging in a knockdown, fifteen round fight. For the moment however, I chose to present a logical argument to Mr. Rhodes. "Let's not be too hasty, Mr. Rhodes."

"Mr. Hughes."

"Wait. Let me advance a slightly different scenario."

"Go ahead."

"Suppose, just suppose there actually is a Michael Dambreau Hughes, and everything checks out except his address. In other words his address is incorrect, perhaps one or two numbers off—but the postal delivery person—knowing Mr. Hughes, delivers the mail anyway. Wouldn't you give that Mr. Hughes the grand prize money?"

"Not if his address did not match with the address that was on the original contest registration form that was mailed to that particular Mr. Hughes."

In frustration, I said, "Say is this the line you give every award winner? Maybe this is all a sham. Maybe The National Readers' Conglomeration doesn't have fifty million dollars, or even fifty dollars to award to some so-called winner."

"Mr. Hughes, if I were you, I'd be careful how I characterize the reputation of The National Readers' Conglomeration. We are organization that is beyond reproach. Any comments that sully the reputation of The National Readers' Conglomeration will be forwarded to our legal department who may choose to institute legal action for slander, libel, defamation, and at least fifteen other intentional torts."

"Look, I don't intend to be bullied by some large organization. You can't treat me this way. I've got rights. I've got—"

There was a pronounced click on the other end.

"Hello? Hello? Hello?" I placed the phone on the receiver, after realizing that Mr. Rhodes had hung up the phone.

As I said, the chance of winning fifty million dollars was worth taking extreme measures. So, I hired a lawyer by the name of Sanford S. Stillwater. I'd be willing to bet that the "S" stood for "shady." Anyway, Stillwater thought that there might be a dollar or two, actually several million dollars, to make from the case, so he gladly accepted the dispute on a contingency basis. I never cared for lawyers, and Sanford S. Stillwater did not instill any warm and fuzzy feelings in me. He was a slimy shark with a serpent's tail. I mean what kind of attorney places advertisements and business cards on utility poles, and inside homeless shelters. Nevertheless, Marcia recommended

Stillwater. Given that he had taken me to the cleaners during divorce proceedings with Marcia, I decided he had the right disposition to handle my case.

For six months, Stillwater battled the corporate behemoth of The National Readers' Conglomeration. He was quite enthused by our chances at the outset. In fact, he thought it quite possible that the group would ultimately settle for several million dollars. He created a lengthy and voluminous paper trail. Once again, I saw visions of the eternal good life. Even after I paid his fee and expenses, there would be enough to buy that 6,000 acre ranch in Montana, and have enough left over for four or five helicopters.

Over time though, as Stillwater became more immersed and knowledgeable in the nuances of sweepstakes law, and my actions prior to the errant notification phone call, Stillwater's enthusiasm waned. There would not be the quick, large settlement that he had originally envisioned. Repeatedly, he asked me, "How much time would it have taken you to have informed the sweepstakes sponsors that your middle name was Devin instead of Dambreau. If you had just done that, then we'd be living large by now."

It was true that had I informed The National Readers' Conglomerate of the middle name mix-up at the beginning, none of this contentiousness would have been necessary. But by the same token, if I had corrected the middle name snafu early in the process, then I would not have needed Stillwater, and he would not have had a chance to receive a settlement contingency.

When all was said and done, we settled for a sum that I am not permitted to disclose. Let me put it this way though, I believe every one made money off my case, except me. After Sanford S. Stillwater deducted expenses, a dozen other charges, and his contingency fee, I received a check that allowed me to buy a few thousand shares in a *can't miss stock*, that went bankrupt in six months.

Streaks

There are only so many frozen dinners you can microwave. There are only so many books you can read. And there are only so many movies you can see. After my separation from Marcia, I drifted into a rut. Even visits with my kids became predictable. I needed some zing into my life, though I wasn't sure what activity or hobby I should try for either the physical challenge or emotional joy.

Stewart, from cubicle 6B, suggested that I try betting on the dogs. "Nothing gets your blood pumping like greyhound racing," he observed.

Before Marcia and the kids, I occasionally spent an afternoon at the track and betted on horses, dogs, and any other animal that ran. Watching from the clubhouse, I insulated myself from activities below. As I recalled, the experience was rather antiseptic, and not particularly exhilarating.

Stewart remarked, "The clubhouse is for the betting elite. No action ever happens up there. You need to mingle with the regulars out near the rail. That's where you want to be. That's what will get your competitive juices flowing."

So I took Stewart's advice and avoided the clubhouse elite. Outside, the atmosphere was indeed different. There was no piped music or champagne. It was people humming and chanting and drinking beer from a plastic cup. Even an hour before post time of the first race, there were hundreds of daily wagers studying stacks of racing forms. Some highlighted certain facts from previous races. Others scratched particular dogs because of poor performances under similar circumstances.

Outside on the rail, my adrenaline surged, fueled by the sights and sounds of racetrack central. I smelled the pungent odor of stale cigars, and unfiltered cigarettes. My shoes were covered with discarded race tickets. I could almost touch the dogs as they walked by. I was eyeball-to-eyeball with the dogs and they did not blink. They were lean with not one ounce of fat. From my vantage point, I could gaze into their eyes and see whether they possessed the necessary desire to win a race.

A man approached. He smiled, then said, "I've never seen you around here. What's your name?"

"Michael Hughes."

"Mike, is it?"

No one, not even my mother or ex-wives called me Mike. I always considered myself a Michael, not a Mike or a Mikey, or a Mickey. Down on the track though, standing among bettors old and young, skilled and unskilled, with teeth and without teeth, it did not seem to matter what I was called—so in that case, Mike would do just fine. "Yeah, that's what everybody calls me," I replied.

"Good to meet you, Mike. My name is Shorty—Shorty Blake," he said extending his hand.

Shorty was indeed short—not an inch over five-foot-two. He wore a cowboy hat, beaded cowhide jacket, large gold belt buckle, and basic cowboy boots. His beard was neatly cropped and completely white.

As we were talking, a rather shapely woman sauntered over to Shorty and said in a quite, sultry and alluring voice, "You want a tall one, Shorty?"

"Sure, sugar. Anything you say."

"I'll be right back."

Shorty noticed that I was without a form or other essentials of a regular bettor. He stroked his beard, then asked, "So tell me, Mike. Do you have a system?"

"A system?"

"Yeah, a system for betting on the puppies."

I had no system; I had no clue for betting on the greyhounds. I could look at the dogs, but could not decipher the code of their stride. In previous trips to the dogtrack, I had never picked any winning dog or combination—I had never won any money—not one cent. I shook my head. "Do you have a system?"

Shorty laughed. "You want to know a secret?"

"What?"

"There is no system that comes from stacks of racing forms, or numerology, or scientific evaluation. Picking winners comes from here and here," Shorty remarked, pointing to his head and heart. "You've got to trust both, and know when each should rule. It's that simple."

"You come to the tracks often, Shorty?"

"Often enough." Shorty inhaled deeply. He smiled, as he savored the aroma of the track. "You might say that it's more than a hobby for me. But I am not addicted to the track. I have other interests. I like to fish, and for pure relaxation, I sketch people and wildlife."

"Really?"

"Yeah, but I pick greyhounds better than I sketch."

"Well, I am a novice when it comes to picking greyhounds."

"That's actually a good sign. Remember—your head and heart—that's all you need."

The woman with the sultry voice returned with Shorty's beer. "Here you go, Shorty."

"Thank you darling," he replied, handing her a dollar for the beer, and five for a tip.

She kissed his forehead. "I'll be back in half-an-hour."

"I'll be here." Shorty watched the dogs move about. "So what does you heart tell you about the first race?"

"I don't know."

Shorty casually mentioned the number six dog, *Wayward Apple*. While I considered the greyhound, in the end, I picked *UdontNO*. The odds board indicated that *UdontNO* was the favorite. A couple of minutes before post time, Shorty's dog, *Wayward Apple* could muster no better than eight-to-one odds. I figured that Shorty was a grizzled veteran who won just enough to keep coming to the track. Recent racing history noted that *Wayward Apple* had enough closing speed to perhaps capture third place (show). But in ten previous races, the dog had not won once. Considering the less than stellar performance, eight-to-one odds for *Wayward Apple* were actually surprising. Nevertheless, Shorty had advised against relying too much on statistics. But, I firmly believed that statistics had value in determining the probability of a dog winning a race. So, for me, logic prevailed over instincts, and I wagered twenty dollars on various combinations with *UdontNO* in the mix. And ignoring Shorty's comments, I did not bet even fifty cents on *Wayward Apple*.

Shorty sipped on a frosty cold brew while he shared stories with a couple of the regulars. He tipped his cap in my direction, and said, "May your tickets be nothing but winners."

"Thanks," I replied. "Same to you."

A minute before post time, and a sea of humanity rushed toward the rail. I claimed twenty-four inches of rail space about eight feet from the finish line. In seconds, dreams would be both fulfilled and dashed.

And they were off. Eight dogs charged out of the gate, chasing a mechanical rabbit.

In a flash, there were hundreds of people lined against the rail, mesmerized by the progress of the dogs.

Hands waved with a frantic purpose, urging one particular dog, or another to charge to the head of the pack.

"Come on seven-four. Come on seven-four!"

Another woman yelled, "Get a movin' *Slow Queen*. I needs a new pair of shoes!"

Yet another person screamed, "It's gonna be my night. Come on lucky three dog. You can beat them others. Come on and win. I know you can do it."

A man in a blue painter's cap and maroon jeans bellowed, "Get in gear *Honey Elope*. Tonight's your night. I've got confidence in you. Come on! Don't get bunched in by them other dogs. You can do it!"

Shorty was on the rail, directly in front of the finish line. Unlike the others, he did not yell or scream or plead with the greyhounds. He watched with a calm, expectant attitude. It was as if he expected to win.

Halfway through the race, *Wayward Apple* was sixth. The dog was roughly ten lengths off the pace. In comparison, my dog, *UdontNO* was third and inching up on the leaders. Several along the rail began shouting for *UdontNO*. I smiled, for I believed that had picked the winner. *UdontNO* was only one length from the lead. My happiness was short-lived. In a flash, *Wayward Apple* shot past the other dogs and claimed the lead.

The man in the blue painter's cap, screamed to the top of his lungs, "Don't do this to me *Honey Elope*! I got my paycheck riding on you!"

Apparently *Honey Elope* did not hear the man in the blue painter's cap, for the greyhound finished seventh. In disgust, the man tore his tickets into a hundred pieces and scattered them like ashes on the pavement. He left, cursing the dog, the track, and the world.

Wayward Apple did indeed win the race. *UdontNO* finished fourth and out of the money. Shorty sifted through his tickets to match various winning combinations. He checked the tote board and saw that his bets had paid off handsomely.

In fact, not only had Shorty won the first race, but also the second, third, fourth, fifth, and sixth race. By my modest calculations, he must have been up at least a couple of thousand dollars. As for me, I had lost the first six races. I had only lost about forty dollars. But it was quite apparent that I picked dogs like I picked teams in major sporting events.

Shorty glanced at a racing form in preparation to place a wager on the seventh race. After a few minutes, he moved to the rail and asked me, "What do you think about *Martian Lasso*?"

The immediate question I asked myself, is *Why would anyone who had just won six consecutive races, ask a novice like me, about a particular dog?* Since I could not answer that question, I guessed that Shorty was just making small talk. With absolutely no idea how to respond intelligently, I chose to answer with an everyman's response, "It's an interesting dog."

Shorty lowered his voice almost to a whisper. "You're right, *Martian Lasso* is an interesting greyhound. But it is also an extremely inconsistent greyhound. *Martian Lasso* won seven races in a row earlier this season, then failed to finish in the money since."

"I see."

Shorty moved a bit closer, as he continued to whisper, "Well, I like you, Mike. As soon as I saw you, I said, there's someone who has potential. And I am happy that you haven't pored over the racing forms all evening. Like I said, they are mostly a waste of money, time, and energy. Anyway, I got a tip for you, box *Martian Lasso* with the number three greyhound *Second Chance Stella*, and the number four greyhound *Kool Cool Cold*, and you will win a tidy sum. I guarantee you the odds at post-time will be better than twenty-five to one."

"Better than twenty-five to one?"

"I guarantee it." Shorty walked off to talk to a couple of the regulars. They congratulated him on his impressive winning streak. One of the women, a lady around fifty decked in tight black jeans and a black frilly vest asked Shorty for a tip on the next race. Shorty mentioned a couple of dogs, though neither was *Martian Lasso*.

Martian Lasso, Second Chance Stella, and Kool Cool Cold. I repeated the names of the dogs, as I waited in line to bet. Shorty had won six races in a row, and he guaranteed me a winning combination in the seventh. I thought about Shorty's streak. Could he pick winners in a seventh straight race? After all, he favored dogs who were no one's picks or choices. Maybe his streak of correct picks had ended in the sixth race. *Martian Lasso, Second Chance Stella, and Kool Cool Cold* appeared to be an odd combination. Nevertheless, Shorty had won six more races than I had won on that evening. I would be absolutely foolish not to follow his advice. So I would simply take Shorty's picks and bet on them.

"Place your bet please," the man behind the window said.

After placing the bet, I returned to the rail. The woman with the sultry voice served Shorty another beer. This time he gave her a ten dollar tip. She hugged and kissed him. "I'll be back before you know it," she remarked.

"I trusted my heart this time, Mike. It was time to do so."

Shorty had been right all evening. Could he pick another winner? In a few minutes, that question would be answered.

At the start of the seventh race, Shorty's three dogs were three lengths off the lead dog. Halfway through the race, they were six length off the lead dog *Dinkie Mite*, and fading fast. Apparently, Shorty's magic had vanished.

Suddenly, and from seemingly out of nowhere, *Martian Lasso* made his charge. Over the final sixty yards, the greyhound tracked down and passed every other dog except *Second Chance Stella*. The two race dogs dueled for position during the final strides of the race. From my vantage point I was not certain who had prevailed.

At the finish, *Martian Lasso* won in a photo finish with *Second Chance Stella* second, and *Kool Kool Cold* third. The final result was exactly as Shorty had predicted.

"What did I tell you? *Martian Lasso* was due. At thirty to one odds, I raked in almost seventy-five hundred. How did you do? Did you clean up too?"

"Yeah, yeah. I scored big. Thanks for the tip."

"Look, if you want, we can go up and cash our tickets together."

"You go on ahead. I'll catch you in a minute or so. I've got to make a call, check on my daughter."

Shorty hesistated, then said. "Okay. But don't take too long. You never want to hold a winning ticket with those kind of odds for long."

"I'll keep that in mind."

Shorty and Wanda briskly walked to the pay-off window. When they were out of sight, I pulled my ticket from my shirt pocket. I winced as I stared at it. I bet on three dogs all right—a sure thing, I thought—but not the three dogs Shorty had suggested, because I felt that all streaks had to end at some time—and it just seem that Shorty's streak had run its course for the evening. I simply did not trust Shorty, and paid the price.

I returned to the rail, and tried to appear and sound upbeat.

"You got any thoughts on the last race of the night?" Shorty asked.

"Not really."

"Nor do I. Sometimes there's nothing to distinguish the dogs. There's no standout, and there's no sleeper in this pack."

Scanning the racing form, I asked, "What do you think about *Carnation Tights*?"

"Not much. At best an average dog. Might sneak in for show, but that's about the best that you could hope for." Shorty studied the greyhounds as the milled around the central stall area. "No, I wouldn't bet anything on *Carnation Tights*. Maybe I just might skip this race. But if I do bet, I might place a small wager on *Quanky*. But I've got to tell you that I am not sure about *Quanky*. The dog could finish last as easily as he could finish first."

Streaks. At some point all streaks have to end. But as I could attest, streaks could last days, weeks, years. Certainly a streak once established could last one night. *Quanky* might not be Shorty's favorite. *Quanky,* however, was Shorty's pick. All night, I had not listened to Shorty's earlier observations and choices. I had resisted his advice and wisdom. However, if Shorty could pick the winners of seven races in a row, then there was no reason to believe that he couldn't pick the winner of an eighth straight race.

Quanky's odds were fifteen-to-one. This was another long-shot pick of Shorty. This was my opportunity to score big, to make a nice bundle. I moved briskly to the betting window. I bet *Quanky* straight up, as part of a perfecta, trifecta, and combo box. I bet *Quanky* in a dozen different ways. When he won, I would reap the benefits of smart betting.

Half-way through the race, *Quanky* was dead last. I was certain that *Quanky* could not see the mechanical rabbit.

Like the others, I called out for *Quanky* to get in gear, and make a move on the lead dog. "Don't wait too long, *Quanky*!" I yelled above the other thousand screaming voices. "I've got faith in you *Quanky*. But you've got to make a move now!"

If at all possible, it seemed that *Quanky* was running in reverse. Perhaps it was just that with each stride, the quickest greyhound lengthened his lead.

Quanky came in sixth. I stared at my ticket. I stared at the dog. He was grinning. How dare he grin after I had placed my faith and a considerable bet on him. I had just bet six hundred dollars on a dog who finished sixth out of eight dogs. I had just lost a month's worth of groceries on a dog who crossed the finish line, thirty lengths behind the winner *Broken Area Code*.

For the first time in the entire evening, Shorty had incorrectly picked the winning dog. What an especially inopportune time for his streak to end.

"Sorry about *Quanky*," Shorty apologized. "But like I said, I had a hunch, but wasn't sure. Anyway, what's the most you lost—maybe twenty dollars? It shouldn't have made any difference, since you won big in the last race. I mean you must have won a bundle on the race featuring *Martian Lasso*, right?"

"Yeah, right." I walked off sadder, but wiser. Trust is a mercurial human emotion. We often say that we have trust in a person, or an event, or an activity. But the fact of the matter is that even in those situations that we say we have trust, there is invariably a smidgen of doubt. That should not be the case. For me, that should not have been the case with respect to Shorty. He was not some school boy amateur, guessing at the answers on a multiple choice test. He was a professional, maybe grizzled and a tad eccentric, but a professional nonetheless whose guesses in dog races were better than my so-called *scientific and deductive* picks. He had warned me against relying on charts, and graphs, and racing forms. *Rely on your brain and guts*, he had urged. But, the inescapable fact was that I ignored him. I suspected that I ignored him because of the way he looked, or spoke, or acted—something about Shorty that I did not trust or appreciate.

In one evening I learned about streaks, people, the human condition, and trust. I was poorer, but wiser. Next month, I picked the Dinosaurs to win the Super Bowl. They lost forty-seven to zero. Some things never change. I should have asked Shorty.

Three-For-One Coupon Day

At least twice a year, my father and mother would visit us. Virtually every day they would travel to a different mall or shopping outlet to scour for super sales and deep discounts. Mind you, these were essentially the same stores they could shop at back home. But they claimed that the prices and values were better in our hometown as opposed to theirs. So they travelled a thousand miles just for the opportunity to save an extra fifty cents on ginger tea.

"You still got that Peabody's grocery store around the corner from you?"

"Yeah, pops." For some reason, my father relished a trip to Peabody's.

"Well, if you don't mind, I'm going to make a trip there this afternoon. I've got a couple of things I need to get."

"Just give a me a list, pops. I can run by the store later."

'No, no, I don't want be any trouble. Anyway, I need to take the car for a spin every day."

"All right."

"Do you want to come along?"

I nodded.

As we walked toward the car, my father abruptly stopped. "Aren't you forgetting something?"

"What, pops?"

"Your coupon folder."

The fact was that I did not have a coupon folder, or anything that even resembled a coupon folder. On occasion I would clip a coupon, if I just happened to have a pair of scissors handy. And from time-to-time I would used the coupons that my father sent. But often he would mail me a couple dozen coupons a week for products that I either didn't use, or didn't know existed. Rather than tell my father to stop sending me the mountain of coupons, I simply thanked him, then dropped them in file thirteen. So, most times, I simply relied on in-store specials, and coupons that the coupon-lady dispensed on the weekends.

"I misplaced it, pops," I fibbed.

"I'll get you another one then. Everyone needs a coupon folder. I'll get you a functional one—one that includes a calculator, so that you can keep track of your savings, item-by-item."

I wondered what type of person would carry a folder full of coupons with them halfway across the country—a compulsive obsessive was my guess—which perfectly matched the description of my father of course.

"Do you have any coupons for Peabody's super soft soap?"

"I don't believe so."

"Really? I'm sure that I sent you a dozen or so of those coupons a couple of weeks ago. Did you use them all already?"

I had not used any of them, for as I already noted, I tossed them in the trash not long after I received them. "Well, I don't recall seeing them. Maybe you sent the coupons to Tony by mistake."

"No, Tony likes Lester's premium soap. I sent him a bunch of those coupons a month ago."

"Maybe I misplaced them."

My attempt at deception accomplished nothing. We drove to Peabody's without further delay.

As soon as we entered Peabody's, my father's eyes lit up, as though it was Christmas morning, and he had discovered that Santa had been extra good to him. He grabbed an in-store weekly circular, and skimmed through eight pages of in-store specials. As he skimmed, he committed to memory every discounted or sale item.

It was painfully obvious that I was coupon novice. My father only bought items for which he had coupons, or that were in-store specials, or that were on sale, or discounted, or temporarily reduced in price. Occasionally, he purchased items with mail-in rebates—but he preferred not having to spend money on postage, and waiting up to ten weeks to receive a check that typically totalled less than one dollar.

My father understood the system which explained his unparalleled success in maximizing his purchasing power. And as he pointed out, it was because of that system that he had saved enough over the years to pay for my first year in college, and a round the world cruise for he and moms.

"I'm going to aisle ten and get some Scarborough tissue. I got a seventy-five cent off coupon."

Something was not right. My father had not purchased that brand of tissue in over fifteen years. He claimed that the tissue was as rough as the back of a wild boar. "You don't even like Scarborough tissue."

"I know. But your Uncle Charlie does. I trade him the tissue for some Chase cola."

As we pushed the grocery cart down aisle sixteen, I placed a jar of Moore's smooth peanut butter into the shopping cart.

"Do you have a coupon for Moore's smooth peanut butter?" my father asked.

"No."

"Neither do I. Maybe you should put it back and wait until you have a coupon, or it goes on sale."

"The kids like Moore's. We ran out yesterday, and need some more. I think I can afford the two dollars for peanut butter."

My father opened the in-store advertising circular, and ripped an uneven portion from page three. "Look, put the Moore's back. Here's a coupon for Peabody's own brand of peanut butter. It's a thirty cents off coupon. Since today is three-for-one coupon day, you'll save ninety cents. That means the peanut butter will cost you only one dollar. That's a great price."

"It is, but the kids don't care for the store brand peanut butter."

"This is not wine. Peanut butter is peanut butter. I bet they won't know the difference."

"Maybe I can convince Millicent to eat the store brand. But I am telling you that Malcolm can taste the difference. Besides, he's quite brand conscious. Once he sees that the peanut butter is not Moore's, he'll never eat it."

"Then tape the Moore's label over the Peabody's label. I'm talking from experience. I've had both. There is no difference."

"He'll know."

"You didn't know."

"What are you talking about?"

"When you were Malcolm's age, you were brand name conscious as well. You wouldn't eat bananas unless you saw the Bennet label on the bananas. But we couldn't always find Bennet bananas. So your mother suggested that I buy the store brand, remove the store label, and replace it with the Bennet label."

So, after forty plus years, my father finally confessed to the mystery of the switched bananas. I always suspected as much, but trusted my parents explanation. Malcolm's tastes and beliefs were largely fashioned by the television and other visual media, such as the Internet. Consequently, I was not certain that switching labels would fool him. I sighed, and responded, "Look, pops. I don't intend to take a chance with the peanut butter.

"All right then, suit yourself. Spend the extra dollar and ten cents on brand name peanut butter that tastes exactly like the store's in-house peanut butter. It's apparent that you've got money to burn."

Anytime I spent money in a manner that my father did not approve, he said *It's apparent that you got money to burn.* The fact of the matter was that I did not have money to burn—sometimes, I did not have any money period. But, for the extra dollar it cost to buy name brand peanut butter, I was also buying peace of mind, and no hassles. To me, that was worth the extra cost, and justified the additional cost. My father thought I was a few coupons short in the brainbasket. He suggested that I at least wait until I could ask Malcolm if he would eat the store brand peanut butter. I declined.

Thirty minutes later, we finished shopping. With a grocery cart filled to the brim with sale, and special items, we gravitated to check-out aisle thirteen.

"And do you have any coupons, sir?"

"We certainly do," my father answered.

My father handed the check-out clerk three dozen coupons.

"My but weren't we busy," the check-out clerk said in a condescending tone.

The clerk questioned at least three of the coupons. But my father's bulldog determination ultimately prevailed. So, on three-for-one coupon day, my father saved fifty dollars and forty-five cents. With part of his savings, he offered to buy me an ice cream cone on the way home. I accepted. When I was much younger, my father treated me every Sunday to a dairy treat at the neighborhood ice cream store. For one brief moment, I relived my childhood.

We returned with our bags of groceries. Malcolm greeted us and offered to help. He removed items from the brown plastic grocery bags, but stopped when he lifted the jar of Moore's peanut butter from the second to the last bag. "Is this your peanut butter, grandpops?"

"No, Malcolm. It's your's."

Malcolm turned to me. "Moore's peanut butter, pops?"

Oblivious as to what was about to transpire, I replied, "Yes, just like you have always requested."

"Pops, I haven't asked for Moore's peanut butter by name in over a year."

At that point I sensed that I was in a single engine plane over the Pacific Ocean with no fuel, and no land in sight. I prepared for the obvious—a figurative crash and burn. "Is there something wrong with Moore's peanut butter son?"

"Well, it's just that I thought you might buy Peabody super smooth peanut butter."

My father curled his lips, as if to say, *I told you so.*

I on the other hand smacked my lips in disgust. Malcolm had never mentioned Peabody's peanut butter before. I reminded Malcolm of that fact, by saying, "You've always eaten Moore's super smooth peanut butter."

"That's because that's all you've bought."

"I thought you liked Moore's brand the best."

"Come on, pops. Peanut butter is peanut butter. Anyway, the school is collecting labels from Peabody store brands. Depending on the number of labels the school collects, Peabody Grocery Stores will donate computers and other equipment from our school wish list."

The next day I went back to Peabody's and ripped out the in-store coupon from the grocery circular. I had missed out on three-for-one coupon day, but still purchased a large jar of Peabody's super smooth peanut butter. I viewed the transaction as saving thirty-three cents on the Peabody's brand. From my father's perspective, I lost the opportunity to save and additional sixty-six cents. That was okay though because *I had money to burn.*

With respect to the different brands of peanut butter, I sampled them both. Unlike Malcolm's pronouncement, peanut butter was not peanut butter. One brand was definitely creamier and smoother and tasted better. But it wasn't Moore's. No the victor was the Peabody store brand.

It figured. Based on that experience, I never missed three-for-one coupon day again, and I never bought name brand peanut butter or bananas again. Both my son and father were happy. That was all that mattered.

Parking Lots

I couldn't end this book without passing along one more story about my father. Not too long ago, I flew home for an extended weekend. My father had scheduled an appointment downtown and asked if I would go with him.

My father asking for assistance? Stop the presses, I think we have the lead story on tonight's newscast. I immediately accepted his offer.

We lived about ten minutes from downtown. Nevertheless, in order to make absolutely certain that he wouldn't be late for his business meeting, my father and I left the house an hour early. Traffic was heavier than normal, but we still reached downtown with plenty of time to spare. Since it was often difficult, if not impossible to find on-street parking, I fully expected my father to park in an enclosed parking structure. But old habits don't die easily, and my father was accustomed to parking on-street as opposed to a parking lot.

My father drove around the block five times and could not find an on-street parking space. I suggested to him that perhaps we should park in a nearby parking garage. He suggested that I have my head examined since only a demented soul would consider paying over two dollars an hour for parking in a garage, when there were plenty of on-street parking spaces offering hour parking meters for fifty cents.

We drove around the block six more times. Spaces occasionally became available, but we were never in the proper position or location to take advantage of the vacated on-street parking space. My father glanced at his watch.

"And what time is your appointment, pops?"

"In about ten minutes."

"Look, pops. I realize that you don't like parking garages and the rates they charge, but under the circumstances, don't you think it might be wise to consider parking there, just this once."

My father scratched his head, then said, "Maybe you're right, son."

My father accepted my suggestion? I immediately considered that perhaps the person who was driving the car was not my father but some sort of clone or perhaps a cleverly disguised look-alike.

My father entered the garage and parked on level five, the green quadrant, purple corridor, northside, space E386. Upon exiting the car, I suggested that we jot down the location of the vehicle. After all, on more than one occasion I had forgotten where I had parked my car in a large garage.

"I don't need to jot down the space number. I know what level we're on, and I will have no problem finding the car when our business is done."

That response sounded more like my father. I tried to quickly scribble the necessary information on a scrap of paper that I removed from my pocket. However, I am dyslexic when it comes to numbers, so I was not sure if I had placed the numbers in the proper order.

Though my father's business meeting went smoothly, it lasted far longer than he anticipated. Almost two hours had elapsed. When my father finished, he walked briskly to the elevators. "Come on!" he commanded, recognizing that I was not keeping up the pace.

"What's the rush?" I asked.

"If the car is parked longer than two hours, then we will have to pay for an additional parking charge."

"Pops, what are we talking about—maybe a dollar or two."

"So, I guess you've got money to burn."

I wanted to burn that phrase from the English language, but no such luck. We reached the elevators, and my father punched the button for level D.

"Pops, I believe you parked the car on level E."

"Believe what you want son, I parked on level D."

Seconds later, my father bolted from the elevator on level D. Though we circled the entire level we found no car.

"We need to get to a phone quick, son. Someone has stolen my car."

"Pops, no one has stolen your car."

"Do you see my car on level D?"

"No."

"Then someone has stolen my car."

"As I tried to tell you earlier. You parked your car on level E."

"Are you trying to tell me that I don't remember what level I parked my car?"

"I scribbled down the level and space number when we parked the car, pops. It's located on level E."

"You expect me to believe that my car is parked on level E as opposed to level D."

"Yes."

"Then why weren't you more forceful in the beginning."

My father might have been thirty years my elder, but was in far better physical condition than me. He raced up the garage stairwell to level E. My father spotted the car, and headed straight for it.

I stopped about twenty feet in front of the car in order to tie my left tennis shoe lace.

"Come on, come on," my father urged. "You can tie your shoes later. I want to get out of here, so that we don't have to pay for another hour."

I complied with my father's wish. The tires squealed as my father backed out of the parking space.

He glanced at his watch, then smiled at me and said, "We're just going to make it." My father drove up to the pay window, confident that he had not overextended his time in the parking garage. Handing the parking attendant the time ticket, he informed the young man, "It should be four dollars."

The parking attendant validated the entry and exit times. "That'll be six dollars," he corrected.

"What did he say?" my father asked.

"He said six dollars. Don't worry pops. I'll take care of the fee."

"Six dollars?" my dad bellowed. "Did that kid say we owe six dollars for parking?"

The parking attendant who was a young adult, as opposed to a teenager as my father had portrayed him asked, "Is there something wrong?"

"Is there something wrong?" my father repeated in disbelief. "You had better believe there is something wrong. You said the fee is six dollars when it should have been four."

"Look, mister. Your ticket indicates that you entered Kinkaid Covered Parking Facility number 16 at four minutes after two. You handed me your ticket for final check-out at six minutes after four. At the entrance to Kincaid Covered Parking Facility number 16 it clearly and precisely states that parking is two dollars per hour or any fraction thereof up to the maximum daily rate of ten dollars. You were in the facility for two hours and two minutes. Consequently, you owe six dollars."

"Well my watch says that we were in your facility for precisely one hour and fifty-eight minutes. So I owe you four dollars instead of six. If your machine says differently, then there must be a mistake in your timing mechanism."

"There is no mistake. Our tickets are dispensed by Waterman 3000 which happens to be the most accurate parking meter timer in the industry. It is accurate to within five seconds per month. And each month it is re-calculated. So the chances that your ticket is incorrect are infinitesimal."

"Well the Waterman 3000 is wrong."

"That's impossible."

"I should have been charged four dollars instead of six."

"Like I said before, the Waterman 3000 is never wrong. You owe six dollars."

"Look sonny, that's impossible. Your time clock must be wrong. Here's four dollars, and be sure to give me a receipt."

"Thanks. Now you owe two dollars more."

"Wha-wha-what?!" my father stammered.

"The parking fee is six dollars. You owe two dollars more."

My father's left eye started to twitch, and it seemed as though a blood vessel throbbed down the right side of his neck. "I'm not paying a cent more. Your time clock is wrong."

By this time, there were four or five drivers behind us, waiting to pay the attendant and leave the parking lot.

One of the drivers honked his horn. "Hey, I ain't got all day," he bellowed.

Another shouted, "Some of have us to get home!"

My father blurted back, "Some of us are conducting business up here, so pipe down and rest your jets!"

Another three cars fell into line behind us. Soon there was a symphony of car horns blaring, and angry voices yelling.

"Am I going to have to call security?" the attendant asked.

"Not if you raise the gate, so we can exit."

The man directly behind us screamed, "I'm writing down the number of your license tag. I'm going to hunt you down and exact my revenge if you don't pay your bill now, and leave immediately."

"Gee, I'm quaking in my boots."

I heard one of the people in the car line screaming at the top of her lungs in what I believe was German. Now, I know very little of the language, but I doubt she was passing along civil greetings, or dinner recipes.

Car horns honked, blurted, chimed, and reverberated. The natives were getting mighty restless, and appeared poised to rush our vehicle.

"I've had enough," the attendant said. "I'm not losing my job over some grizzled retiree." He pressed the speaker on his walkie-talkie. "This is station number six. I need security to come to station number six."

My father smiled. He felt that summoning security would resolve the matter in his favor.

I on the other hand felt that we were a couple of minutes away from a potentially embarrassing confrontation. Since discretion is the better part of valor, I chose to play peacemaker and pay the additional two dollars.

"You should have never given that scalawag two dollars. I bet he keeps the money and has a grand old time."

"Right, he probably blows the wad on a burger and fries at Funky Burgers."

"There is no need to get sarcastic."

"It was two dollars, pops—not two hundred."

"If you save two dollars, it eventually becomes two hundred. Maybe that is why I have money, and you never to seem to have any."

I couldn't argue the fact that my father's frugality led to a sizeable retirement nest egg. But my actions prevented anarchy at the parking lot. And there was something to be said for preserving peace and tranquility among the populace on that day.

Thanksgiving Biscuits

Don't get me wrong. I love my life now. But I have a soft spot in my heart for my first Thanksgiving with my first wife Marcia. Neither one of us had a job. Our collective savings was just over a thousand dollars. But none of that mattered. What mattered was that we were together, alone, and in love. There was a hint of snow in the air, and holiday music filled the airwaves. And so that first Thanksgiving was special in many ways—not the least of which for the biscuits that Marcia baked. More on the biscuits a little later. But let me first describe some other details of that first Thanksgiving.

Marcia and I had married the week before Thanksgiving. We were newlyweds still getting used to marriage, and living under the same roof. Our love for one another was complete and fulfilling, but little by little we discovered personal traits and habits that somehow had been masked during the courtship ritual. I learned never to scramble eggs with a fork, and Marcia discovered that it was best to always place the cap back on a tube of toothpaste. We survived that first argument, and maintained our first wedding promise that we would never go to bed angry with one another.

That first Thanksgiving was about more than just parades and football games. It was about family. In our case, the wonderful feeling about being part of new family, and the sadness of being apart from the families that had been the center of our lives from our first breaths. We spent the morning of our first Thanksgiving just spending quiet time in bed. We reminisced about the first time we met, and about our courtship. We snuggled and cuddled and enjoyed each other's company.

Around noon, we ventured from the bedroom. I thought that Marcia might change her mind, and tell me that she wanted to go to her folks for Thanksgiving. So on my return from getting the morning newspaper, I stopped and filled the gas tank. Marcia almost wavered, almost took me up on the offer to visit family for Thanksgiving. But in the end, she chose to prepare a quaint Thanksgiving dinner.

It was just the two us, so we thought that on that first Thanksgiving as man and wife, a whole turkey might be too much to cook, and too much to eat. But we believed it was important to remain as traditional as possible in our holiday food fare, so Marcia suggested that we feast on turkey wings. Marcia found the perfect turkey wing recipe in our only cookbook which was a wedding gift from her cousin Rudy.

While Marcia prepared the turkey wings, biscuits, and other fixings, I tackled the egg nog. I used my father's secret recipe. Besides the two of us, only my brother Tony knew the special ingredients. I felt fortunate indeed to have been entrusted with such a treasured concoction. Though it was my first time preparing egg nog, I was certain that when I finished my batch, it would be comparable to my father's.

I followed the recipe to perfection. Where it said a dash, that's how much I placed in the bowl. When the recipe called for a pinch of nutmeg, that's how much I sprinkled in the egg nog. I followed the directions exactly, yet something was not quite right. When I finished, the egg nog did not look like my father's egg nog, and did smell like my father's egg nog. I sprinkled a dash more nutmeg. Ah yes, that's how I remembered pops egg nog. It was generously flavored with nutmeg.

At the other end of the kitchen, Marcia seemed to be laboring with the biscuits. There was milk, and flour, and ice water, and a biscuit cutter spread out along the counter. Marcia appeared to measure the ingredients, but the proportions did not seem to be correct. After all, I thought more than a teaspoon of water should have been mixed with a cup of flour. Even though no one would ever confuse me for a chef, I offered my assistance to Marcia. She politely ushered me out of the kitchen and suggested that I watch a football game, or read a book, or engage in any other activity, so long as it did not require my presence in the kitchen.

For the next few minutes, I heard Marcia singing and humming Thanksgiving songs and other tunes of the season. Then the singing abruptly stopped. I thought I heard a dish crash to the floor, but I wasn't sure.

About an hour later, with the pleasant aroma of turkey wings filling the apartment, I peeked into the kitchen to spy on Marcia. She was still preparing biscuits. I noticed that the wastebasket was full with paper towels, and egg shells, and other partially empty or damaged boxes of food.

"Need any help?" I asked.

Marcia shot back a look that was not filled with love. "Why are you asking that? Do you think I am having a problem? Because if you think I am, then you're wrong. Everything is all right. I just want everything to be perfect. So I scratched the first couple of batches of biscuits. But everything is all right now. I don't need your help. Watch the second half of the game, or take a nap."

Early on in our marriage, I didn't know when to leave well enough alone. I offered, "I don't mind helping you, really."

Her upper lipped quivered. "I said, I don't need any help." Marcia's eyes were stone cold killers. I could sense that the stress of fixing biscuits was affecting her demeanor and civility. It would not be the end of the world if we did not have any biscuits. But I realized that if I suggested that in Marcia's agitated state, I would be sleeping on the sidewalk outside our apartment or worse.

"All right then, I'll go back to the game. I can hardly wait until dinner."

Time passed, and I heard more commotion in the kitchen than when a cat scratches its claws on a clean blackboard. Blenders whirred, knives chopped, eggs broke, and potatoes whipped.

"Dinner's ready," Marcia panted.

Marcia's hair drooped. At no time during our courting, engagement, wedding, or first week of marriage had Marcia's hair drooped. In fact, I could not remember even one strand of her hair being out of place. But on that first Thanksgiving, Marcia's hair drooped, and sweat rolled down her face. And for good measure there was a trace of flour that streaked above Marcia's left eyebrow.

I surveyed the kitchen table. In the center was gravy. But it was different than I remembered. The gravy wasn't lumpy like my mother's, and the color was more orange than brown. Nevertheless, I knew that it was made with love. I also felt that in time, the lumps would appear, and the color would be more natural.

It was the biscuits though that appeared mishapen, and well, quite inedible. I tapped my bride's biscuits on the corner of the kitchen table. One biscuit left a dent in the wooden table. Another removed the varnish from the table.

I offered another silent prayer.

Marcia prepared our plates. Determined that I stuff myself, Marcia crammed and piled food on every square inch of the plate.

I chewed and chewed and chewed, but did not seem to make much headway with the biscuit. Marcia fixed her eyes on me. I tried to soften the bread product with a couple of swigs of water. The biscuit turned into a cementy paste.

"Well how are they?"

Fifty-one and one-half chews later, I swallowed. There were still gritty little pieces of biscuit attached to the roof of my mouth, and other bits wedged between my teeth. After taking another sip of water, I replied, "The turkey wings are fine, maybe just a touch dry. But for the first time, they taste wonderful."

"No, not the turkey wings. The biscuits. How are the biscuits?"

I knew that Marcia had asked about the biscuits the first time. I thought that I had skillfully avoided answering what I considered a loaded question. It was quite possible that my future marital relations hinged on my answer to Marcia's question—*How are the biscuits?* I considered the possible responses, and sadly realized that none of them were particularly palatable. For all practical purposes, Marcia should have known the answer already. When it takes a jack-hammer to separate biscuits, then that should be a tip-off that the bread product should be accompanied by a skull and cross bones. Yet, Marcia asked, so she must have been looking for praise and lies. I remembered the words of my mentor LN Hayes, "*Only an adulterer tells his wife that her cooking is bad.*" Truth or deception? I chose deception.

"How are the biscuits?" Marcia asked again, with a trace of impatience.

"They're quite good—they have a lot of body to them." As soon as I uttered the last phrase—*have a lot of body to them*, I cringed. That was the type of response that was sure to get me a night or two on the sleeper sofa.

Marcia sort of rolled her eyes. Still, she chose not to attack my response. Instead, she asked, "Were the biscuits as good as your mother's?"

Perspiration popped up on my forehead. I was in a no-win situation. One of the last pieces of advice my father gave me before I married Marcia was to avoid at all costs, and under any circumstances getting sucked into a comparison of how mother and wife cook, clean, or do anything else in relation to one another. With victory not on the horizon, I would settle for a tie. I answered timidly. "They were the best biscuits that you have ever baked."

"Thank you for being honest with me," Marcia said. For the first time in over six hours, Marcia smiled. Of course, it was the first time that Marcia had baked biscuits. But she seemed appeased at the response, and at the time, that was all that mattered.

I actually ate two biscuits. All it took was four glasses of ice tea, and seven ten-ounce glasses of water.

Cleaning the kitchen took our collective efforts. All the discarded ingredients and paper plates, and other utensils were crammed into a large plastic waste bag. I toted the bag to the dumpster. As I returned to the apartment, a pre-teen boy with a red wagon approached.

"Happy Thanksgiving, young man. What can I do for you?"

"Happy holidays to you too, mister. My name is Thad Burton. I'm a student at Daybrook Middle School. I'm selling holiday wreaths for our Art Club. Do you want to buy one?"

"How much are they?"

"Ten dollars, mister."

"That's pretty pricey for a wreath."

"It's for a good cause. We're going to buy art supplies and books. And we intend to take a trip to the art museum at the State capital in the spring."

I had exactly ten dollars in my wallet. Well, I wouldn't be buying coffee and a doughnut for a few days, but so what—the holidays were upon us, and the wreath would spruce up our spartan apartment. I paid for the wreath.

"Thanks, mister," the boy said, as he wheeled his red wagon full of wreaths to the next apartment. "And have the most joyous of holiday seasons."

"And happy holidays to you, young man."

Marcia examined the wreath. As wreaths go it was plain—no fancy designs or bows, or ornaments. Marcia smiled anyway. She said the wreath had character—that its pine and cinnamon scent was a perfect complement to the holidays. It was nothing special, yet I suspected that it would always be treasured by us.

We placed the wreath on the fireplace mantel. There were no other decorations to detract from its almost majestic presence.

The fire illuminated the entire room. With no furniture, we propped our sleeping bags on the far side of the fireplace. Marcia and I snuggled. The wood crackled, and in the background, holiday music gently rolled through the apartment. We snuggled for what seemed an eternity. On that night, there was no one else in our universe. Every now and then, I would cast an eye towards the holiday wreath. Between the fire, and the moonlight, the wreath seemed to sparkle. The sparkle from the wreath warmed our hearts as much as the robust fire.

The fire sparked its last flame around midnight. *Silver Bells* slipped into *The Twelve Days of Christmas* slipped into *The First Noel.* I sipped egg nog, as I hummed a tune of the season.

And I have had better days, and happier moments. But I do not think that I have had a better Thanksgiving before or since that first one with Marcia.

Throughout life, there are *firsts* that are to be cherished—first day at school, first kiss, first love, the delivery of a first child, and in my case, first Thanksgiving with my spouse.

For one day, out of thousands of days in my life, I understood completely the meaning of giving and sharing. I understood about accepting those who were different from me. And as I look back on that day, I realize, hopefully not too late in my thousands of days of life, that life, in spite of all its obstacles, is good and precious, and should be savored each and every day, and never squandered. For a day past, is a day that will never be recreated. And for me, that first Thanksgiving symbolized life and love, without any strings. I wish there had been more.

I Should Have Seen It Coming

At the outset, let me state that it is precisely because of the events chronicled in this story that I was urged, rather forced to change the names of everyone associated in the book including my ex-wives and kids. So instead of specifically referring to my six kids by their correct names, I chose two generic names, Millicent, and Malcolm to represent all my children. I even had to assume a new name in order to protect national security.

With that preface let me close my book with these words, never let family read a manuscript ahead of time, especially if they are prominently featured in it. As a courtesy, I gave a copy of the draft manuscript to my ex-wives, and children to read. I was seeking praise, and gracious comments. What I actually received was a vitriolic diatribe concerning misstatements, inaccuracies, and other shortcomings chronicled in the book.

My agent had warned me against seeking feedback from relatives, so she was unsympathetic when I mentioned their reaction. She informed me that I had a deadline to meet, or that I would have to return my advance.

"Don't worry. I'll have the completed manuscript to you in two days," I said in an attempt to reassure my agent who had heard that story before.

I returned to my computer. While it might take longer than two days to complete the revisions to the manuscript, I felt confident that it would be finished within a week. I smiled knowing that in a week or so I would be signing a major book publishing deal. At last, everything was proceeding according to schedule. The frantic knock on my front door shattered my momentary tranquility.

I opened the door, and found Marcia, Millicent, and Malcolm angrily waving copies of the manuscript in my face.

"You made it sound like I was a butcher!" Marcia bellowed.

"You're exaggerating," I responded.

"Exaggerating? That's a laugh. You exaggerated and worse throughout the story on plants."

"The story is basically true."

"You never mentioned that they lifted the ban after two years."

"It would have detracted from an otherwise humorous story."

"Look, I am up for board position on the Wagner Foundation. If they read this book, they will think I am totally unqualified to be on the board."

"There are nothing but snobs on the Wagner Foundation Board."

"And that's what I want."

Before I could respond, Malcolm joined the negative chorus. "And I've got a beef with you, pops, too. I made a B minus on the state capitals test not a C minus."

"The story reads better with you making a C minus, rather than a B minus."

"Well, I've been talking it over with my lawyer, and he says that what you have done to me is a plain, yet brutal, character assassination."

"Character assassination? Wait a minute—You've hired a lawyer?"

"That's right, pops. Shelly Cason. She's the best defamation attorney in the country. I had no choice. I've got to protect my interests."

"What interests? So you made a B minus instead of a C minus. I was just using a little literary license."

"What is literary license to one is a lie to another."

My son had a point. But as LN Hayes always said, the truth was just too boring. Still, I was having a hard time accepting the fact that my son had hired an attorney, or for that matter could afford to hire an attorney.

"Tell me son, how could you afford an attorney?"

"Now don't get all bent out of shape, pops. But K.C. and I have made a pretty penny betting against your picks in every major sporting event."

"K.C. encouraged you to bet?"

"Actually, it was my idea, pops."

"When I found out just how much money K.C. was making off each bet, I decided that I wanted a piece of the action. Face the facts, pops. You are terrible and pathetic at picking winners for major sporting events. Of all the stories in the book, that one on Streaks was the most accurate. Anyway, it took me no time to make a bundle off your incorrect predictions."

"I can't believe that you would do this to me."

"Believe it pops. Anyway, as I was saying, my lawyer says that you have portrayed me in an exceptionally negative light. She says that you make me look like a simpleton. More importantly, pops, my lawyer says I have a rock solid case against you for intentional infliction of emotional distress."

"You would sue your father, your best friend?"

Malcolm cleared his throat. Staring out the window, he remarked, "Best friend is such an overworked phrase, pops. I mean, I am not sure, if any one of use knows how to define the term *best friend*. But I can assure you that you one of my closest friends. You're probably right up there in the top ten—and if not, then certainly in the top twenty. When you think about it, pops—being in the top twenty of my closest friends is not so bad. And as for suing you, I am shocked that you think that I would resort to filing a legal action against you."

"So I have nothing to worry about."

"Really pops, suing you would be a last option, a last resort. But you know attorneys. They never want a client to say never. For what it's worth, though, Shelly Cason says that you might want to consider hiring your own attorney."

Hire my own attorney? Actually that might not be a bad idea, though the attorney would be representing me on criminal as opposed to civil charges. I guessed that this was payback from Malcolm for not getting a fancy bike for his tenth birthday.

Millicent confronted me with a different set of demands.

"Daddy, the book has to be changed as it relates to me."

"And what do you propose?"

"These are my suggested editing changes."

I quickly scanned Millicent's copy of the manuscript. "You want to be called Melissa?"

"I've always wanted to be called Melissa."

"But your name is Millicent."

"I've never wanted to be a Millicent. Melissa better reflects who I am. Besides, if any of the stories are turned into a TV movie, or television series, I want to be known as Melissa."

Unannounced, Pierre the mime barged into my office and rapped his knuckles on my desk—actually he created the illusion of doing both. Still, it was apparent that he was upset. Of all the individuals noted in my book, Pierre was perhaps the last individual that I thought I would ever see again. So when he entered my den, I was truly surprised.

"Do you mind telling me how Pierre learned of the manuscript?"

Malcolm answered. "It's a small world, isn't it, pops? Full of unforeseen turns and coincidences. Anyway, as luck would have it, Shelly Cason represents Pierre the mime. When she read the manuscript and found a reference to Pierre, then she felt obligated to contact him and set forth her concerns."

Pierre stormed around the room. He was furious—well as furious as a mime can get. He tossed imaginary wads of paper in my direction. He stamped his feet on the wooden floor—although with a mime, the stamping is an illusion.

"All right, all right. What will it take to make everything all right with everyone?"

Pierre the mime handed me a personal note. There were a number of symbols in the letter that I guess only a mime could decipher. But the gist of the note was that Pierre wanted script approval if the book was made into a movie. I rubbed my temples, and exhaled. Who ever heard of giving a mime script approval of any movie screenplay.

The note went on to say that Buddy Carvell also wanted script approval of any movie screenplay.

Melissa, I mean Millicent, handed me another sheet of paper. "These are actresses who I do not want to portray me in any movie or series."

The list contained over two hundred names. "You've crossed off virtually every actress in Hollywood and New York."

"I know. I want an unknown to play me—someone not jaded by the establishment. A fresh face who can capture the essence of me."

"You're too young to have an essence."

"Oh, daddy!" Millicent said pouting.

Sure I had contemplated perhaps signing a network deal to develop a TV sitcom on my life's misadventures. But Millicent, going Hollywood on me was a bit disconcerting. I had an everlasting image of Millicent as a foot shorter than me, with ponytails, and braces, and a smile that would melt ice. Replacing that image with one of Millicent projecting an essence, whatever that might be, was one that I intended to resist with all my might.

Marcia, feeling neglected observed, "If you were going to write a humorous story about us, why didn't you write the one about me and the school bus."

"You mean the time that you left your wedding ring on the school bus?"

"No, not that time."

"Or the time that you ran into the school bus?"

"I never ran into a school bus."

"Yes, you did, moms. Remember when I was in first grade," Malcolm offered.

"I almost hit the school bus," Marcia corrected. "No, I was talking about the time that the school bus got stuck in mud."

"You're not serious?" I asked.

"I most definitely am serious."

"That story is boring, dear. If I include it in the book, I may be sued for cruel and unusual punishment."

Marcia gave me that look that signaled that I had entered the danger zone. "Well that's the story I want you to include in your book. Otherwise, I want you to delete all references to me."

"But Marcia, you have to admit that the plant story was funny."

"Yes, if you consider being humiliated as being funny."

Yes, I guess I did considered being humiliated as funny. Anyway, we were both humiliated in that story. I played no favorites, and intended to keep the story in the book, just as I had initially written it.

Next it was Malcolm's turn to seek changes in the book.

"And what do you want, son?"

"You know," he replied sheepishly.

"If I knew, I wouldn't ask. What do you want?"

"Money, pops. You know, I'm not trying to make a mint off you, and retiring before I reach twenty is certainly not my goal. But in order to compensate me for the emotional trauma that I have and will suffer as a result of this book being published, I believe that a negotiated settlement, in the low seven figures is appropriate."

"This is a joke, right?"

"Shelly, said I should never joke when it comes to money, pops. Look, I know you carry liability insurance. Let your insurance company worry about the money."

"Maybe I should bill you for your room and board, and meals over the years son. That would probably reach the low seven figures."

"All right, all right, pops. Though it is against Shelly's advice, I am willing to make a compromise offer. I am willing to drop the threat of a lawsuit in exchange for an addition to the book to include a story about me having a romantic relationship with a pre-approved movie star or celebrity.

"Forget it, son."

"Look pops. I'm trying to be reasonable."

There was a knock on the back door.

"Excuse me." I sprinted to the back door, and opened it. Standing in front of me was Sam Waterstone, the last person I thought I would see again.

Waterstone, stepped just inside the hallway, and closed the door. "I thought we had an understanding," he said grimly.

"What are you talking about?"

"The manuscript. You wrote extensively about Coogan."

"Say how did you find out about the manuscript?"

"You really aren't that bright, are you?"

"So what you told me about Coogan was really the truth?"

"Look, I don't have time to rehash sensitive and classified information."

"Coogan said you were a prankster. This is just another gag, right?"

Waterstone pulled me closer. "You realize," he said in a perturbed whisper, "that you may have compromised the entire operation."

"I don't believe you."

"Quite frankly, I do not care whether you believe me or not. The issue on the table right now, is whether you publish your offensive and damaging tome in the next several weeks. I am telling you that you can't."

"You don't have that kind of authority."

"That's where you are wrong. I have all the authority that I need. But if I reveal myself to your editor now, then my effectiveness for future missions is compromised. That is why I want you to contact your editor and delay printing of your book until all references to Coogan can be deleted."

"This is ridiculous, Coogan revealed the whole charade, and the real reason that he didn't want anyone to know his first name."

"Coogan told you that his first name was Claymore right?"

"As a matter of fact he did."

"That's a code name. If you include it in the book, it will wreak havoc with our North American operations. As it stands now, it is quite likely that some enemy intelligence forces have received word concerning Coogan's existence and location."

"Coogan must have paid you a bundle."

"This is not some sophomoric prank, Hughes. This is deadly serious."

"You know, you were more convincing at the airport."

"Damn it, man! Lives are at stake."

Waterstone reached into his jacket pocket. I did not get the impression that he was going to give me a gift certificate to a steak restaurant.

Perhaps Waterstone was delusional, and had actually convinced himself that Coogan was part of the Federal Witness Protection Program. I decided to humor him. "All right Waterstone, you've convinced me."

Malcolm interrupted the conversation. "Hey pops! It's Shelly Cason—you know, my attorney. She wants to speak to you."

"Don't think this is over," Waterstone remarked. "If the book is published with references to Coogan, the consequences will be swift, drastic, and not to your liking."

Malcolm called out again. "Pops, do you want me to tell Shelly to call back?"

I was about to respond to Waterstone, but like Houdini, he had vanished in the blink of an eye.

"I'll be right there, son." I returned to my office, and spoke to Attorney Shelly Cason. "I believe that everything has been taken out of context," I told her, attempting to calm fears, and soothe ruffled feelings and egos.

Shelly Cason ignored my comments, and pursued her own agenda. "Mr. Hughes, I hope that you have reconsidered including certain stories and materials that are presently contained in the latest draft of your manuscript."

"You've got some nerve lady, contacting me, after you've brainwashed my son against me."

"And you have some nerve writing such an unflattering memoir on your family and acquaintances."

"They're humorous vignettes."

"They are career-damaging, life-altering, reckless fabrications."

"You are exaggerating."

"The only person exaggerating, and grossly at that I might add, is you, Mr. Hughes."

"Listen, Ms. Cason—"

Attorney Cason interjected, "Not only do I represent Malcolm, and Pierre the mime. But I also represent Buddy Carvell, Brendan J. Bucknell the Fifth, and Timmy Hudson.

Timmy Hudson? How could he, after I sent him ice cream? In fact, how could any of them cast their lot with an attorney of such questionable tastes and ethics? "You represent all of them?" I asked with a tinge of disbelief.

"Yes, I do. But, I did not call you concerning any of those clients."

"Then what is the purpose of this phone call?"

"It's to let you know that I also represent a Mr. Bear. You know him as Big Woofin Bear. He was a former acquaintance of yours. As I understand it, the two of you parted on less than friendly terms. Mr. Bear has read selected passages of the stories in which he is featured. While you may be able to win sympathy from your family, Mr. Bear is prepared to contest publication of the book. He considers the book out-and-out character assassination."

"You represent a bear?"

"Don't tell me that on top of all your other sins, that you are blatantly anti-bear?"

Wait a minute, Shelly Cason couldn't be representing big woofin bear. This had to be a dream. I rubbed my eyes and opened them. I was still staring at my family, and Waterstone, and Pierre the mime. I must have imagined that I rubbed my eyes. It was time to wake up from this nightmare.

I awoke, and raced to the bathroom. I stared at the mirror.

All was right with the world. I was four times divorced with six children.

I was a happy, not terribly wealthy, middle-aged, divorced man. But I was not facing the wrath of everyone who was mentioned in my book.

I should have seen it coming. I should not have eaten that midnight snack last night. My mother always warned me not to eat after seven in the evening. Some nights I remembered. But whenever, my stomach rumbled, I conveniently forgot my mother's words of caution.

The phone rang. Almost midnight and the phone rang. Only one person would call me so late at night. I answered the phone and said, "Evening, pops."

"I was thinking about you son, and decided to just give you a call."

I belched. "Excuse me."

"What's wrong son?"

"It's just a little indigestion."

"What did you eat?"

"I'm not sure," I fibbed.

"You don't know what you ate?"

"I think it was steak and onions."

"Did it have any sauce on it?"

Some things never change. And that's the way it should be.

The End

0-595-26019-5